ELIZABETH FAIR
BRAMTON WICK

ELIZABETH MARY FAIR was born in 1908 and brought up in Haigh, a small village in Lancashire, England. There her father was the land agent for Haigh Hall, then occupied by the Earl of Crawford and Balcorres, and there she and her sister were educated by a governess. After her father's death, in 1934, Miss Fair and her mother and sister removed to a small house with a large garden in the New Forest in Hampshire. From 1939 to 1944, she was an ambulance driver in the Civil Defence Corps, serving at Southampton, England; in 1944 she joined the British Red Cross and went overseas as a Welfare Officer, during which time she served in Belgium, India, and Ceylon.

Miss Fair's first novel, *Bramton Wick*, was published in 1952 and received with enthusiastic acclaim as 'perfect light reading with a dash of lemon in it ...' by *Time and Tide*. Between the years 1953 and 1960, five further novels followed: *Landscape in Sunlight*, *The Native Heath*, *Seaview House*, *A Winter Away*, and *The Mingham Air*. All are characterized by their English countryside settings and their shrewd and witty study of human nature.

Elizabeth Fair died in 1997.

By Elizabeth Fair

ELIZABETH FAIR

BRAMTON WICK

With an introduction
by Elizabeth Crawford

DEAN STREET PRESS

A Furrowed Middlebrow Book
FM14

Published by Dean Street Press 2017

Copyright © 1952 Elizabeth Fair
Introduction copyright © 2017 Elizabeth Crawford

First published in 1952 by Hutchinson

Cover by DSP
Cover illustration shows detail from
Farmhouse and Field by Eric Ravilious

ISBN 978 1 911579 33 5

www.deanstreetpress.co.uk

INTRODUCTION

'DELICIOUS' WAS John Betjeman's verdict in the *Daily Telegraph* on *Bramton Wick* (1952), the first of Elizabeth Fair's six novels of 'polite provincial society', all of which are now republished as Furrowed Middlebrow books. In her witty *Daily Express* book column (17 April 1952), Nancy Spain characterised *Bramton Wick* as 'by Trollope out of Thirkell' and in *John O'London's Weekly* Stevie Smith was another who invoked the creator of the Chronicles of Barsetshire, praising the author's 'truly Trollopian air of benign maturity', while Compton Mackenzie pleased Elizabeth Fair greatly by describing it as 'humorous in the best tradition of English Humour, and by that I mean Jane Austen's humour'. The author herself was more prosaic, writing in her diary that *Bramton Wick* 'was pretty certain of a sale to lending libraries and devotees of light novels'. She was right; but who was this novelist who, over a brief publishing life, 1952-1960, enjoyed comparison with such eminent predecessors?

Elizabeth Mary Fair (1908-1997) was born at Haigh, a village on the outskirts of Wigan, Lancashire. Although the village as she described it was 'totally unpicturesque', Elizabeth was brought up in distinctly more pleasing surroundings. For the substantial stone-built house in which she was born and in which she lived for her first twenty-six years was 'Haighlands', set within the estate of Haigh Hall, one of the several seats of Scotland's premier earl, the Earl of Crawford and Balcarres. Haigh Hall dates from the 1830s/40s and it is likely that 'Haighlands' was built during that time specifically to house the Earl's estate manager, who, from the first years of the twentieth century until his rather premature death in 1934, was Elizabeth's father, Arthur Fair. The Fair family was generally prosperous; Arthur Fair's father had been a successful stockbroker and his mother was the daughter of Edward Rigby, a silk merchant who for a time in the 1850s had lived with his family in Swinton Park, an ancient house much augmented in the 19th century with towers and battlements, set in extensive parkland in the

Yorkshire Dales. Portraits of Edward Rigby, his wife, and sister-in law were inherited by Elizabeth Fair, and, having graced her Hampshire bungalow in the 1990s, were singled out for specific mention in her will, evidence of their importance to her. While hanging on the walls of 'Haighlands' they surely stimulated an interest in the stories of past generations that helped shape the future novelist's mental landscape.

On her mother's side, Elizabeth Fair was the grand-daughter of Thomas Ratcliffe Ellis, one of Wigan's leading citizens, a solicitor, and secretary from 1892 until 1921 to the Coalowners' Association. Wigan was a coal town, the Earl of Crawford owning numerous collieries in the area, and Ratcliffe Ellis, knighted in the 1911 Coronation Honours, played an important part nationally in dealing with the disputes between coal owners and miners that were such a feature of the early 20th century. Although the Ellises were politically Conservative, they were sufficiently liberal-minded as to encourage one daughter, Beth, in her desire to study at Lady Margaret Hall, Oxford. There she took first-class honours in English Literature and went on to write *First Impressions of Burmah* (1899), dedicated to her father and described by a modern authority as 'as one of the funniest travel books ever written'. She followed this with seven rollicking tales of 17th/18th-century derring-do. One, *Madam, Will You Walk?*, was staged by Gerald du Maurier at Wyndham's Theatre in 1911 and in 1923 a silent film was based on another. Although she died in childbirth when her niece and namesake was only five years old, her presence must surely have lingered not only on the 'Haighlands' bookshelves but in family stories told by her sister, Madge Fair. Another much-discussed Ellis connection was Madge's cousin, (Elizabeth) Lily Brayton, who was one of the early- 20th century's star actresses, playing the lead role in over 2000 performances of *Chu Chin Chow*, the musical comedy written by her husband that was such a hit of the London stage during the First World War. Young Elizabeth could hardly help but be interested in the achievements of such intriguing female relations.

CHAPTER ONE

THE MORNING was wet and it must have been raining all night, for a pool of water had seeped under the back door of Miss Selbourne's cottage. When she came downstairs to let out the dogs that slept indoors, these dogs, frolicking ahead and then running back to encourage her, made wet footmarks all through the kitchen and across the uncarpeted floor of the little hall. It was a pity, for yesterday had been Mrs. Trimmer's day for "doing" the hall and the kitchen, and now they would not be done for another week.

Miss Selbourne might, of course, have fetched a cloth and wiped away the dogs' footmarks. But a life devoted to dogs makes one indifferent to the state of one's house. After tut-tutting mildly at Agnes and Leo she drew back the bolts and prised open the back door, which was sticking badly as it always did in wet weather. Agnes and Leo ran out and bounded down the garden to the kennels to mock the less privileged dogs who were still confined in their sleeping quarters. A confused babble of barks and yelps marked the beginning of the day.

Miss Selbourne lit the oil cooker, put the kettle on, and returned to the foot of the stairs.

"Tiger, Tiger!" she called.

Tiger was not, as strangers assumed, another dog, but Miss Garrett, her friend and partner. Tiger was a heavy sleeper—a useful accomplishment in such a noisy house as this—and it was often necessary to go upstairs and shake her into consciousness. But this morning was different; perhaps the importance of the day had penetrated into Miss Garrett's sleeping brain, as the thought of a journey or a visit to the dentist will rouse us more effectually than an alarm clock. Miss Selbourne heard heavy bumps, a prolonged coughing, and the squeak of an opening door. She returned to the kitchen.

Shortly afterwards Miss Garrett joined her. Miss Garrett was one of those people who can do nothing until they have had a cup of tea. It was for this reason that Miss Selbourne had to get up first. Even Miss Garrett's tongue did not work freely till the tea was brewed. She simply nodded to her friend and sat herself heavily on the edge of the kitchen table. The table creaked; Miss Garrett frowned at the dogs' wet footmarks; Miss Selbourne poured out the tea.

"Well, old thing," said Miss Garrett at last, putting down her cup, "it's not much of a day."

They looked out. The view was rather obscured by an over-grown Virginia creeper and heavily shadowed by the trees that bordered the lane. It was difficult to make a good weather fore-cast from the kitchen window.

"Of course, it's quite early yet," Miss Selbourne said hope-fully.

"Been raining all night. It's bound to make the ground mud-dy. I told them!" said Miss Garrett triumphantly, passing her cup for a refill, "I said to them right from the beginning that that field was bound to be muddy."

"You were quite right, Tiger. And they knew you were right. But I suppose it was the only ground they could get."

"Oh, bosh! What about the playing field? Or the flat piece on Marly Common? Now that would have been perfect. If only they'd given me a free hand!"

"Perhaps they will, another year." But even Miss Selbourne's loyalty could not blind her to the fact that the playing field was always in use on Saturday afternoons, and that Marly Common was three miles from Bramton. Tiger's schemes were always ex-cellent; it was just in the practical details that she failed. But for that, what might she have accomplished! She was so clever, so ambitious, so like a man in her freedom from convention and petty-mindedness.

Like a man too in other ways, in her indifference to her ap-pearance, even in her appearance itself. In the small crowded kitchen her size and her mannishness were exaggerated; it was as though one saw her through a magnifying-glass. Perhaps the disappointment of the wet morning had affected Miss Sel-bourne, who was so accustomed to Miss Garrett's company that usually she could hardly be said to see her at all. But now Tiger's bulk, her massive chest and shoulders, her big thick legs, made bigger and thicker by corduroy trousers, her square strong hands and square weatherbeaten face seemed for a moment quite overpowering. It was only for a moment; the next instant Miss Selbourne got her back into focus.

Tiger was a big woman; she looked strong and hearty, but she had a weakness—she looked able to take care of herself, but she needed love and attention. She needed to be petted and cared for, like the dogs, and like them, she needed to be groomed. I must remember to see that Tiger washes her neck before the show, thought Miss Selbourne. Her ears, too, and her fingernails.

"Well, Bunty, we can't sit here all day," Tiger said breezily. She stood up, giving herself a good shake as if she were a dog that had been out in the rain. "Gosh, what a day, she remarked. "I bet you the Hanson girl cries off." But in spite of these gloomy words it was plain she was in a good humour, for she continued:

"I'll do kennels."

"Oh, no, you've got a long day ahead of you. I'll do them this morning." In these small contests in unselfishness Miss Selbourne was usually the winner, but today Miss Garrett prevailed.

"So have you, old thing. Besides, I'm dressed and you're not, and I think it's my turn." Miss Garrett remembered that it was her turn only when she was quite willing to undertake a task, so Miss Selbourne was able to let her go without misgivings. She herself picked up the kettle and went upstairs to dress. From her bedroom window the day showed some improvement. The rain had lessened, the clouds looked higher, and a breeze was stirring the larches on the hillside. "Bank Cottage is so sheltered," Miss Selbourne used to say when people commented on the curious position of her little house. Sheltered was a pleasing adjective; it forestalled another which did not please her. But sometimes, looking out from her bedroom window, she admitted to herself that Bank Cottage was rather shut in.

It stood in the trough of a narrow valley running north and south. The long, thin garden was bordered on one side by the lane and on the other by the railway embankment. A row of elms grew along the lane; beyond the railway embankment to the east was a rising hillside covered with larches. The embankment towered above Bank Cottage like a rampart, and when a train passed everything in the house vibrated to its passing. But fortunately there were few trains. The single line was a branch from the junction at Bramworthy to the village of Bramton; it had been built in the early days of steam's triumph and was now almost superseded by an efficient bus service which connected Bramton more directly with the outer world.

It was the embankment, rather than the trains, that people were conscious of when they visited Miss Selbourne. It was the embankment that cut off the morning sun and made the garden appear so disproportionately narrow. In spring the embankment was gay with primroses, but in summer the dry grass was sometimes set on fire by passing trains, and then Miss Selbourne and Miss Garrett had an anxious time. Behind the house, where the garden merged into a tussocky paddock, were the kennels, wooden buildings vulnerable to fire, and more than once they had had to remove the precious dogs till the danger was over. On hot summer evenings, although both believed in early bed and early rising, they sat up until the last train had gone by.

But now, though it was summer, there was no danger of destruction by fire. The house could safely be left. It was really a good thing, thought Miss Selbourne, that it had been such a wet night. For this was the day of the show, the Bramton and District Dog Show, and although the Hanson girl was coming in to look after the dogs that were not going to the show, she was not really the person to cope with an outbreak of fire. As she reached this conclusion Miss Selbourne heard the slam of the back door, and an instant later the sharp barks and scuffling excitement of Agnes and Leo as they chased each other round the hall, and Tiger's voice shouting, "Sit, sit! Sit down till you're dried. Bunty, where's the towel got to?"

At the same moment the cuckoo clock at the head of the stairs sprang into action with a whirring of wheels. The doors opened, the cuckoo popped its head out and began its seven cuckoos. A subterranean rumbling which quickly increased to a dominant roar heralded the passing of the first train. "Very punctual to-day!" shouted Tiger from the kitchen. She meant that the train was punctual by the cuckoo clock, not that the cuckoo clock kept good time by the train.

Miss Selbourne put a clean handkerchief in her cuff, pushed the window wide open, and went downstairs.

The train could be heard, but more distantly, from the houses that made up the hamlet of Bramton Wick. The lane crossed the little river and turned westwards up the hill. It was known as Wick Lane, and where it joined the upper road along the ridge was the commercial centre of Bramton Wick, consisting of a post office and general store, a roadside cafe, and an unobtrusive inn. It was too small to be classed as a village, and the buildings were neither picturesque nor ugly. There were a few cottages near-by, but Bramton Wick (commonly called Wick, to distinguish it from Bramton proper) was a straggling place; the newer houses which had been built between the wars were strung out along the ridge, and set back among trees, so that they hardly seemed to belong to the small settlement at the crossroads.

In one of these houses, some twenty years earlier, Major Worthy had settled down to spend the years of his retirement. Having been fortunate enough to marry a woman with a little money, he had been able to retire comparatively young.

Curtis, as his wife explained to every newcomer, had never really got over the last war (and by this she meant the war of 1914-18), and in particular still suffered from the effects of the sunstroke he had got in India. For years she had worried her-self nearly demented over his delicate health, till at last she had been able to persuade him to give it up—for what was success compared to one's health? And so they had come here—for the best doctors in London could do nothing for Curtis, but one of them suggested that in the country, somewhere really quiet, he would be as well as he could hope to be anywhere. Of course, he would never be completely fit, but that was partly his own fault. He was too active, he could not bear to be idle.

"If he would only rest more—!" Mrs. Worthy would exclaim, and from the direction of her loving, anxious glance the visitor would realize that the man digging the border or sawing up logs, whom one had judged by his clothes and wrinkled leathery appearance to be an unusually energetic hireling, must be the victim of sunstroke and World War I.

"Gwennie!" Major Worthy said peremptorily. There was a faint inaudible reply from the kitchen. "Gwennie!" he called again, and this time his wife appeared in the doorway and he was satisfied that she really had heard him.

"Breakfast ready?" he inquired. "It's eight o'clock." He looked at his watch and at the hall clock, and then, more gloomily, at the barometer. "Glass has gone down again," he informed her. "Not much hope of a fine afternoon. Not a day for your best bib and tucker."

"I know, Curtis. Isn't it a shame? Oh, I don't mean my clothes, but isn't it a shame if it's going to be wet for the dog show? I was talking to Miss Selbourne yesterday—or was it Thursday? Yes, it was Thursday—and she told me they were expecting a great many people, but I don't suppose they'll come if it's wet. I'm afraid the guarantors will lose all the money they put up."

"More fools they. Catch me putting up money for a show in a little place like this. What about breakfast?"

Major Worthy spoke abruptly, but not unkindly. Staccato remarks were his normal mode of expressing himself, and his insistence on punctuality was perhaps a relic of his army career. When breakfast was on the table he sat down without the least appearance of haste to examine his letters. Mrs. Worthy, whom a lifetime of devotion had prepared for such contingencies, produced a padded tea-cosy for the teapot and a small replica of it for the boiled egg. There were three places laid at the table, and two boiled eggs—she herself had only toast—but the other egg had to wait out in the cold. She had not foreseen, when she bought the little egg-cosy at the church restoration bazaar in the year before the war, that she would have another dilatory man at her breakfast table.

Presently Major Worthy looked up. "Where's young Jocelyn?" he asked. This was a question which hardly needed an answer, nor did he pay much attention when his wife said, "I expect he's still having his bath." The short phrases that composed much of Major Worthy's conversation were spasmodic, meaningless, a mere overflowing of his abundant energy. Like the whistling escape of steam from a safety-valve, they filled the surrounding air with noise but required no response.

Mrs. Worthy was sufficiently aware of this to know that sudden silences and abrupt changes of subject need not be ascribed to ill-humour. She waited for Curtis to finish his letters. She was placid, but alert.

"Well, don't I get any breakfast this morning?" he said at last, and at this she unhooded the teapot and filled the cups. Then she gave him his egg, first slicing off the top and putting salt on the side of the plate. She got up and walked round the table to set the egg in front of him, and while she was up she bent over the toast-rack and selected the most evenly browned slice for his plate. Her duty was now done, since he preferred to butter the toast himself, and she returned to her place and prepared to begin her own breakfast.

Before Major Worthy had finished his egg the door opened and young Jocelyn appeared. "Good morning, dear," said Mrs. Worthy. "Afternoon," said Major Worthy. "We shall have to get you an alarm clock, young feller."

Mrs. Worthy looked anxious. People did not understand Curtis, that it was only his manner, that he was not really rude, or angry, or avaricious. And young people (by this she meant Jocelyn) were so sensitive. She was sorry for young people, whom the war had deprived of money and prospects and ambition, but not sorry enough to sympathize if they annoyed Curtis.

By misunderstanding his uncle, Jocelyn had before now succeeded in annoying him to a quite unnerving degree. It was a relief when he ignored the offer of an alarm clock and simply said good morning. He took his seat at the table, she passed him his egg (restraining herself from uncapping it), and the meal continued. Major Worthy fired off remarks, Mrs. Worthy answered them, and Jocelyn ate in silence.

"Weather's looking up a bit," Major Worthy decided, rising to his feet and shaking crumbs of toast all over the carpet. It had stopped raining some time ago, and now they could all acknowledge it.

"Perhaps it will be fine after all. Jocelyn, I did tell you about the show, didn't I? I don't suppose you'll find it very interesting but it will be—well, it will be a little gaiety, won't it?"

A little gaiety was perhaps what Jocelyn needed.

"Yes, Aunt Gwennie," Jocelyn agreed politely. He had the common masculine attribute of being, after a meal, better-tempered and more amenable to kind thoughts, and it was under their influence that he added: "I suppose you're not showing Binkie?"

"I think Binkie's too old. Of course, he doesn't look it but actually he's nearly ten. We've had him since he was eight weeks, and oh, when I think what a dear little pup he was! He came to us from some dear friends of your uncles who went in for breeding dogs after the last war—they didn't, I'm afraid, make a great success of it and after a time they gave it up, but they still kept dogs—one does, you know, when one's once had a dog, and of course they had had a lot of dogs. They gave Binkie to us as a Christmas present, and he arrived in a little wooden box. He was so small. I said to Curtis, he's much too small to travel alone. Of course, by that time we'd got him out of the box and he was running all over the place. Oh, he was a dear little thing!"

"Who's a naughty pup then?" Major Worthy interjected suddenly. Jocelyn looked round, but Binkie was not in the room.

"Yes, wasn't he naughty? He tore everything up, he nearly drove Mabel, that was the maid we had then, frantic. Of course, he's settled down now, he's quite grown-up and sedate." She paused, and Jocelyn said quickly:

"I thought of going into Bramton this morning."

He had only just thought of it, while he was wondering how to detach himself from Aunt Gwennie without attaching himself for the whole morning to Uncle Curtis. It was so unlike him to decide on a definite action that Mrs. Worthy was surprised, and wondered if he could have made some friends in Bramton, since there seemed no other reason for his going there.

"Of course, dear." She hesitated. Should she tell him to take the car? But apart from his using the petrol, she did not like the way Jocelyn drove the car. It was not the way the car was accustomed to being driven; too often he forgot that it was not a jeep or whatever he had learned to drive in the Army. But before prudence and kindness had finished their argument the question was settled by his saying: "I thought I'd walk in to get some exercise. Then I can come back on the bus."

"If you want exercise I can give you plenty in the garden," his uncle offered as he crossed to the door. "Finest exercise in the world. Nothing like it. Look at me."

Jocelyn looked at him. Fortunately Major Worthy had his back to the room and did not notice it. But Mrs. Worthy noticed it, and decided that it would do Jocelyn no harm to walk both ways. She had been going to offer him his bus fare. Now she merely asked him if he knew the way.

"You mean across the fields?" he answered, obligingly intelligent for once. "Well, I cut off at the crossroads, don't I, and straight down to the river? There's a footbridge somewhere—"

"And it brings you out into the lane, and then you go under the railway, I mean the lane goes under the railway, and up the hill on the other side, and it brings you on to the Bramworthy road just by the gates of Marly House. That's much shorter than keeping this side of the river. If you went *this* way—"

"But I won't," Jocelyn said ruthlessly. "I'll go the other way. Down to the river. By the way, who lives in that house you pass going down to the river? A rather pretty house with oodles of creeper all over it?"

Starting mentally from the front gate, Mrs. Worthy arrived at the first cottage along the road. Thatched, decrepit, certainly ivy-covered. "Why, that's Mrs. Trimmer's cottage. You're not very observant, Jocelyn"—she was still angry with him—"for, don't you remember, we passed there the other evening when Mrs. Trimmer was just going in? You know her, she comes here twice a week to scrub the passages and I stopped that evening—was it last Tuesday?—and spoke to her. I wanted—"

"Oh, I don't mean that old shack. I mean the big house on the way down the hill. The garden slopes down to the footpath."

When he said "the big house," she thought of Endbury or Cleeve Manor or Marly, all houses undeniably bigger than her own. It took her a few seconds to realize that he must mean Woodside, and then she protested that it was not a big house at all. Perhaps it only looked big because it was long and low, or perhaps the creeper made it look bigger. There were only four bedrooms and all of them quite small. And it might be pretty but it was certainly damp.

Jocelyn waited, not too impatiently, for every minute's delay made it less probable that he would have time to walk into Bramton. Finally, when his aunt had described three different houses similarly affected by damp, he repeated his question.

"Who lives at Woodside?" she echoed. "Why, some people called Cole. They have been here for years, but somehow we don't seem to know them very well."

Binkie was chasing a fugitive hen across the garden. Clara was waiting to make the beds. And there was her frock to iron out for the afternoon, and the lunch to cook. So there was no time to tell Jocelyn any more about the Coles.

CHAPTER TWO

IT WAS FORTUNATE that Woodside was quite a small house, and that the general shortage of servants made housework a permissible employment for gentlewomen, for they could hardly have afforded a resident maid. Mrs. Cole did not mind the housework, but she would have hated admitting that she was much poorer than her neighbours and therefore an object for their compassion or patronage.

She did not mind the housework, but she was remarkably bad at it, and could comfort herself only by remembering that after all she had not been brought up to cooking, dusting, and polishing, and that she had come to these tasks late in life. Her two daughters, who were very fond of her, made her increasing years an excuse for letting her do as little as possible, for they would not have hurt her feelings by pointing out the dust she overlooked or the dreadful solidity of her puddings.

Mrs. Cole, who was secretly aware of their true reasons for sparing her, tried to show her gratitude by praising and admiring everything they did, as though no one else had ever done it half as well. Perhaps, too, by making them out to be so wonderfully talented, she disguised her own inadequacy; it was not that she was really so incompetent, it was just that she could not reach their level.

During the war, they agreed, she had done wonders. Gillian's marriage, Laura's absence—first at school and then in the Land Army—had left her unprotected; like the personification of a slogan she had had to sink or swim, and she had swum. Those days were now past, and as if in reaction from their prolonged activity Mrs. Cole showed signs of becoming an old lady. She had always had a tendency to dramatize her life (with herself, of course, in the leading part), and now she had begun, as it were, to rehearse her final role, though she was not yet word-perfect.

For dramatically-minded characters costume is important, and Mrs. Cole, to her daughters' regret, had taken to wearing soft-soled slippers, peculiar old skirts, and a large hand-knitted Shetland shawl which enveloped and concealed—or so she believed—all the deficiencies of her warm but shapeless jerseys.

"If you wear your shawl in July, what will you wear in the winter?" Laura inquired.

"I know, darling, but it's such a miserable morning. It's been raining all night."

"But it isn't raining now, Mummy."

"At my age one feels the cold more," replied Mrs. Cole, huddling into her shawl.

Gillian came into the room dressed in a manner that seemed designed to mark the difference between crabbed age and youth. Her short-sleeved cotton frock had reached the stage of being fit only for the garden, a stage which Gillian's clothes attained with uncommon speed, in her own eyes, although her sister always thought her the height of elegance. Had it been Laura, Mrs. Cole would have hinted that the frock was too young, or too bold, or too flimsy, but Gillian somehow contrived to forbid such criticism. Her marriage had established her independence; her widowhood made it permanent. Mrs. Cole, a widow herself, could not but feel that her elder daughter had finally outgrown the nursery.

It was a pity, for of the two Gillian had always been the more impulsive, the more wayward—not that this was Mrs. Cole's adjective—and the more stubborn. She had been the one who needed guiding and checking. Laura had been shy and retiring; what *she* needed was encouragement. Thinking this, Mrs. Cole travelled back into the past, for when she thought of her daughters in the present tense it was only to admire and applaud them.

"Is anything happening this morning?" asked Gillian. Housework and gardening were not events, and Laura and her mother understood this.

"Toby said he might come over," said Mrs. Cole, who had asked Toby to lunch, but had not yet told them so.

"This morning? I thought he said he had to come over for the dog show."

"I suppose that means he'll come this morning and stay for lunch."

"Toby is always doing that," said Gillian. "I expect Lady Masters encourages it. She's so madly economical."

"But equally madly devoted to Toby. She can't really want him to lunch out."

Gillian disagreed. "It's the sort of love that thrives on absence. She sees him as an ideal son, but it's much easier to see him like that when he isn't there."

"Oh, Gil, but why? Toby's a nice creature. What more could she want?"

"Perfection," said Gillian. "Someone to show her off. Someone more like the heroes of all the novels she reads, and more dashing and up to date. Toby is so sunk in the past."

Laura knew that Gillian found the past very boring. Reminiscences of childhood are often boring, and perhaps Toby Masters, who had known them all their lives, was too apt to bring up old jokes and anecdotes and to cling to traditions that even Laura found tedious. The blackberry picnic, the excursion to Bramworthy Fair, and other highlights of their childhood had been revived by Toby since his return to Endbury. She understood what Gillian meant by saying he was sunk in the past.

"I think," Mrs. Cole interposed, "that Lady Masters wants someone to show off Endbury. She's never really got used to living in a place like Endbury."

This time Gillian and Laura exchanged sympathetic glances. They would not contradict their mother; they knew she regarded Lady Masters, in her secret heart, as an interloper. They had once lived at Endbury themselves.

As well as being their family home, it was a fine old house and locally famous. Mrs. Cole had gone to it as a bride and had lived there for the whole of her short married life, which had been a very happy one. Robert Cole was not a man who worried much about the future, and Laura sometimes wondered what would have happened if her father had not died young. She pictured them still living at Endbury, in increasing discomfort and poverty, eking out an inadequate income with paying guests or showing people round the house at half-a-crown a head.

Fortunately—if it were not blasphemous to think so—the death duties had made it impossible for them to remain. Laura and Gillian had been quite small when their father died, and fortunately again they were both girl-children, which had made it easier for Mrs. Cole to listen to her trustees and agree to the sale.

Mrs. Cole had not been able to cut herself off from a district where people knew who she was, and old Mr. Corton's offer of Woodside had been gratefully accepted, so that she was within easy calling distance of her successor at Endbury and had somehow found it incumbent on herself to introduce Lady Masters to the countryside.

Not unnaturally, her opinion of Lady Masters was coloured by jealousy, regrets, and a faint tinge of malice, but Lady Masters did not perceive this, or perhaps she simply ignored it; she had a bland manner and a considerable talent for ignoring unpleasant conclusions. Laura and Gillian were the right age for Toby; they spent a lot of time at Endbury; they saw it from two points of view, as Toby's home and, through their mother's eyes, as a house with a splendid past and a diminished present. But they had never felt possessive about it, and nowadays they could privately congratulate themselves on not having fifteen bedrooms to dust or a crypt-like kitchen to cook in.

It was different for Mrs. Cole. Though she had been a beauty she had not married till she was over thirty. She told her daughters that this was because she was both irresolute and fastidious, but her contemporaries had thought her flirtatious and their mammas had condemned her as "fast." In any case, Endbury (and, of course, Robert) had justified her delay. She had been married in the spring of 1919, Robert was newly demobilized, the future seemed bright as a dream and Endbury the perfect setting for her beauty. Robert was extravagant and easygoing; for a few years they had spent money lavishly, restoring the gardens, improving the house, entertaining their friends, as if they were still in the Edwardian age to which they both belonged.

When one looks back, the remembered garden is always sunlit. So it was with Mrs. Cole; she looked back at Endbury and saw it as it had been in those first years, and she felt—for feeling, not thinking, was her specialty—that she had been defrauded.

It was therefore useless to argue with her about Lady Masters, who, simply by living at Endbury and by being a rich widow instead of a poor one, had come to represent the intricate and incomprehensible evils that had evicted Mrs. Cole.

But Toby escaped this antipathy. Mrs. Cole rather liked him, and moreover it had occurred to her that it would be something of a triumph, or rather, a restitution, if he should one day marry one of her daughters. She was not a matchmaking mother. The idea lay at the back of her mind, to be taken out and looked at occasionally. When it had first presented itself she had united him with Gillian, who had left school and could not have the coming-out dance she deserved. Then the war had started and

Gillian had married someone else, and Laura was still too young to marry, so the idea was shelved. Now Gillian was a widow and Laura of marriageable age, and either of them would make a wonderful wife for Toby. But beyond asking him to luncheon occasionally, and being a charmingly sympathetic listener herself, she did not interfere.

However, it would not have been right to let Toby be falsely accused of cadging a meal, and she now confessed to her daughters that he had been invited. Laura pointed out that it was a pity she had not said so earlier, because he would get sausage pie again. Gillian said sausage pie was good enough for Toby.

In spite of this lack of enthusiasm, Mrs. Cole thought that Gillian looked more cheerful. She was always careful not to question Gillian's moods, and now, having helped to clear away breakfast and partially tidied her own room, which could never be perfectly tidy because there was always small piles of clothes that needed mending or might perhaps be sent to the poor but which in fact rotated slowly between the chairs and the cupboards, she put on her gum-boots, exchanged the shawl for an old Land Army jerkin of Laura's, and thus protected against the English summer hurried out to the garden. For Mrs. Cole was an incorrigible gardener, and once out of doors she soon forgot that she was verging on old age.

Gillian did her share of the housework efficiently and quickly. As she explained to Laura, she did not want to stay in and have to spend the morning talking to Toby if he should arrive, as he too often did, before he was really expected. Laura replied that it was her day for cooking so she could not talk to him either.

"Mummy will talk to him," said Gillian. "He's really more suited to her than to either of us."

Laura did not dispute it, but she no longer accepted all Gillian's opinions as being infallible. Gillian was careless and impulsive, content with generalizations and half-truths. Toby had a calm, serious manner which perhaps made him appear a suitable companion for the old, and, of course, he enjoyed reminiscences of the past. But really it was easy for anyone to get on with him, and though Gillian did not choose to remember it he had been their closest friend for years. Gentle, faithful, reliable, he had grown up with them like a brother, or at least like the brother of one's imagination.

But since he was not their brother, and since Laura's imagination had developed with her years, it had become natural to wonder if one would like to marry Toby.

She had not discussed this with Gillian. Gillian would be too demanding; she would want to know if Laura was in love with Toby, and whether she was prepared to share Endbury with Lady Masters. These, Laura felt, were questions for the future.

At present the whole thing was simply hypothetical, an interesting possibility, no more.

Gillian decided to go for a walk, and as they had no dog to exercise and she needed an excuse for neglecting Toby, she was easily persuaded to take the papers to the Misses Cleeve at Box Cottage. The Misses Cleeve, who were believed to be very badly off, could not, owing to their position, be solaced by gifts of money or food, but it was hoped they would benefit by reading the two quarterlies to which the Coles subscribed.

Box Cottage was on the Bramworthy road close by the gates of Marly House. Gillian walked down the lane. It was quiet in the valley, sheltered from the wind and pleasantly warm. She walked rather slowly, thinking of nothing important. She wondered if she could afford a new summer dress or if she should save up and join the golf club at Bramworthy next year. That she could not play golf did not matter to Gillian, for there would be men who would enjoy showing her how to hold the clubs. There were always men who enjoyed showing you how to do something.

Though Gillian was not an acknowledged beauty like her mother, she was a very pretty young woman. She had fine eyes and a good profile. Her mouth was too large for classical perfection and her face too sharply pointed, but since she was fortunate enough to live in an age when triangular faces were fashionable it did not matter. She could look amused, amiable, and intelligent, and she could also look shy and helpless as the occasion demanded. Both she and Laura had inherited their mother's fair curly hair, but as they persisted in cutting it short they would never be able to boast that it had hung down to their waists and needed twelve hairpins to keep it up.

As Gillian approached the place where the lane and the railway ran parallel she was roused from her meditation by the shrill barking of several dogs. Ahead of her she saw a dilapidated car drawn up in front of Bank Cottage. It seemed to be full of dogs, and when she got nearer she saw that Miss Garrett and Miss Selbourne, each clasping a dog, were trying to put them into the car without letting the other dogs out. They hailed her with joy.

"Come and give us a hand. Can you open the door and grab Pippin, while I slip Blue Girl in?"

"Better let her hold Blue Girl, old thing. Pippin's so bad with strangers."

"Perhaps that would be better," said Miss Selbourne, thrusting Blue Girl into Gillian's arms. Blue Girl was a thin serpentine dog who clawed and wriggled, but Gillian preferred her to Pippin, who had bitten her the last time she had visited Miss Selbourne. When they had got both dogs into the car, Miss Garrett clapped her on the shoulder.

"That was topping," she said heartily. "I can see you're good with dogs."

This was almost the highest praise that Miss Garrett could utter.

"I suppose you're off to the dog show," Gillian remarked. At once, as if the sun had gone behind a cloud, an expression of gloom and anxiety came upon the faces of Miss Selbourne and her friend. Forgetting Gillian's presence, they resumed the argument that had gone on since half-past nine that morning.

"Really, Tiger, it must be you—yes, really. You're on the committee and you'll be more useful."

"Useful!" echoed Miss Garrett gruffly. "I'm no use—an old crock who can't walk twice round the ring. No, no, Bunty, you go. You can *show* them better than I can." She looked with noble renunciation at the bounding dogs inside the car.

"*Please*, Tiger!" said Miss Selbourne in a tearful voice. But Miss Garrett still shook her head, and the argument might have continued indefinitely if Gillian had not interrupted to know what it was about.

The Hanson girl had let them down, telephoning to say she had a cold and Auntie said three miles was too far on a bicycle in the rain. Not that it was raining by that time, commented Miss Selbourne, while Miss Garrett sniffed to show what she thought of colds. And since they had at present two nursing mothers with young puppies that could not be taken to the show, as well as Agnes and Leo who were really more pets than show dogs, someone would have to stay at home to look after them.

"And worse than that," cried Miss Selbourne, "we had a letter this morning from Mr. Greenley saying he would call in this afternoon—of course, he must have forgotten about the show—to look at a puppy he was thinking of buying as a present for his niece."

Gillian understood her distress. Customers were important, and the prizes at the Bramton and District Dog Show would hardly compare in importance with such a customer as Mr. Greenley. For Mr. Greenley was a very rich man.

"I'll hold the fort," she said. "That is, if you'll trust me," she added pleasantly. "Then you can both go to the show."

There was a moment's hesitation and then Miss Garrett moved forward. Gillian was on the alert and dodged the congratulatory thump. "Good chap," boomed Miss Garrett. "You know what it means to be a pal. There's nothing like a war for teaching people to stick together."

Gillian knew that Miss Garrett and Miss Selbourne had first met when they were driving ambulances in France in 1917. Sometimes it seemed as if the two wars had coalesced in Miss Garrett's mind, she would treat Gillian as a contemporary and allude to shell holes, mud, and billets, forgetting that Gillian's warwork had been done on a typewriter in a London office and that a quarter of a century separated these dissimilar experiences.

But there was no time to explore Miss Garrett's mind, for owing to their protracted arguments the two ladies were already late in starting. Hastily they showed Gillian the kennels, the dogs, and the dishes containing the dogs' dinners and recon-

stituted milk for the nursing mothers. No meal had been prepared for human consumption, but there was a cracked morsel
of cheese, a stale loaf, and a soft lump of margarine on a tin plate
which exactly resembled the dogs' plates. Miss Selbourne produced these without apologies and Gillian accepted them without demur. She listened carefully while they explained which
litter Mr. Greenley was to be shown and which puppy he was,
if possible, to be persuaded to buy. "Fifteen guineas," said Miss
Selbourne, and added, as she had added so many times, "they're
worth all of that."

"He can afford it," Miss Garrett said more explicitly.

They promised to call at Woodside and explain Gillian's absence. As soon as they had left, to an accompaniment of wild
barks from the show-going dogs and frenzied howls from Agnes and Leo in the kitchen, Gillian went upstairs to inspect their
bedrooms. They had insisted that she should make herself at
home; she wished she had asked Miss Selbourne whether she
had any powder or lipstick put away for party occasions, for
there was none in sight. A closer search revealed a small box of
curiously pink powder on the window ledge of Miss Selbourne's
room and a lip-salve which disappointingly proved to be greasy
and white. After examining the brushes and combs Gillian decided, for hygienic reasons, not to comb her hair.

Jocelyn Worthy's walk into Bramton had dwindled into a
walk down to the river and back. He saw the car coming up the
lane and heard it stop at Woodside. At this time he was loiter-
ing on the part of the footpath that gave a view of the sloping
garden where he had seen Gillian yesterday. Since Jocelyn had
come to believe that there was no one under fifty in Bramton
Wick his glimpse of Gillian had made him determined to get
to know the people who lived at Woodside, but he was not sure
how to go about it. He had brought Binkie with him, hoping that
he might stray into the garden and have to be rescued, but the
garden proved to be well fenced and Binkie had been brought
up to walk to heel.

In any case, the garden's only occupant this morning was an oddly-dressed old woman—he classified women quite simply as being old if their hair was grey—who had her back to him and must have been deaf or something, for she paid no attention to the whistles and shouts with which he pretended to recall Binkie from a bramble patch.

Mrs. Cole always ignored the existence of the footpath. It was seldom used; she had often told Miles Corton that he should close it altogether, as he could easily do by removing the footbridge across the river, which would soon teach people to go round by the lane. Her landlord listened politely and ended by reminding her, if Laura or Gillian had not said it first, that the footpath was a right of way.

Mrs. Cole accepted this without believing it, which was the reason why she constantly renewed the attack. Her landlord was a busy man, he farmed his own land, he was saddled with Marly House, and he was still too young to understand how much old people liked privacy. If his father had been alive she was sure the footbridge would have been taken away.

CHAPTER THREE

IN ADDITION TO being Mrs. Cole's landlord, Miles Corton owned a good deal of land round Bramton Wick. He was well liked by his tenant farmers and the men he employed, but among other residents in the district he was not altogether popular. His dark and rather arrogant face made people say he was bad-tempered. They also said that he was a proud man, and that "he made you feel he had no time for you."

The last remark was probably true; Mr. Corton had very little time to spare from the strenuous business of farming and estate management. This morning he had had an early appointment at some outlying fields beyond Bramton Wick, where he had to meet the tenant farmer and a technical expert sent by the County Agricultural Committee to discuss a new drainage scheme. It was not, of course, the right time of year for the work, but the appointment had been made by the expert, who believed in looking well ahead, and the farmer had asked his landlord—in the character of the prisoner's friend—to support him.

Mr. Corton had driven over and had spent a couple of hours in the fields, where the expert had explained the complicated and expensive scheme he recommended, and the farmer, an inarticulate old man whose only argument for having his own way was that he had known the fields all his life, had repeated stubbornly that Higher Cowfold would do very well when the ditches were cleaned up and that Lower Cowfold would never be dry nohow on account of all the spring-es up along the edge of the wood.

The expert, whose scientific training had not included a course in tactful persuasion, had driven off in a huff, and Mr. Corton had spent another forty minutes looking at his tenant's livestock, at the end of which old Cayman had agreed that it might be worthwhile trying to improve the Cowfolds and had exacted a *quid pro quo* which his landlord could ill afford. Altogether it had been an unprofitable morning and Mr. Corton was not in a very good humour as he reached the Wick crossroads, where a near-collision with another car did nothing to improve his temper.

The other car came out of the lane at a good speed, swerved adroitly to avoid him, and went by with two wheels on the bank. He had time to see that it was Miss Selbourne's car and that it was full of dogs.

"Women drivers!" said Mr. Corton inevitably, and having a poor opinion of the Continent he added, "That woman thinks she's still in France." For since he was also Miss Selbourne's landlord he was constrained to call on her sometimes and had once spent a long hour discussing with her the best route for an ambulance convoy from Rouen to Calais.

With his mind still running on field drainage schemes he remembered, as he approached Woodside, that Mrs. Cole had asked him how she could drain the boggy lower part of her garden where she wished to plant some flowering shrubs to hide the public footpath across the fields.

Miles Corton had inherited many responsibilities from his father, and Mrs. Cole was one of them. Old Mr. Corton had been a great admirer of hers, and when she had to leave Endbury he had let Woodside to her at a ridiculously low rent. He had sent estate workmen—the carpenter, the plumber, and the handyman from the Home Farm—whenever anything at Woodside needed attention, and his head gardener had sent fruit and early vegetables, and also young Handley or young Joe to assist her in the great work of reconstruction which she immediately undertook in the neglected garden.

Those spacious days were now past. There was no longer a plumber or a carpenter at Marly, the handyman was past work, the head gardener in his grave, and the hothouses falling to pieces for lack of paint and empty of peaches and nectarines. But the tradition remained. Mrs. Cole, who would have been too proud to accept public charity, felt no compunction in asking her landlord for advice or help if it were of the kind he could be expected to supply. She made up for this by giving him plenty of advice in return for his own, and would have given him help too if she had felt he needed it. On his side, Miles Corton did what he could, partly out of respect for his old father's memory, and partly because he liked Mrs. Cole.

He liked her, that is, when he was in a good temper. At other times he found her very annoying.

It was not perhaps the right morning for him to visit Woodside, but from a perverse sense of duty he stopped the car at the gate. The house was screened from the lane by birch trees and rhododendrons, so it was not until he had walked up the drive that he saw another car standing outside the door. Recognizing this car, he turned aside and went round the end of the house, looking for Mrs. Cole, who was almost certain to be somewhere in the garden. He soon found her, but she was accompanied by the owner of the car.

The usual greetings were exchanged. "Nice to see you again," said Toby Masters. Toby Masters was a slim, fair young man who looked even younger than he was. Miles nodded to him, but he did not feel it was particularly nice to see Toby. There was something about Toby's boyish charm which never failed to irritate Mr. Corton.

"Come and look at the garden," said Mrs. Cole, as if he had not looked at it a hundred times before. He explained that it was the boggy bit he had come to see, and she began telling him all over again of her plans. Before they could inspect the boggy bit they had to look at the new roses. They had been expensive, and now Mrs. Cole was not sure she had not preferred the old General MacArthurs she had pulled up to make room for them.

"I liked them too," said Toby. "They'd been here for years. I remember Gillian coming to tea when she was about twelve and bringing my mother a great armful of them. They were a gorgeous colour."

Miles thought at first that it must have been a superfluous present, for the rose garden at Endbury was famous. Then he remembered that Lady Masters was ruled by her gardener and could never pick the flowers, and he understood that Mrs. Cole, by sending Gillian with a great armful of roses, was mocking Lady Masters for her helplessness. Thinking of this subtle jest he warmed towards Mrs. Cole, and began to discuss with her the possibility of moving the rock-garden down to the lowest slope of the ground, where the flowering shrubs, when they were big enough, would give shade and enable her to grow several plants she could not grow at present.

But it all depended on the draining of the boggy bit. They had now reached this part of the garden, where the ground fell steeply towards the fence. Mrs. Cole was still wearing her gum-boots and Miles had already spent a long morning in sodden fields. They went down the bank and began poking about in the choked ditch at the bottom. Toby Masters, who was wearing highly-polished brown shoes and his best grey flannels in honour of the dog show, turned back to the house.

Laura had finished the cooking. The sausage pie was in the oven, and she had had time to change her dress. She had just finished laying the table when she looked up and saw Toby coming across the lawn.

"Where's Mummy?" she called through the open window. Mrs. Cole had taken Toby away—for he had arrived, as usual, long before they were ready for him—and had promised to keep him amused till lunchtime.

"She's paddling about in that very wet bit. I thought I'd come and give you a hand."

"Thank you, but it's all done," said Laura, who knew from experience that Toby was very unhandy, though well intentioned. "Come in and have some sherry."

Mrs. Cole sometimes complained that sherry was an unnecessary extravagance, and in her periodic attempts at economy she would deliberately forget to order it. However, there was just enough left in the bottle to fill two glasses. Remembering that her mother did not drink and that Gillian would be out, Laura decided that one glass would be enough for Toby and she would have the other herself.

"Is Miles Corton lunching here?" Toby asked.

"Not that I know of. Why—did Mummy say something about it?"

"Well, he's here. I left him with your mother, down in that wet bit."

"Oh," said Laura. She looked at her untasted glass of sherry and put it back, rather regretfully, on the tray. "I suppose he came to see about draining it, and she'll probably ask him."

Toby looked more serious than usual and she hoped he was not thinking that she disapproved of all invitations issued by her mother. But Toby did not quickly perceive implications of that sort. Toby's mind, which was of the steadfast variety, was still occupied with Miles Corton.

"He's an odd chap, isn't he? Never goes anywhere, never does anything."

"He's always so busy. He farms his own land, you know—the Home Farm the bailiff used to have. I mean, he really works at it. And he's short of labour. I don't suppose he has much time for other things."

"I should like to farm," said Toby. "In fact, I'm seriously thinking of it."

Since he had come out of the Army, Toby had thought seriously of many careers and had tried several of them. Finally, he had opened a bookshop in the county town of Bramchester, in partnership with a man he had met in Italy. This man, Lady Masters explained, was quite brilliant; he had the real business brain and a great technical knowledge of bookselling. This excused, by implication, his rather peculiar appearance, and certainly he seemed to be a very hard-working man.

"You haven't chucked the shop?" asked Laura.

"Oh, no, I'm just taking a short holiday. We're slack at present, but I rather think I've been overdoing it lately."

He sighed. He was nervous about his health. Laura blamed Lady Masters for this, who had fussed over and cossetted him when he was a small boy. To divert him from his ailments she said that farming must be very healthy, even if there wasn't much money in it.

Toby said that Miles Corton certainly did not seem to make it pay.

"I don't know why he goes on living at Marly," he said. "It must be hideously uncomfortable. Why doesn't he do up the bailiff's house and live there?"

"Oh, well," said Laura, "the Cortons have always lived at Marly. You wouldn't like to give up Endbury, would you?"

"That's not the same thing. You know we haven't always lived at Endbury. That argument, the feudal-ancestral one, is pretty dead nowadays. I do love Endbury, and I wouldn't care to leave it, but that is because of what it means to me. It's very beautiful. I suppose it's a symbol of happiness in my life."

You can dream about your past there, she thought. Aloud she said: "Couldn't that be what Miles feels about Marly House?"

"Of course not. To begin with, Marly is not at all beautiful, and then, as I said, it must be hideously uncomfortable." Evidently Toby's aesthetic appreciation of Endbury was combined with a certain insistence on comfort. And even Lady Masters's economical regime would offer more comfort than the cross old cook-housekeeper could provide for Miles Corton in a house which was, as everyone admitted, not at all beautiful and completely unmodernized.

"He's not married," Toby continued. "It would be different if he wanted to hang on to it for his children."

Laura laughed. "Neither are you married, Toby."

"Oh, but I shall marry some day," he said seriously. "Now old Miles seems to have settled down to be a bachelor."

In the interest of hearing that Toby intended to marry, Laura forgot to point out that Mr. Corton was not, after all, more than ten or a dozen years older than herself. It was the first time Toby had spoken of getting married, but from the way he looked at her she was suddenly convinced that it was not the first time he had thought of it. And, of course, when he said that Miles had settled down to be a bachelor he was implying that Miles could have married at any time. She saw the significance of this. Miles could marry whom he pleased—but Toby could not.

"Before you get married," she said lightly, "you will really have to decide whether you are to be a farmer or a bookseller.

Toby gave a rueful grin. "Or a butcher or a baker or a candlestickmaker. But honestly, Laura, don't you think farming would suit me?"

The return of Mrs. Cole and Miles Corton prevented her from answering. Knowing that Gillian would be out, and that therefore there would be enough food to go round, Mrs. Cole invited her landlord to stay for luncheon. She was a little surprised, though pleased, when he accepted.

"Have some sherry," said Laura. "Look, I poured it out, it's on the table. No, Mummy doesn't take it."

"What about you?"

She was just going to say that she had had hers when she realized that Miles, who was more observant than Toby, had noticed there were only two glasses.

"I don't—"

"Nonsense, of course you do. Drink it up," he said firmly, rather as if he were offering her a dose of medicine.

"I'm afraid it's the last of the bottle."

"And you poured it out for yourself."

She could not deny it, but really it would have been much easier if he had just drunk the sherry without making a fuss. She thought she preferred men to be unobservant like Toby, who was discussing flowers with Mrs. Cole and had not noticed anything.

At luncheon they talked about the dog show and Toby said he thought of buying a dog. He regretted that Gillian would not be coming to the show, as he wanted her advice on what sort of breed to get.

"Is Laura not an authority on dogs?" asked Miles.

That was not what Toby meant. He had wanted them both to be there. He liked to have plenty of advice, and friendly laughter and discussion, and perhaps to be teased a little about his choice. Gillian and Laura together could do this better than Laura alone. But he could not say this; instead he said rather stiffly that Laura wasn't very keen on dogs.

Miles was not shocked by this heresy, but he asked why Laura went to dog shows. Mrs. Cole pointed out that there was not a great choice of entertainment in that part of the country and it did Laura good to get out.

"You make me sound like a crotchety invalid," Laura protested. "And anyway, I have lots of interesting things to do."

Mrs. Cole sighed. She did not like to think that Laura was wasting her life, but this fear sometimes assailed her on nights when she could not get to sleep early, and it was then that the idea of her marrying seemed most agreeable.

Now, as she listened to their talk and laughter, the vague idea expanded and grew stronger. Hitherto she had thought it would be nice if Toby should marry one of her daughters—either Laura or Gillian was to reign at Endbury. But from this moment Laura became the heroine of the dream; and the dream itself, put into words and admitted to conscious thought, became a clear hope for the future.

She would have been surprised had she been able to see how nearly Laura's thoughts matched her own. Since Toby had said he intended to marry "some day," Laura's mind had been busy. The more she thought of it, the clearer it became to her that this day depended entirely on Toby's mother.

Of course, she had always known he was under his mother's thumb. But not until now had it occurred to her that poor Toby simply could not afford to marry unless Lady Masters approved. True, Endbury belonged to him; but the money which maintained it belonged to her. Toby had practically nothing of his own, as he had once told her when they were discussing a career for him, and although he was an only child and would one day inherit his mother's wealth, that day was unpredictable. In the meantime he had a large house on his hands, and a business which had not yet begun to pay its way.

Laura was not romantically in love with Toby, nor was she so foolish as to suppose that he would defy his mother, renounce Endbury, and settle down to a hard-working life in some uncongenial job in order to marry whom he pleased. Toby was not such a lover of liberty; she knew him too well to believe that such actions were possible for him. But she liked him. If she wanted to marry Toby, and if he wanted to marry her—these were still vague questions for which she could find the answers later on—the thing to do would be to convince Lady Masters that she would be a suitable and agreeable daughter-in-law.

Lady Masters was a possessive mother, but she was also clear-headed and practical, and her plans for Toby's future might well include matrimony.

Laura wandered off into a daydream in which, by some unspecified act of nobility or heroism, she became the admired of all and the only person Lady Masters wanted for a wife for Toby. From this she was recalled by Toby himself, who turned to her and said he had a message from his mother: would she and Gillian dine with them after the dog show? They were to go straight back to Endbury and not to bother about changing. This invitation showed at once how much there would be to live up to if one were to satisfy Lady Masters. At Endbury they still dined in the evening, at Endbury, unless excused, one was expected to wear the right kind of clothes.

"Will she mind about Gillian's not coming?" Laura asked Toby said they would ring up from the post office at Bramton to let her know. ("So that the food won't be wasted," Gillian would have pointed out. . . .)

Since the Coles had neither a car nor a telephone their social life was even more restricted than is usual in the country, and Laura would in any case have found this occasion a pleasant break in the monotony of evenings devoted to reading and backgammon. But now it had a greater importance. She even wished that they had been "changing," so that she could have worn her one evening dress and looked grand and dignified. But as this was not to be she ran upstairs and borrowed a fine white hemstitched handkerchief out of Gillian's top drawer. Gillian had often told her that handkerchiefs, stockings, and gloves were the things to judge, and be judged, by; and Gillian's outlook resembled that of Lady Masters in many ways, though it would not have done to tell her so.

"Ready?" asked Toby as she came downstairs.

"Yes, quite. I just went to get a clean handkerchief."

Toby looked at her with positive affection. "That takes me right back to the past," he said. "You and Gillian being pursued down the drive by your mother, with clean handkerchiefs flapping in her hand, whenever you set off for anywhere, and me with the jumper of my sailor suit simply bulging with them at dancing classes. How frightfully important clean handkerchiefs were!"

Laura laughed and agreed, without mentioning the present importance of a clean handkerchief. It did not occur to her that the moments when it was most evident that Toby was fond of her were always those in which, by some gesture or allusion, she recalled the shared and treasured past.

CHAPTER FOUR

Mr. Thomas Greenley, had he but realized it, was as much of a rarity as the odd exotic plants and depressingly ugly orchids with which he filled the greenhouses and the borders in his splendid garden at Cleeve Manor. True, he was neither ugly nor exotic; his fame did not consist in his having been discovered on a windswept ledge of the Himalayas or in the gloomy fever-ridden swamps of some Amazonian jungle and transported at great expense to a situation where the mere fact of his survival was a cause for wonder and congratulation.

Compared with his plants he was commonplace and practically static. But he had other qualities not less remarkable than theirs, qualities indeed more easily assessable by his neighbours, few of whom were capable of judging a plant except by its beauty, its usefulness, or its size.

Mr. Greenley was very rich, comparatively young, and unmarried.

The difficulty was that hardly anybody knew him. When he had first bought Cleeve Manor, home of the three old Misses Cleeve who now lived at Box Cottage, rumours of his wealth and the fact that he came from London and had no connexion with anyone in the county caused him to be branded as an upstart, perhaps a profiteer, seeking to establish himself in an isolated district where neither his ancestors nor his former associates could be held against him. It somehow got about that he was married (perhaps because Cleeve Manor seemed so unsuited to a bachelor), and mothers of families, who might have been tempted by his wealth and the thought of their unmarried daughters, remained aloof.

Had Mr. Greenley wished he could, of course, have overcome this opposition, which in any case dwindled as soon as it was known that no Mrs. Greenley existed. But he showed no particular desire to fraternize with his neighbours. He did not shoot, he did not fish, he had apparently little interest in country pursuits. Moreover he was often away from home, for he was still actively engrossed in the business—variously supposed to be armaments, stockbroking, or simply money-lending—which provided him with his wealth.

He came down to Cleeve Manor usually at week-ends, and usually alone. He never went to church. Very few people managed to become acquainted with Mr. Greenley, and those who did reported that he was pleasant, but dull, and that if asked to do anything he invariably excused himself by saying that he was a busy man. It was evident that Mr. Greenley had not been brought up on the principle of *noblesse oblige*.

When he wanted anything he set about getting it in the simplest possible way. He wanted a puppy for his niece, so he wrote to Miss Selbourne, who advertised each week in the local press, to say that he would call on Saturday afternoon to buy a puppy. He intended that after he had chosen it Miss Selbourne herself should be responsible for delivering it at Sunningdale, where his niece lived.

It was about four o'clock when Gillian heard the car stop outside in the lane. She walked slowly down to the gate, letting Agnes and Leo run ahead so that she could see Mr. Greenley's reactions to dogs. Mr. Greenley's reactions kept him on the far side of the gate. This was reassuring, as it probably meant that he knew no more about dogs than she did herself.

"Good afternoon," she said, and went on to explain who she was and the reason for Miss Selbourne's absence. He had of course forgotten about the dog show. He said with formal politeness that he hoped she had not stayed away from it on his account.

"I was rather glad of an excuse for staying away," Gillian assured him. "I think dogs are only bearable in small quantities. The more there are, the sooner one gets bored."

This pleased him. From the little he had seen of his neighbours he had supposed that everyone living in the country was insanely devoted to dogs, silly, destructive animals in his opinion, and he had been prepared to endure a spate of enthusiastic nonsense from some weather-beaten female in a white coat and a hard felt hat. For Mr. Greenley pigeonholed his fellow creatures, and for each category he had a mental picture, a stock figure as it were, to which he expected the reality would correspond.

"Perhaps I shouldn't say that," Gillian continued. "It's not very businesslike, is it, when you've come here to buy a dog?"

She laughed, and Mr. Greenley laughed too, for no particular reason.

"Even one dog would bore me," he said boldly. "I'm getting this puppy for my niece."

"You'd better come up to the kennels and choose it. These two are quite tame. They'll jump up at you, but they won't bite."

The conversation had been conducted across the rickety little gate. Gillian now opened the gate and Mr. Greenley came inside. Agnes and Leo hurled themselves upon him with wild barks of enthusiasm, but he felt that Gillian knew what she was talking about and he bore it without flinching.

As they went along the muddy cinder path to the kennels Gillian was able to inspect him more closely. He was tall, clean-shaven, and younger than she had thought at first. Not a bad-looking man, she decided, if it had not been for his clothes. He was wearing a thin tweed suit of the loudest check imaginable, a light-coloured background patterned with lines of orange, blue, and brown. As if that were not enough he had chosen a tie and socks whose pale blue matched and accentuated the blue line in the suit, and there was a horrible hand-kerchief, orange—as far as she could see—with a blue border, poking out of his breast pocket.

Really, thought Gillian, it would be an act of charity to make friends with the man and tease or cajole him into modifying those dreadful clothes, which did not suit him in any way. With that colourless, rather solemn face and the high forehead from which his hair was already receding, he could not afford to be so flamboyant. He was like a caricature of an English country gentleman. Probably, she decided intelligently, he dressed like that only because he or his tailor thought that was how one ought to dress in the country.

She was quite right. Mr. Greenley, whose town clothes were as conventional as those of any other man, had depended too much on his mental picture of an English country gentleman when choosing tweeds for his country suits. But since he was so rich no one had questioned his choice, and if he noticed the difference between himself and the other men he met in the country he probably attributed it to their greater poverty.

It did not take long to select a puppy, and Gillian had no difficulty in selling the one Miss Selbourne wanted to get rid of. She almost felt she was taking an unfair advantage of Mr. Greenley, who readily accepted her suggestion that it was the prettiest and the liveliest, and did not notice that it was slightly undershot. But when she told him that it would be fifteen guineas his expression hardened. Mr. Greenley's business instincts were very highly developed, and it was not in his nature to accept a price without bargaining.

"A lot of money for a little dog," he said shortly.

At this Gillian's compunctions vanished. She forgot that he knew nothing about dogs. She remembered that he was a rich man who could well afford fifteen guineas.

"It's worth *all* of that," she answered firmly, in a good imitation of Miss Selbourne's voice. "In fact it may be worth a good deal more. You must remember that these are pedigree dogs. They are all registered at the Kennel Club. I don't suppose that matters much to you," she added, with a frank smile which recalled their earlier agreement on the subject of dogs, "but it does explain why they cost fifteen guineas."

Mr. Greenley was a little shaken by the smile, but he rallied.

"I don't suppose it will matter much to my niece," he objected. "She's only eleven."

"Of course she might be just as happy with a mongrel pup," Gillian agreed. "But then she'll take it about with her and show it to everyone, and people who know about dogs will realize that you've given her a handsome present."

She could not have found a more convincing argument. Mr. Greenley liked his presents to be thought handsome. He said cautiously, "Well, I still think it's a lot of money," but he said it in a tone that showed he intended to buy the puppy.

"I'm sure you won't regret it."

"Then I'll have it. Not," he added hastily, "to take away with me." He explained that his niece's birthday was in three weeks time, and Gillian said that was a good thing as the puppy was still a bit young to leave its mother, and gladly undertook, on Miss Selbourne's behalf, to have the puppy sent to Sunningdale and to write to Mr. Greenley's sister so that she could arrange for it to be met. In all this she showed herself sensible and efficient. Miss Selbourne would have dithered and Miss Garrett would have agreed to anything and forgotten such important details as the date and the address. It was fortunate for them that Mr. Greenley had come on the afternoon of the dog show.

It was fortunate for Gillian, too. If she had met him in any other way Mr. Greenley would have pigeonholed her as "young woman living in the country," and she would have been a type, not an individual. But now he had noticed two things about her. She did not care for dogs. She could drive a bargain. For he shrewdly suspected that the puppy was not worth the fifteen guineas she had unblinkingly demanded. Added to these, she was, as he had seen from the beginning, a very pretty and amusing young woman.

Gillian took him into the house to write the cheque. She had not spent the morning idly. The living-room was tidier than it had been for months, and all the muddy footmarks, human and canine, had been wiped off the floors. Gillian disliked what she called "squalor," and felt that she could not appear at her best in a room where the mantelpiece was thick with dust and the flowers had died three weeks ago but still hung drooping in slimy vases. She had also cleared a sheaf of bills and letters off the writing-table and had even unearthed a fairly clean piece of blotting paper. Naturally, Mr. Greenley did not notice these changes, but he felt he was with someone who was alert and intelligent, intelligent enough, that is, to please him, for he did not desire a high degree of intelligence in women.

While he was writing the cheque Gillian slipped into the kitchen and put the kettle on. At her casual offer of tea Mr. Greenley opened his mouth to say that he was a busy man. But the absurdity of his being busy on a Saturday afternoon in the country struck him more forcibly than it had done on other occasions. He accepted, and was again pleasantly surprised when she produced the tea quickly, without fuss and without the apologies to which he had become accustomed on the rare days when he took tea in other people's houses; for it seemed as if he had an unfortunate knack of being there when there was no cake, or a stale one, or on the day when the baker did not call.

Gillian gave him tea and gingerbreads. She did not explain to him that there was no bread and butter because the bread was hopelessly dry and she had used the margarine to make the gingerbreads. Instead she talked cheerfully and amusingly, telling him a little about the importance of the dog show and a little about herself and where she lived.

Presently Mr. Greenley was doing the talking. He told her about his niece and his nephews and his difficulty in remembering their birthdays and his sister's annoyance when he overlooked these important dates. His sister lived only for her children and could not understand that a busy man like himself had other things to think about. He told her about his sister's house at Sunningdale, which was very comfortable and yet not quite what it should be considering what it cost to keep up. Perhaps her servants were a lazy lot. The garden, said Mr. Greenley, frowning, was a disgrace.

"The gardener's an obstinate old idiot. I often tell her she ought to get rid of him. Of course, he won't take orders from a woman, that's the real trouble. My sister," he explained, "is a widow."

"So am I," said Gillian, looking sympathetic but amused. "And I feel for her. Gardeners can be terrible tyrants when they know you don't know, or even if they think you don't know. We haven't a gardener at Woodside, only an odd man sometimes to do digging, but even he always wants to dig what we don't want dug."

He asked who looked after the garden when the odd man was not digging, and Gillian explained that her mother was gardener-in-chief and she and her sister junior, very subordinate gardeners.

"If you care for gardening," said Mr. Greenley, "perhaps you would like to come over to Cleeve some day and have a look at mine. Of course, it may not interest you. I am"—his voice became a little pompous—"a specialist. Alpines and orchids are my greatest interest, and I flatter myself I am rather successful with them at Cleeve."

"I should love to see them," Gillian replied seriously. "But you mustn't think I'm an expert gardener. You would have to explain everything to me."

She looked at him hopefully, trustfully, and he found himself saying that it would give him great pleasure to show her round. After that he said it was time for him to be moving, and she did not try to delay him, but walked down to the gate at his side and made him laugh by describing how she had come to the rescue of Miss Selbourne and Miss Garrett. She confessed that she had expected he would be a man who would talk about dogs for hours, and in return he told her that he had resigned himself to the thought of listening—though not for hours—to some fool of a woman who hadn't an idea in her head beyond dogs. Each of them felt complimented by the evident fact that they were superior to these fictitious characters.

At the gate he shook her by the hand and said he would ring up next time he was at Cleeve.

"I'm afraid you can't. We haven't got a telephone. Or a car," she added regretfully.

Mr. Greenley was slightly disconcerted, which caused him to say impulsively: "Good Lord, what a life! How do you manage?"

He immediately regretted it. Experience had taught him that it was better to ignore other people's poverty. If their attention was drawn to it they were apt to take offence, or worse still, to become plaintively sorry for themselves.

But Gillian simply laughed. It was not the heroic laugh of one who puts a brave face on things. It was a pretty laugh, bubbling and infectious.

"You look so surprised, as if I'd said we hadn't got any sheets or blankets on the beds. It's horrid of me to laugh, for really it just shows you must have a very kind heart. But we manage perfectly well. We've got bicycles."

"Bicycles," he murmured.

"Lovely bicycles—mine is quite new. You'll see it when I come over to Cleeve. But you'll have to send a postcard when you want me to come."

"You can't come that distance on a bicycle."

"Indeed I can. I often go to Bramworthy, and it's no farther than that."

"Nonsense," he said decisively. "I'll drive over to fetch you. How about next week?" Mixed with the surprise of finding he had a kind heart was the surprise of finding that he really wanted her to come. She had made him laugh. She was a sensible young woman, having his own views about dogs. And she did not make a fuss about being poor, nor did she try to insinuate that there was no virtue in being rich. Instead, she said gaily:

"Of course, that would be lovely, much better than cycling, though I hope you haven't suggested it just because you feel you ought to. Do you suffer from a sense of duty?"

"No," he answered. It was true, but it was a thing he usually kept to himself, feeling, and perhaps rightly, that for a man in his position a sense of duty was a useful attribute.

"Neither do I," said Gillian. "And now I'm sure you want to be off, and I must go and feed those bitches again."

He reminded her that they had not yet settled upon a day for her to come over to Cleeve Manor. He suggested next Saturday; Gillian said it would have to be Sunday. Sunday then, at three o'clock.

She watched the car out of sight. The car had a wide, opulent behind, better suited to park gates and sweeping drives than to the narrow, dusty lane. She looked at her watch and was gratified to discover that it was nearly half-past six. She thought of Miss Selbourne and Miss Garrett, of Laura and Toby and all the other people at the show, and she decided that the impulse which had led to her spending the day at Bank Cottage had been a good impulse.

Upon this cheering thought she returned to the cottage, to wash up the tea things and put the living-room back the way its owners had it, which meant collecting the letters and bills, the cushions with their feathers bursting out at the seams, the dog's basket, and several old bones and rubber balls from the dark hole under the stairs where she had hidden them. Half an hour later, when she had begun to listen for Miss Selbourne's return, she remembered that she had also hidden Agnes and Leo, after they had served their purpose as an introduction to Mr. Greenley. She had lured them into an empty compartment of the kennels, while Mr. Greenley was looking at the puppies. It was fortunate that there was just time to release Agnes and Leo before their loving owners returned, for to find their house pets callously relegated to the kennels might well have prejudiced such fanatics as Miss Selbourne and Miss Garrett. As it was, their arrival was curiously subdued, even the dogs barked less loudly, and Gillian quickly realized that they must have had an unsuccessful day.

It took her a little longer to realize that they were not on speaking terms.

"Was everything all right?" Miss Selbourne asked, when they got into the house; for their first duty had been to put the dogs to bed.

"Oh, yes."

She gave them an account of the afternoon. The cheque was on the mantelpiece, with the address the puppy was to go to and the date it was to be sent off. Gillian picked up the cheque and handed it to Miss Garrett, who had thrown herself into an armchair by the fireplace in a manner that explained why all the chairsprings were broken. But Miss Garrett rejected it with a flapping motion of her hand. "I'm not the boss," she said gruffly. So Gillian gave it to Miss Selbourne, who put it back on the mantelpiece.

She hardly liked to ask how they had got on at the show, for it was obvious that they had not got on well. She said it was time she was moving, remembering that this was Mr. Greenley's formula for departure. But Miss Selbourne, though she might be tired, cross, and tearful, was still conscious that they were under an obligation to Gillian, and that the laws of hospitality applied even to people like herself who—as Tiger had recently told her—put their miserable little bank balances first and golden opportunities second. She offered Gillian a drink. Gillian thought it would be a good thing if they all had a drink, and as her acceptance would provide the occasion she accepted.

Miss Selbourne went to a drawer in the writing table, took out a key, went to the corner cupboard, and produced a bottle of whisky and a bottle of gin. Gillian was surprised and impressed. While she was congratulating Miss Selbourne and hearing the involved story of how one could buy whisky sometimes from a chemist in a remote village the other side of Bramworthy, the atmosphere seemed quite normal. Their voices, a passing train, the whimpering dreams of Leo, provided the usual amount of noise. But gradually, like rising mist, a cold silence crept over the room.

Gillian took her glass and sat down on the sofa. Miss Selbourne took hers, but she did not sit down. She remained by the table, which was behind Miss Garrett's chair, and she looked apprehensively at Miss Garrett, who was lying back in her chair with her eyes shut but with a wakeful brooding look on her face.

Gillian was one of those happy people who can quickly determine not only what is best for themselves, but what is best for others. What was best for Miss Garrett at this moment was whisky. Since it was now clear to her that Miss Selbourne and Miss Garrett could not address each other, she felt justified in dealing with the situation herself.

"Let me get you your drink," she said to Miss Garrett, and to Miss Selbourne: "Do sit down, I'm sure you must be awfully tired, too." Miss Selbourne retired to a rather distant chair, and Gillian poured out a generous measure of whisky and handed it to Miss Garrett, who sniffed at it suspiciously before raising it to her mouth and swallowing most of it in one long gulp.

Conversation became a little easier; that is to say, both Miss Selbourne and Miss Garrett talked to their guest, who answered them in turn and sometimes by repeating what one of them had said drew a reply from the other, which could in its turn be transmitted to the original speaker.

When this had gone on for half an hour Gillian decided that she had done as much as she could towards reconciling them, and that time must do the rest. She took her leave. Miss Selbourne came down to the gate, and once out of Miss Garrett's hearing was able to tell her, in a hurried, indistinct whisper, how dreadfully disappointed Tiger had been over the judging. There had been something else, too, an offer of partnership, a suggestion that they should combine with some woman who had a large house and wanted to share it, an idea that if they had five times as many dogs they would make five times as much money. But, of course, she pointed out sadly, one might easily lose five times as much, and it was not a thing one could agree to on the spur of the moment.

It was rather difficult to hear her, and Gillian could only offer general sympathy. Their whispering was interrupted by the appearance of Miss Garrett at the front door, who shouted impersonally that Agnes had been sick in the hall. Feeling sure that this mishap would draw them together, Gillian went off down the lane.

CHAPTER FIVE

THE ROSE GARDEN was at the far side of the lawn. It was a paved garden. The roses grew in long beds round the sides and in square beds set in the paved walks. The silvery-grey stones, still warm from the afternoon sun, looked luminous now in the fading light, and the flowers made pools of colour in the dusk.

The garden was enclosed by a low stone colonnade, and beyond it at one side the ground fell gently away to a view of distant fields and woods; on the other side, across the smooth lawn, was the east front of the house, the Queen Anne front which was reproduced in nearly every book about the beauties of the county. At one end, approached by three shallow steps, was a small open-fronted temple or summerhouse, from which one could look down the length of the garden to the background of dark yews and silver firs. The colonnade and the pillared temple were wreathed with climbing roses, and their scent, filling the air, was the scent of Endbury itself.

In the little temple, which was familiarly known as the Stone Shelter, Lady Masters liked to have her coffee on fine summer evenings when it was not too cold. She was not a person who felt the cold very much, but Laura was glad she had not had to put on a thin frock to dine at Endbury that night. She wondered how Lady Masters got her old parlour maid to carry the coffee right across the lawn. But, of course, Lady Masters got things simply by always having had them and by taking it for granted that she always would have them.

The coffee, which was tepid and anaemic, was put on a small table between them and Lady Masters poured it out.

"You take sugar, Laura?" She opened her bag and found a small bottle from which she fished out a tiny pellet for Laura's cup. "This saccharine is much better than the ordinary kind," she said. "I get it from my chemist in London."

Many articles of everyday use were magically improved by being used by Lady Masters; her approval, like a royal warrant, set a seal of virtue on certain kinds of soap, tea, and cosmetics; Gillian even declared that there was a special sort of hair dye, obtainable only from "my hairdresser in London," which gave to Lady Masters's coiffure its peculiar purplish-brown lustre.

"It's wonderfully sweet," Laura said of the coffee. She had dutifully praised the economy soup, and had the recipe of the stale-cake trifle, but it was so difficult to admire the coffee that she was glad of this remarkable sweetness.

After they had drunk the coffee, Toby remembered that he wanted to fill his cigarette case, and he ambled off across the lawn. Laura hoped they might all go, but Lady Masters declared it was too fine an evening to spend indoors.

"You're not cold, Laura?" she asked benevolently.

"Oh, no."

Laura wondered if one got used to the cold. The rooms at Endbury were nobly proportioned, but they needed a great deal more heating than their present owner allowed. Lady Masters approved of fuel rationing; she said it taught people to be careful.

But this was summer. Her thoughts were running too far ahead.

"And you enjoyed the dog show?" It was less a question than a statement, and she hastened to agree with it. Conversation with Lady Masters was largely question and answer, but the answers had to be the right ones.

"But Toby did not get a dog after all," said Lady Masters.

"No. I'm not sure if the dogs were for sale. You see, they were there to be judged, and—"

"My dear child, of course they were for sale. People who breed dogs have to sell them. That is how they make their living."

"I suppose so," Laura said humbly. "I wonder if Toby really wants a dog."

"I think it would be a good thing if he got one."

"But would he have much time for it?"

"Naturally the dog would have to stay here—a bookshop is not the place for young dogs. But Toby comes home nearly every week-end." Lady Masters added cryptically: "That is why I think he should have a dog."

Laura could not follow her. Did she mean that Toby needed a dog to complete the picture of the young squire in his home? Or was the dog to occupy him, to take him out for brisk walks and give him something to think about?

She suggested that a spaniel would be nice.

"Not a spaniel. They always get too fat. Not a white dog, because of the hairs, nor an Airedale, because they fight. And I abhor those silly little dogs that yap and trip you up."

"What about a Great Dane?"

"My dear Laura, how should we feed it? None of the really big ones would do. I shall have to think about it."

With a gesture which swept a dozen breeds into limbo, Lady Masters dismissed the subject of dogs.

"And now, Laura," she said. "Tell me—do you think Toby is getting discouraged about his bookshop?"

It was gratifying to be asked a question like that, but Laura did not know how to reply.

"I don't know," she answered. "He hasn't said anything to *me* about it."

"Oh, naturally. If it was anything definite, anything he needed advice about, he would have spoken to me. But his general
attitude? Toby, you know, is a sensitive creature. One can often
guess what he is feeling."

Lady Masters prided herself on understanding the young,
and which of the young should she understand better than
Toby?

"I really don't know," Laura said again. "I think perhaps he's
been a bit depressed lately. But I haven't seen much of him," she
added hastily, for she did not want to get Toby into trouble for
being depressed. Lady Masters did not approve of people who
hedged and she observed rather coldly that Laura and Gillian
saw Toby almost as often as she did herself.

"Though I expect," she continued more kindly, "that even
with you two he makes more effort to hide his feelings. And, of
course, poor boy, he's had such a difficult time since he came out
of the Army." Just for a moment, hearing an unusual despond-
ency in the familiar clipped voice, Laura had a glimpse of another Lady Masters, and guessed that it might be his mother and
not Toby who was having the difficult time. It was this glimpse,
so brief and unexpected, that moved her to say quickly:

"I think if only Toby would keep on with a thing he would be
all right. I mean, it doesn't matter what the thing is—the bookshop will do—so long as he keeps on with it. He needs—he just
needs to get past a certain point, then he'll be all right. He'll
settle down."

She had momentarily forgotten about the need to show herself as a docile and commendable person. She half expected to be
snubbed. Lady Masters was not the sort of woman to welcome
advice, and it was the first time she had ever discussed Toby.

But after a thoughtful pause Lady Masters said: "Do you really think that?"

"Yes, I do," she answered more boldly. "I think Toby doesn't
know what he really wants to do, and so he will go on trying first
one thing and then another unless he is—unless you make him
stick to something."

"Dear Laura, I am not a tyrant to 'make' Toby do this or that. I do not believe in coercing young people," Lady Masters declared. "I am very fond of young people and I understand them. And my poor Toby has wasted such a lot of his youth fighting a war. Do you think I could bear to tie him down for the rest of his life in some niche which does not suit him?"

"But he'll just go on wasting his youth," argued Laura, suddenly stubborn. The thought of Toby's being tied down in a niche did not depress her unduly.

There was another long pause. It was almost dark now, and Lady Masters turned her head and peered at Laura, who realized that her choice of words had been unfortunate. Lady Masters was a possessive mother, but she could not bear to be thought possessive. Outsiders must not suggest that she ruled Toby. Persuasion and advice were permissible; maternal tyranny was not.

"Ah, well, youth is the season for trial and error," Lady Masters said at last. "All young people make mistakes, and hold strong views without much reason behind them." She spoke with determined good humour, as one would speak to an argumentative child. It was hardly possible to pretend that it was Toby who held the strong views.

"I can't think what's happened to Toby, but really it's getting too dark to sit out here. Shall we go back to the house and find him?"

The subject was closed. Side by side they walked back across the lawn.

Laura felt uncomfortable for the rest of the evening. Lady Masters was as benign as usual, but it was plain that no alliance had been established. She had not expected to conquer Toby's mother in one evening, but she had hoped to make a beginning. It seemed they were back on the old friendly footing that had existed since her nursery days, in which she was simply a subordinate figure, "dear Laura" or "dear child," whose existence was taken for granted. And probably if Lady Masters thought of her at all now it would be as someone who criticized and argued—almost worse, she felt, than being a dear child in the shadowy background.

It was not very late when Toby drove her home to Woodside. The moon was rising and the night was clear. A soporific peace lay on the countryside, and so quiet was it that they could hear the river splashing over its little waterfall at the head of the valley, as they lingered outside the gate. Usually Laura made her farewells quickly or took Toby into the house with her to talk to Mrs. Cole and Gillian, but tonight she made the beauty of the evening an excuse for staying at the gate where they could look across the moonlit valley to the Marly woods.

"Nice day, wasn't it?" Toby said placidly. "The dog show I mean."

"Oh, Toby, don't let us talk about dogs any more."

"Were you very bored?" He spoke in what Gillian called his "hurt" voice, and she answered hastily:

"Of course not, I loved it, I only meant that I've been talking about dogs all day, even to your mother after dinner."

"Mama is thinking of buying a dog for me."

Laura looked at him incredulously. Then she laughed. She had always thought he belonged to the cult which holds that Mothers are Sacred. In her present state of mind it was an enormous relief to discover that Lady Masters was not invulnerable.

"I suppose that was why you wanted to buy a dog for yourself, today."

"Well," he said doubtfully, "I thought it would be nice to choose my own dog."

She laughed again, but she realized that too much frivolity would be out of place. She suggested that he might buy a dog in Bramchester.

Gillian was in her bedroom engaged in one of the routine inspections of all her clothes with which she whiled away her spare time. Coming in to tell her about the borrowed handkerchief, Laura was struck anew by the extreme neatness of everything in Gillian's room compared with her own. Gillian's possessions were always tidy, her stockings darned, her gloves clean, and she herself, even when wearing her oldest clothes, could achieve an effect of trim elegance that was quite beyond

Laura. Laura attributed this to Gillian's having been married and lived in London.

"I knew you'd been in," Gillian said calmly, "because you left the drawer open. Yes, of course it's all right. But haven't you got any of your own?"

Laura said most of her good ones had got lost and the others did not look as white as Gillian's.

"It's because you send them to the laundry or let Mrs. Trimmer wash them. The laundry loses them and Mrs. T. makes them grey. You should wash them yourself."

She went on to tell her sister how to make them white, but Laura forgot to listen. She was thinking, not for the first time, that Gillian was far more suited to be Lady Masters's daughter-in-law than she herself. This did not mean that she would be the right wife for Toby, but it occurred to Laura that if Lady Masters should look to the Cole family for a bride for her son, Gillian would be her choice. It was a saddening thought.

"And it's really quite easy and doesn't take much time," Gillian concluded.

"Don't you think it's time we asked Lady Masters to tea again?"

"Oh, surely not," said Gillian, showing no surprise at this change of subject. "Haven't you seen enough of her lately?"

"It isn't that I want to, but I've been three times to Endbury since she was here, and you lunched there that Sunday. We must keep our end up."

Gillian said they had better ask their mother. Since Mrs. Cole was in the habit of agreeing with whatever her daughters suggested—except on the subject of gardening—it was hardly necessary to seek her approval. But the tradition that she must be consulted was stoutly maintained by both Gillian and Laura.

"Make it next Sunday," Gillian continued. "I shall be out."

She had already told her family about her meeting with Mr. Greenley at Bank Cottage, but she had not yet told them that she was going to be shown the gardens at Cleeve Manor. Now she explained to Laura, in a casual way, that on Sunday she was having tea with Mr. Greenley and seeing all the peculiar orchids and other exotic plants which were his only interest in life.

"It will be very difficult to think of the right responses," Laura sympathized. "What a pity Mummy isn't going, she's so good at talking about gardens. She'd know all the proper things to say."

This was as annoying for Gillian as it had been for Laura to hear that Toby was more suited to her mother than to herself. But she concealed her annoyance and replied that anyone could cope with an enthusiast; one just had to look intelligent and admiring and make a few exclamations at intervals. This was really a brief and curtailed summary of Gillian's whole doctrine of behaviour.

"Is he very fat and bald?" asked Laura, who seemed to have got it into her head that Mr. Greenley was a fatherly old man.

"Not at all fat, and not yet bald. He's not as old as you think, and would look quite nice except for his frightful clothes."

She went on to describe the clothes.

"Oh," said Laura.

Unlike sisters in fiction, they were not in the habit of confiding to one another the romantic secrets of their young hearts. Laura had had few such secrets to confide, and she had known instinctively that Gillian would not lend a sympathetic ear to the account of her deep attachment, which had lasted nearly six months, to a young man staying at the Vicarage for Latin coaching, or the even more unprofitable affection she had expended on film stars, the photograph of a school friend's brother, and the heroes of books.

Gillian herself had married young, and undoubtedly she had loved her William, but she had not talked of her love to Laura. Her marriage had taken her away from home; William had been killed in the early part of the war, but Gillian had stayed on in London, with her job as a good excuse for being there. It was not until the war was over that she returned to Woodside. By that time, it was only reasonable to suppose, her affection and her grief for William had diminished. She kept his photograph on her dressing-table; she had once told Laura that she had married much too young, but that she would never regret it because she and William were the right age for each other. It was difficult to know what to make of this.

But although Gillian kept her emotions to herself, Laura understood her well enough to know that she would not waste her life dreaming about a vanished past. And lately Gillian had been getting bored, and had even talked about going back to London and getting another job. Laura did not want this; it was much more fun having Gillian at home. So she was glad to hear that Mr. Greenley was moderately good-looking, in spite of a tendency to baldness and a deplorable taste in dress.

"I suppose he has a palatial establishment and a butler."

"I shall know after Sunday. By the way, I left all the papers at Bank Cottage."

"What papers?"

"The papers I was going to take to the Miss Cleeves. I never got there."

"Could you rescue them, and then, if you like, I'll take them on?" She knew that Gillian did not care for the Misses Cleeve. Indeed, it was rather difficult to like them.

"No," Gillian said firmly. "They must do without the papers. I've spent enough time at Bank Cottage for one week. Oh, Laura, if you could have seen that place! All dogs' hairs and mud and last year's dust. And yet I can't help liking them."

"I feel rather sorry for them."

"Why?"

Gillian often told her sister that she made a virtue of being sorry for other people, and to counteract this weakness in Laura she resolutely shut her own eyes to the need for pity.

"Why should you feel sorry for them? They don't notice the dust and the squalor. They've got the beloved dogs and they've got each other. Of course they quarrel, but then they have all the fun of emotional reconciliations."

"They're hard up."

"I bet they're not as hard up as we are. They've got a car and a bottle of whisky. Or rather, they had a bottle of whisky," Gillian said accurately.

"Well, I can't help feeling sorry for them. It's such an uncomfortable place for a house."

"Oh, rubbish, Laura! Dozens of women live like that, with cats or dogs or parrots, all over the country, and they are perfectly happy. You might easily be one yourself some day."

Gillian believed in having a realistic outlook, but this was carrying it too far. Laura was still young enough to see a wide gulf between herself and Miss Selbourne, but even the most distant prospect of a life whose interests centred on dogs or cats or parrots was not agreeable to contemplate. She said crossly:

"I couldn't bear it. I'd sooner die young."

"Or you might marry," suggested Gillian.

Gillian had a practical mind and a rooted distaste for desperate remedies.

CHAPTER SIX

BANK COTTAGE and Box Cottage were both on the Marly estate. They were not far apart, and both were occupied by middle-aged or elderly spinsters. Visitors to the neighbourhood sometimes found this confusing, but none of the residents could have confused Miss Selbourne or Miss Garrett with the Misses Cleeve who lived at Box Cottage.

The Misses Cleeve, who were the last survivors of a well-known local family, had the sort of importance that a tribal deity might have for a tribe which had only recently been enlightened by missionaries. They were as much part of the landscape as the obelisk on Gibbet Hill or the New Bridge built by their ancestor in 1723 to put Bramton on the map. Though they had left their family home many years ago, their name gave them a ghostly right of possession; as long as they were alive Mr. Greenley would still be "the man who bought Cleeve Manor." They could be pitied or derided, but they could not be ignored.

There were three of them and they were all remarkably like toads. Perhaps the fact that they had lived together for so long was responsible for their close resemblance to one another (as people grow to resemble the horses or dogs they cherish), for the ancestral memory of the village proclaimed that the second Miss Cleeve had once been good-looking and the youngest had had red hair. No trace of these deviations remained; the pattern was set by the eldest Miss Cleeve and repeated in her sisters. Their hair was perhaps more abundant than hers, they were more mobile and less majestic, but it was difficult to tell them apart until you spoke to them. After that it was easy, for although they were all a little peculiar, Miss Myrtle was indisputably the victim of religious mania and Miss Cleeve herself was almost stone-deaf.

One afternoon in the week following the dog show Mrs. Worthy, who had been shopping in Bramworthy, stopped her car outside Box Cottage. The back of the car was full of parcels, horseflesh for Binkie, fish for the rest of the household, fertilizer and lawn sand for the garden, library books and knitting wool for herself. Kneeling on the front seat she delved among these parcels until she found the melon. Meanwhile, Jocelyn sat beside her and continued to gaze rather bleakly in front of him. He held strong views about his aunts driving and was wondering whether he should say he would walk on or whether, if he waited, she would let him drive home.

"I shan't be very long," said Mrs. Worthy.

She took it for granted that Jocelyn would wait for her. Although he had been with them for less than two months, he had already become a responsibility. She had grown used to planning for him, to mending his clothes and sending him out for walks, and listening, with her mind on something else, to his stories about his Army service: dull stories about the food in the Naafi or one of the chaps in his hut, which did not compare with his uncle's tales of the ferocious Boche or the man-eating tiger. So now, without giving him time to speak, she shut the door of the car and hurried up the little path to Box Cottage.

Jocelyn was so used to having his mind made up for him, whether by his sergeant-major or his aunt, that he slouched back against the seat and closed his eyes.

"So kind," muttered Miss Cleeve, fondling the melon. "Really very thoughtful of you, Mrs. Worthy, and quite a little change for us. We never get much fruit unless people are kind enough to bring us some. I don't know how it is, but this garden won't grow fruit."

"The land will not be fruitful unless the Lord bless it," said Miss Myrtle Cleeve, speaking in a loud voice and fixing Mrs. Worthy with a penetrating stare.

Since Miss Cleeve was deaf she could ignore her sister's interruptions, but Mrs. Worthy found them embarrassing. She did not know whether to reply or whether to continue the conversation on ordinary worldly lines. She attempted a compromise by asking if they had yet heard the new vicar of Bramton preach.

"No," said Miss Cleeve, "peaches will never grow out of doors. At least, I never heard of them in this part of the country. Of course, at home they grew in hothouses. Papa was very fond of them."

Mrs. Worthy was now involved in two separate conversations, one with Miss Cleeve about hothouse fruit and one with her sister about the works of the Lord, and since neither of her interlocutors paid any attention to the other she was soon in difficulties. Fortunately an interruption occurred.

The third Miss Cleeve, christened Matilda, but known to friends and foes alike as Pussy, appeared in the doorway ushering in a large and well-dressed caller who carried with her a chip basket containing three peaches. Miss Cleeve peered through her pebble glasses at the advancing figure. "It never rains but it pours," she said, but whether she referred to the fruit or the visitors was uncertain.

"Dear Miss Cleeve—something which I hope will cheer you up." With a generous gesture, Lady Masters proffered the peaches and was slightly disconcerted to find that her hostess was already clasping a melon.

"Dear me, I have been forestalled," she said blandly. Her gaze flickered round the room to discover the melon-bringer and for an instant it was uncertain whether she was going to recognize Mrs. Worthy. But neighbourliness prevailed.

"How nice to meet you," she said. "It seems weeks since we met." This was quite true. "You keep very much at home, Mrs. Worthy."

"The petrol—" Mrs. Worthy said vaguely.

"Ah, yes, the petrol!" The petrol explained everything. Lady Masters turned back to Miss Cleeve.

"I was just telling Mrs. Worthy she should go out more," she shouted, bending down and addressing her at pointblank range.

"I hear you, I hear you!" Miss Cleeve gave a sudden cackle of laughter. "I expect they can hear you over at Marly House."

Mrs. Worthy would have been discomposed, but Lady Masters did not blench. "So long as *you* can hear me, dear Miss Cleeve," she said, still speaking in a good-humoured bellow. "And now tell me how you are?" She sat down and prepared to listen.

Meanwhile, the two younger Misses Cleeve had pinned their other visitor into a corner of the room. Miss Myrtle said little, but gazed at Mrs. Worthy with a luminous, unfocused look as though she were seeing something beyond or inside her. This made it difficult for her to listen sympathetically to the stream of ill-natured gossip which flowed from Pussy's lips.

Pussy did not allow her sequestered life to cramp her style; what she could not discover she invented. She knew that Mrs. Trimmer's eldest daughter was expecting again and it was another man this time; she knew that Miss Garrett had shouted at Colonel Forbes, who was judging at the dog show, and had been ordered out of the ring; she knew that Miles Corton was so hard put to it for money that he was thinking of selling Marly House at last.

Finally, turning to Lady Masters, Pussy said baldly:

"I hear your son doesn't care for bookselling after all. Pity he doesn't settle down and get married."

Lady Masters, whose voice was still pitched to the eldest Miss Cleeve's level, said "What?" so loudly that the vases shook and a dried flower fluttered slowly from a withered votive offering hanging below a semi-sacred picture.

"They tell me he's never to be seen in his shop—leaves it all to that squint-eyed partner or office boy, or whatever he is. But I hear he's quite fond of the shop next door where there's a pretty little gal selling dogs." Pussy looked so inoffensive that these remarks acquired an added poignance, as if a child had suddenly affronted its parent with some frightful home truths. Mrs. Worthy tried to look as if she had not heard, a difficult feat in so small a room. But at the back of her mind was the thought that it would be something to tell Curtis at tea.

She could not help admiring Lady Masters. The smile she turned on Pussy was almost serene, and she answered her as calmly as though they had been discussing the weather.

"I think a lot of people go into Toby's shop and expect to find him waiting behind the counter to serve them. They don't realize that he's probably slaving away in the funny little office they've got upstairs."

"Or next door," said Pussy with a titter.

"Or next door," Lady Masters agreed calmly. "After all, you can't expect old heads on young shoulders, and young people never realize what a ridiculous amount of gossip and tittle-tattle goes on in a place like Bramchester. Personally, I'm very glad if Toby is making some friends. I think he deserves a little gaiety after six years of war."

Mrs. Worthy was afraid Pussy was going to point out that the war had ended some time ago, and she said quickly:

"I feel just the same about my nephew. He needs a little gaiety, but then it's so difficult. So few young people in the neighbourhood—nothing to do—and really I can't often let him take the car over to Bramworthy, although he's very fond of dancing and he tells me they have very good dances at that country house hotel—what is its name? Oh, Evergreens, of course, how stupid of me. Jocelyn says they have dances there on Saturday nights, but then the last bus leaves at nine-thirty, and really with the petrol—"

"Yes, I feel very sorry for young people. Is the young man in the car your nephew, Mrs. Worthy? I did not know you had a nephew."

"Actually Jocelyn is my husband's nephew, the son of his brother Armitage, who died quite soon after the last war, and Curtis has always been very good to Mary—that was my sister-in-law—but she died at the beginning of this war, and, of course, to Jocelyn too."

"I see," said Lady Masters. She turned back to Miss Cleeve and explained loudly that Mrs. Worthy's nephew was in the car outside.

"Bring him in," said Miss Cleeve. But Mrs. Worthy had noticed the time; Curtis would be kept waiting for his tea, and he was already annoyed because she and Jocelyn had lunched in Bramworthy, though this had been inevitable because the dentist could only see her at half-past twelve. It had not, of course, been inevitable that Jocelyn should accompany her, but she never liked leaving him alone with Curtis in case he annoyed him. With all this passing rapidly through her mind she became a little vague, and ceased to pay any attention to Pussy, who was now recounting a curious story she had been told about the new vicar of Bramton.

Miss Myrtle Cleeve had walked out of the room before Pussy began her tale. She was known to be odd, and no one took any notice of her departure. Mrs. Worthy said good-bye to Miss Cleeve and Pussy, with a long involved explanation of why she had to hurry home, and it was not till she was outside the front door that she realized that Lady Masters was accompanying her.

"I seized my opportunity," Lady Masters whispered, "or else I should have been there for the rest of the afternoon. Poor creatures."

"One feels so sorry for them."

"Yes, indeed. And it is so difficult—one can do so little for them. I see you and I have the same idea of what is suitable."

"Fruit," said Lady Masters. "People who would be deeply affronted if one gave them soup or bread can always bring themselves to accept fruit. What a beautiful melon you found for them. It quite put my poor peaches in the shade."

Mrs. Worthy, who knew what was right and proper, immediately began to disparage her melon and praise the peaches.

She was agreeably surprised to find Lady Masters so friendly, for hitherto they had been the merest acquaintances. When they reached the car she was distressed to see that Jocelyn had gone to sleep. But Lady Masters only laughed.

"How alike they all are," she cried. "Like puppies!" With a playful but somehow condescending gesture she tapped lightly on the window and Jocelyn woke up with a start. Rather grumpily he got out of the car, and was introduced by Mrs. Worthy.

"It's quite exciting to find another young man in the neighbourhood. I quite thought my Toby was the only one for miles. You must come over to Endbury and meet him."

Jocelyn, rumpled and blinking, did not appear to great advantage, and Mrs. Worthy could not but reflect that neither she nor Curtis had ever been asked to Endbury. But perhaps Lady Masters entertained only for her son. This took her thoughts straight back to Toby Masters and Miss Pussy Cleeve's insinuations, and she thought she perceived a motive for Lady Masters's excessive friendliness. Whether it was gratitude for her tact in diverting the conversation or whether it was a form of hush money, Mrs. Worthy felt that the motive was suspect and the friendliness insincere. And while they stood here talking, Curtis would be fuming for his tea.

"Come, Jocelyn," she said sharply, "it's getting late and I promised Uncle Curtis we would be home by five."

Few people had ever taken leave of Lady Masters so abruptly or, as it were, by proxy. But her talent for ignoring the unpleasant enabled her to carry it off.

"I mustn't keep you," she said graciously. "I expect poor Captain Worthy is longing for his tea. But you will come to Endbury, won't you? I'll telephone."

With smiles they parted. Mrs. Worthy started the car, destroying all Jocelyn's hopes of driving, and pulled out into the middle of the road, where she settled down to her usual speed of twenty-five miles an hour.

"Why did she call me Captain Worthy?" Jocelyn asked sulkily. "You haven't been saying I was a captain, have you?" He knew his aunt was not reliable in military matters.

"She didn't mean you, she meant your uncle."

"Surely after all these years she must know he's a major. And why did she keep on about her son and this Endbury place? I thought you said they were three old maids."

It was obvious Jocelyn thought he had been speaking to one of the Misses Cleeve.

"But I introduced you," Mrs. Worthy protested. "You must listen, Jocelyn. That was Lady Masters."

"You said, This is my nephew Jocelyn. I hadn't a clue. Who is she, anyway?"

Mrs. Worthy told him. She described the beauties of Endbury, which she knew only by hearsay, and she mentioned that Toby Masters had a bookshop in Bramchester.

"I think he comes home for week-ends," she said. "I expect she'll ask you over one Sunday—if she remembers. That will be very nice for you," she added, thinking that at least it would take him out for a few hours and save the Sunday joint.

"Aunt Gwennie?"

"Yes, dear?"

"Has Uncle Curtis said anything about the future?"

Mrs. Worthy sighed. They were almost home, it was late, and she did not feel it was the right time to discuss his future. "No, Jocelyn, I don't think he has decided anything yet."

"Did you ask him about South Africa?"

"I didn't think you were serious about South Africa."

"I wasn't," he replied. "I just thought it might be something to do."

That was the trouble with Jocelyn. The only ideas he had were quite childish, and when you pointed this out to him he would say he wasn't seriously thinking of it; it was just an idea. The idea of growing fruit in South Africa rubbed shoulders with the idea of being an interior decorator in London, and for both he was equally lacking in aptitude and enthusiasm. She would not have been surprised if he had suggested being an engine-driver or an explorer, and naturally she could not worry Curtis with these vague fantasies. It was not as if Jocelyn were longing to start work; indeed, it was seldom that she could get him to discuss the future, which made it all the more annoying that he should bring it up now when she was tired and anxious only to get home and give Curtis his tea.

"I'll talk to your uncle," she promised. "But I don't think he would like you to go to South Africa, and anyway, you know nothing about growing fruit and it would cost a lot of money. Couldn't you think of something to do in England—something, I mean, that you really could do? You see, Uncle Curtis is a very practical man, he would have had a wonderful career if it had not been for his health—I remember a general we knew in India—oh dear, what was his name? General—General—"

"Auchinleck?" Jocelyn said helpfully.

"No, dear, I'm talking about the last war. Anyway, it doesn't matter, but he told me that Curtis was a most methodical man, quite unusually methodical. Practical people are always methodical, you must remember that. So as I was saying—"

But the negotiation of the narrow turn into the gateway of Tor Quay silenced Mrs. Worthy, and then Jocelyn had to get out to open the garage doors. The discussion of his future must wait, for Major Worthy was standing at the door of the house and one glance showed her that something had happened to upset him.

Leaving Jocelyn to take the parcels out of the car she hurried towards Curtis. As she approached he looked twice at his watch, the second glance serving as it were to confirm his suspicions about the first.

"Here we are!" Mrs. Worthy cried brightly. "Such a tiresome afternoon—"

"Dentist take all your teeth out?"

"No, dear, that was this morning, but it was only a stopping."

"Thought you must have gone back for another dose."

"I'm afraid we are a little late, but I had to call at Box Cottage and Lady Masters was there, and—"

"Do I get any tea?"

Mrs. Worthy fled into the kitchen. They were not really very late; experience told her that this was something more than the justifiable annoyance of a man who has been kept waiting for a meal. She was not surprised when Major Worthy appeared in the doorway and waved a small printed ticket at her.

"Know anything about this?"

"What is it? If you could put it down, Curtis, and let me look—no, my glasses are in my bag. Could you read it to me, dear, and then I'll know if I know. Or wait, I'll just finish the bread and butter and then I'll get my glasses."

"Some charity!" said Major Worthy. He snorted. Mrs. Worthy said, "Oh, dear!"

If there was one thing Curtis disliked more than another it was a charity appeal. It was bad enough when they came by post, but then he could assuage his anger by tearing them in pieces and throwing them into the waste-paper basket. But sometimes people with tickets or little flags to sell, for missionary whist drives or church-school dances or other deserving objects, came to the house, and then it was her place to act as a buffer between Curtis and these well-meaning but misguided individuals.

Usually she bought tickets without telling him, for she did not like him to be thought grudging. Nor did he enjoy meeting the sellers of tickets, for it was one thing to express his feelings about a printed appeal and another to express them to some insistent woman jangling a collecting-tin. In such a case the feelings had to be restrained until he could release them on Mrs. Worthy, and it was clear that this was what had happened this afternoon.

"Oh, dear, who was it? What is it for?"

"Charity," Major Worthy repeated, as if all charities were equally opprobrious. "Some damned dance as usual."

"Is it in the village?"

"Can't even garden in peace. Said to her: 'It may be all right for you, but do I look as if I wanted to bumba?'" He laughed triumphantly. Jocelyn, who had come in with the parcels, laughed too. Major Worthy believed that his nephew had no sense of humour, and the discovery that he could see a joke after all put him in a better temper.

"What did she say?" Jocelyn asked with unusual interest.

"Said it was for a good cause. Phui!" exclaimed Major Worthy, blowing this last comment down his nose like an impatient horse.

"Well, it was kind of you to buy tickets, dear, and I'm sure she will be very pleased. Who was it?" Mrs. Worthy saw that the kettle was just coming to the boil. Tea would be ready in a minute, and after a cup of tea Curtis would feel much better. She was grateful to Jocelyn for laughing at the right moment, grateful but surprised, for, like her husband, she had thought poor Jocelyn had no sense of humour.

"One of the Coles, never know them apart. Tea ready?"

"Just give it a minute to draw properly. I expect it would be Laura Cole. The other one, Mrs.—dear me, what is her name? Anyway, the one who was Gillian Cole—doesn't do much in the village."

Hearing this, Jocelyn gloomily resigned himself to the probability that the girl he had seen in the garden was the married one. That was the way life treated him.

"Is the dance in the village?" repeated Mrs. Worthy. She was used to repeating her questions. Major Worthy believed that all women were much too inquisitive and should be discouraged, and since he was a methodical man he stuck to the rules even when the subject was a trivial one.

"Bramworthy," he answered tersely.

"Oh," said Mrs. Worthy, "now I remember! It should be very good, I forget what it's in aid of, but Mrs. Walker told me all about it. They've got a band coming from Bramchester and Malleys are doing the catering, and I promised her I'd take tickets because—oh yes, it's to help the Conservatives, so I knew it would be all right. Not that you and I will need to go, Curtis. I told her that. Our dancing days are over, I said. But Jocelyn can go—you can take the car, Jocelyn, and I must think of someone to ask as your partner. Let me see—"

"There's only one ticket," Jocelyn pointed out.

"Only one!" said Major Worthy. "One's enough, isn't it? D'you expect me to send the whole village? Come along, Gwennie. Do I get any tea, or don't I? Phui!"

CHAPTER SEVEN

MARLY HOUSE, which everyone denounced as both hideous and uncomfortable, stood on high ground on the Bramworthy side of the valley. The drive joined the Bramworthy road nearly opposite Box Cottage, and Wick Lane formed the southern boundary of the park. It was not a large park, and since some of the fine old trees had been blown down and others felled during the war, the house was easily visible from the lane.

It was a large, dilapidated, and perfectly plain house, rather like a child's drawing except that there were more windows. The door was exactly in the middle and the windows were spaced at equal intervals. The roof was hidden behind a parapet; and although this made it look as if the roof had been forgotten it also made the house look too tall and rather topheavy. The third story and the parapet had been added by Miles's great-great-grandfather; he it was who rebuilt the outside of the house, making all the windows the same size and removing various excrescences which offended his tidy mind. Unfortunately he neglected the interior, which remained much as it had been in the mid-eighteenth century.

Miles's grandfather had modernized it to the extent of installing a bathroom, drains, and an extravagant hot-water system. This had been done round about 1885, and since then civilizing influences had left Marly House untouched; for old Mr. Corton, Miles's father, believed that what was good enough for his ancestors was good enough for him. Miles was less rigid, but, as everyone knew, he had no money. So at Marly House there were still candles in the bedrooms and oil lamps downstairs, rats in the cellars, a Chinese paper in the drawing-room, and draughts everywhere.

Miles Corton would have been surprised to know that he was thinking of selling Marly at last. The Misses Cleeve were his nearest neighbours, but he was not in the habit of telling them his plans. However, he was forced to see a good deal of them, for not only was he their landlord, but he supplied them with milk and vegetables and took them to church on Sundays and sometimes to Bramworthy on market days. Or rather, he always took Miss Myrtle Cleeve to church and he never took her to Bramworthy if he could possibly avoid it. The other Miss Cleeves could please themselves.

On this Sunday, Miss Myrtle and Pussy Cleeve accompanied him. The parish church was at Bramton. Two generations ago the inhabitants of Bramton Wick had wished to have a church of their own and had got as far as erecting an ugly temporary building of corrugated iron, known as the Tin Church, where a curate from Bramton officiated on alternate Sundays.

But since the decline in church-going and the increase in cars and bicycles, the Tin Church had become redundant, and nowadays no one except Miss Myrtle thought that Wick needed a separate church. She, who as a child had read *The Daisy Chain* and pictured herself as a ministering angel, still hoped that one day through her efforts a new building would rise up, a stone building in the ornate Puginesque-Gothic style she so much admired. To this end she badgered the Vicar of Bramton, kept a collecting-box in the dining-room at Box Cottage—since her sisters would not allow her to keep it in the drawing-room, where visitors might be embarrassed—and wrote, whenever she thought of it, to the Bishop.

The Vicar of Bramton was new to the living, and at the end of the service he came to the door of the church and shook hands with his parishioners as they filed out. An old rector whom he had served as curate had told him that this was a good way of getting to know their faces.

It may be that the old rector had a brusquer manner than his imitator, or perhaps his parishioners were not so garrulous. The vicar soon found that this method of getting to know people took much longer than he had expected, and inside the church there was a certain amount of shuffling impatience among the people clustered about the door. The chattier members of the congregation lingered in the porch where the vicar had taken his stand, thus preventing the exit of those who would have been quite content with a brief handshake.

It was a fine chance for Miss Myrtle. The previous vicar had been difficult to talk to; he had developed a wonderful knack of avoiding, without seeming to avoid, her; he had always had meetings, visitors, or Boy Scouts requiring his instant attention. Of course he had done his duty, calling at Box Cottage once a month, but at Box Cottage her sisters had no compunction about interrupting or overruling her, and it had been hard to gain his interest.

Now as she came out into the porch she saw the face of the new vicar turned towards her, and she grasped at his outstretched, welcoming hand. Pussy, who had dropped her hymn book, was a little way behind.

"Good morning," the vicar said heartily. "Now this is—? I know your face already, but I can't put a name to it yet."

He laughed to fill in the gap, waiting to hear what her name was.

"Wick is a godless place," said Miss Myrtle. "How can the people worship if they have no church?"

"I beg your pardon?"

"The people of Wick have no church. They walk in darkness. We must labour to build them a church. The Bishop approves of it, but it is for us to bring it to pass."

Wick, thought the vicar. Wick, Wick. Where was it? He had been taken by surprise, and he was still so new to the district that he thought of Bramton Wick as being just a part of Bramton, so it did not occur to him that this was where the church was to be built.

"An appeal should be launched," said Miss Myrtle.

She had a compelling stare. Also, she still clasped him by the hand and he could not very well shake himself free.

"We must see about that," he replied, temporizing; for after all, she had said that the Bishop approved of this scheme and he was the last man to wish to offend a bishop. "Perhaps you would come and talk to me about it one day."

But she had heard that delaying phrase before.

"The work will not wait. The need is urgent. How can the godly rest when misery, want, and ignorance are at the very gates?"

"Quite, quite," he put in, with an ill-advised attempt to combine his two manners, the sacred and the secular. It was not successful, and she paid not the least attention.

"For years I have laboured at this task."

Two or three people squeezed past her and escaped from the porch, and some new faces appeared at the church door. But the vicar was still imprisoned by the firm handclasp and the unwavering stare. By now he had realized that she must be a little eccentric; if she had laboured at the task for years it could not be a new foible of the Bishop's. He felt defrauded and aggrieved.

"Let me tell you the story of Wick," she said. "Many years ago . . ."

There was a small disturbance at the back of the porch, a murmur of apologies as Pussy forced her way to the front. Miss Myrtle had a high-pitched voice, easily recognizable; it had penetrated to Pussy's ears and Pussy had come to put a stop to it.

"Excuse me," she said. "May I pass? Oh, thank you, Mrs. Walker." She arrived at Miss Myrtle's side and gripped her elbow. "Come along, Myrtle. Mr. Corton is waiting for us." So easily, so quickly, did she detach her that the vicar wondered why he had not done it himself. Automatically he extended his hand again, but she ignored it and with a brisk little nod she swept Miss Myrtle away. They are remarkably alike, he thought with dismay, foreseeing that he would have to be doubly on his guard in the future.

Miles Corton, who had been one of the first to leave the church, waited in the sunshine of the broad, empty street. Bramton, a sleepy place at any time, was now so quiet that it might have been under an enchantment. Only the voices and footsteps of the departing congregation broke the spell. Pigeons cooed in the churchyard elms; in the yard of the Cleeve Arms, across the street, an old man sat on a bench puffing at his pipe and watching the congregation with a superior air. Presently some people came to the cars parked in the middle of the street and drove away. Soon only Miles's car was left, and three or four bicycles leaning against the railing round the Cleeve Monument.

Laura Cole appeared at the lych-gate. She saw Mr. Corton standing by his car and came across to speak to him.

"Are you waiting for the Miss Cleeves?" she said. "They'll be ages. Everyone is having a nice chat with the vicar. I suppose he wants to get to know us."

"He should do it at some other time."

"Yes, think of all the Sunday joints. What about yours? I suppose Mrs. Epps is there—and I'm all right, it's Gillian's day for cooking. Oh, dear—" she broke off with a change of voice.

"Why, 'oh dear'?"

"Because I made a vow I would not talk about food or cooking or housework. Have you noticed how everyone talks about them all the time?"

"Not to me," Miles replied gravely. Laura laughed to herself. He was not a man from whom one would demand sympathy for domestic troubles.

"Then you're lucky and I won't break your luck."

But having said this she could think of nothing else to say. Everything seemed to be related to the banned subjects. She looked back at the lych-gate. A few more people came out, but not the Miss Cleeves.

"Well," she said, "I'd better be getting on."

"Are you alone?"

"Yes, I've got my bicycle."

"Then I can give you a lift to the corner of Wick Lane. It will save you the hill."

"But I've got my bicycle."

"Plenty of room on the back. You needn't worry about the car," he said, smiling. "It's quite used to bicycles."

Gillian would have said frankly that it was not the car she was worried about, but Laura was too kind-hearted to say this. They walked across to the Monument to fetch the bicycle. She hoped it would not get scratched.

The Monument was a square pedestal bearing the statue of a man in robes and a curly wig, holding in his hand a model of the New Bridge. On the side of the pedestal was an inscription.

In Pious and Honoured Memory
Of
Sir Alexander James Cleeve, Bt.,
Of
Cleeve Manor in this County.
A Just, Sagacious and Humane Man
Who
By his Liberal hand
And
By the exercise of his Abundant talent:
By draining the Marshes:
By building the New Bridge:
Brought prosperity to Bramton
And
Earned the Gratitude of his fellow men.
This Monument was erected by the inhabitants of Bramton
And
The Gentry of the Surrounding District.

Although both Laura and Miles were familiar with this inscription they lingered to read it again. The time-worn stately tribute to Sir Alexander James Cleeve never failed to touch Laura's heart, and now, forgetting the difficulties of talking to Miles, she said impulsively:

"When I read that and think of Pussy and Miss Myrtle and old Miss Cleeve I want to cry."

Miles grunted, not unsympathetically. She felt that he had understood her, though her words seemed to hang in the air like a foolish parody of her thoughts. He was still studying the Monument, standing with his head thrown back in the full sunlight of the empty square. Looking at him, Laura found herself matching him against the figure on the pedestal. Cleeve and Corton, dead benefactor and living man. The comparison, she thought, was not ridiculous. Miles was a tall man, he had strong features and an expression which, if not exactly sagacious or humane, suggested authority and intelligence. It was a face that could have looked out from the frame of a family portrait. Or perhaps . . .

At this instant Miles, conscious of her scrutiny, turned his head and asked why she was staring at him. Before she could stop herself she continued her musing aloud.

"I was just thinking you would look very well as an effigy on a tomb."

These arresting words, spoken slowly and clearly by the demon who sometimes prompted her, reduced her to unexpected blushes. Miles appeared considerably startled and stared at Laura as closely as she had stared at him.

"I mean"—she struggled to explain—"I mean, I was looking at the statue, and then I was looking at you—comparing you with the statue—" The explanation was hopeless; she looked neither at Miles nor at the statue, but gazed miserably at the ground, feeling the blush burning her cheeks, wishing she could seize her bicycle and hurry away from the accursed spot, but, as in a dream, rooted to the place where she was standing.

"I see," Miles said at length. "Thank you, Laura." But Laura was still dumbstruck and scarlet. He stepped forward and took hold of her bicycle. "We'd better get this on the car," he said calmly. "Here they come."

The frightful moment was over; the voices of the approaching Misses Cleeve released her from the spell.

Laura wished to sit in the back of the car. Miles was equally determined that neither Pussy nor Miss Myrtle should sit in front. This clash of wills was settled by the Misses Cleeve themselves, who scrambled into the back of the car, one after the other, with more agility than Laura had anticipated. She sat screwed round in the front seat, joining in their conversation with assumed interest. It was not necessary to say much, since the Misses Cleeve had plenty to say; the new vicar and the new church at Wick were the themes for a closely interwoven duet which continued until they reached the gate of Box Cottage.

There they found getting out of the car more difficult than getting in, and while Miles was extricating them Laura went round to the back and removed her bicycle from the luggage grid. The strap that had kept it there left a smear of grease on her gloves, and she at once noticed a new scratch on the handlebars.

But these minor mishaps did not matter compared with the necessity of getting away before she and Miles were left alone together. She felt ridiculously apprehensive lest he should re-open the subject of his resemblance to Sir Alexander James Cleeve.

Miss Myrtle, still flushed with the success of her approach to the vicar, left them abruptly and walked into the house, uttering no word of thanks or farewell. But Pussy lingered at the gate. Pussy liked company and considered herself a sparkling conversationalist. She blamed her sisters for the fact that so few people called at Box Cottage and that the few who came stayed such a short time.

Pussy's conversation was compounded of scandal about those who were not listening to her and malicious digs at those who were. Of the three sisters, she alone considered that being a Miss Cleeve gave her the right to sneer at those who were not Miss Cleeves, those upstarts whose ancestors were not commemorated on the marble tombs and worn brasses in Bramton Church.

Miles, of course, was not an upstart, but Pussy had other reasons for disliking him. He was their landlord, they were under an obligation to him, and she could not bear that a Cleeve should be under an obligation to anyone.

It was fairly clear that Miles did not enjoy holding the gate open and being made late for his lunch. This alone, apart from her love of conversation, would have encouraged Pussy to prolong her farewells. But she particularly wanted to speak to Miles; she had heard that his housekeeper, Mrs. Epps, had taken to drink, and the simplest way of learning more about this, or alternatively of doing Mrs. Epps a bad turn, was to ask him about it.

She began with a winning smile and an invitation to come in and try their parsnip wine.

"You too, Laura. Or do you only drink—what's that vulgar stuff—gin?"

"I hardly ever drink gin, it's too expensive," Laura answered. "I'd love to try your parsnip wine, but not just now, I'm afraid. It's getting late, and I—"

"Poor Laura, it's always 'getting late' when you come to Box Cottage," said Pussy, applying the screw.

Laura could not like Pussy, but she felt sorry for her, and her morbid fear of hurting people's feelings made her open her mouth to say that after all she couldn't bear to miss the parsnip wine.

But Pussy was speaking to Miles.

"On second thought, I withdraw the invitation. Parsnip wine is hardly your drink either, is it? I must save up and get a bottle of brandy, and *then* perhaps you'll honour us with your presence."

Miles Corton had a remarkably poor opinion of parsnip wine in general and of the Château Box vintage in particular, but it did not please him to be told he was addicted to brandy. He said shortly that he was practically a teetotaller these days. At this Pussy gave a cry of surprise.

"*Not* a brandy drinker?" she exclaimed. "Then where did the empty bottles come from? My dear Miles, it must be Mrs. Epps! I've heard rumours, you know, but then she's always seemed such a respectable woman—although once or twice lately, meeting her in the road, I've just *wondered . . .*"

Seeing that neither Miles nor Laura was going to ask about the empty bottles, she hurried on.

"I just happened to notice, the day the men came to collect for the salvage drive, what an extraordinary number of empty bottles they had, and all of them brandy bottles! Of course, it wasn't anything to do with me, but I was so surprised! I asked them where they all came from, and they said they came from Marly House."

With her head on one side Pussy peered up at Miles to see how he was taking it. He said nothing, and from the obstinate quality of his silence it was plain he was not going to gratify Pussy by confirming or denying her insinuation. A vague feeling that by standing up for Mrs. Epps she would be standing up for Miles against Pussy caused Laura to intervene.

"Probably the bottles had been there for years. I expect Mrs. Epps had a grand clearing-out for the salvage drive."

"Oh, no," said Pussy, "they were quite new bottles. Grocer's brandy, you know, not *good* brandy." Forgetting that this was the brandy she had accused Miles of being addicted to, she went on to say that Mrs. Epps's brother had drunk himself to death on methylated spirits, so what could you expect?

Laura, who had led a sheltered life, had never heard of anyone drinking methylated spirits, and said so, adding that it must taste horrible. "No worse than some of the other concoctions people pour down their throats," Miles rejoined unkindly. He was seldom unkind to the Misses Cleeve, whatever he thought of them, and this jibe at the parsnip wine escaped Pussy altogether, for she was still going on about Mrs. Epps's brother and the way these things ran in the family.

"You'd better be careful, lock up the wine cellar and so on, just in case. After all, you never *know*."

"No," he said, "but you can always find out from the salvage men."

Pussy put on her innocent little-girl look, the look which made her impervious to sharp answers or contradictions. She was not subdued; on the contrary she was inwardly elated, since it was plain to her that she had succeeded in exasperating her landlord. But before she could follow up her triumph Miles let the gate swing to and turned away, as if he did not care whether Pussy went back to Box Cottage or not.

"Jump in," he said to Laura. "I'll run you home."

"But I've got my bicycle."

Miles had only just noticed that she had removed her bicycle from the luggage grid. He looked at her and then said: "There's still plenty of room on the back."

It was an echo of their earlier conversation. That was how it had begun—the bicycle, the Monument, the effigy on a tomb. Laura suddenly realized that Miles too was thinking of that earlier conversation. He was laughing at her, she thought; and to her annoyance she felt herself blushing again. It was true that Toby often teased her, in what she imagined to be a brotherly way, but being teased by Miles—and in front of Pussy, too—was quite different. She could squabble, argue, and laugh with Toby on terms of perfect equality, but Miles made her feel a schoolgirl again, defenceless and absurd.

"Thank you," she said hastily, "but I'd rather cycle." Oh, dear, that was not what she had meant to say. It was a sort of shorthand contraction of her reasons—that it would be quicker than turning the car, that Miles would be wasting his petrol and upsetting Mrs. Epps by being late for lunch, and, of course, the inadmissible reason that she did not want to be teased.

However, it was too late to explain. Miles looked momentarily disconcerted, then he turned to say good-bye to Pussy, who was now inside her front gate, but still an intent spectator. Laura had a feeling that Pussy was interpreting their behaviour in her own extravagant idiom.

"Good-bye," she called, wheeling her bicycle into the road. "Good-bye, Miles. Thank you for the lift."

Coasting down Wick Lane, lapped in the calm beauty of a perfect summer day, she quickly forgot her confusion. By the time she turned under the railway bridge she had begun to laugh at herself and to wonder just what Pussy would make of it. Pussy's fertile fancy was capable of anything; perhaps she would construe Laura's blush and Miles's annoyance as Romance—not, of course, flawless, but brought to an untimely end by a quarrel. Pussy was a specialist in broken romances.

Laura had been so well brought up that her thoughts led on quite naturally from romance to marriage. She quickly forgot about Miles and Pussy and the disagreeableness of being teased. Instead, she remembered that this was the afternoon Lady Masters was coming to tea.

CHAPTER EIGHT

MRS. COLE sometimes felt vaguely uncomfortable about Mrs. Worthy. They were of the same generation, they lived not far apart, and she really ought to ask her to tea far more often than she did. Only there was the garden, which took up so much of her time, and on Mrs. Worthy's side there was an even greater encumbrance, although perhaps it was wrong to think of Major Worthy as an encumbrance when it was obvious that his wife, like a well-trained Eastern slave, regarded him as the light of her eyes and the lord of her life. No one else had ever been able to see Major Worthy like this, and Mrs. Cole disliked him as much as it was possible for her to dislike anyone.

She was not going to ask Major Worthy to tea. She had had him once and he had stamped round the garden criticizing everything, objecting to the slope of the ground, the shape of the lawn, and the profusion of evergreens; he had told her that creepers made the house damp and that the lilacs were in the wrong place. After tea he had taken out his pipe and without asking permission had proceeded to smoke it, filling her drawing-room with a cloud of peculiarly rank blue smoke. Mrs. Cole had no real objection to tobacco smoke, and she was prepared to admit that some of his criticisms were just; but she found his manners unbearable.

She rather liked Mrs. Worthy, which made her feel the more guilty about neglecting her. It did not occur to her that Mrs. Worthy might ask *her* to tea occasionally, for she quite understood that Mrs. Worthy was not a free agent. None of the Coles had ever been to tea at Tor Quay, and they had learned from Mrs. Trimmer, whose work as a "daily" made her a valuable source of information, that Major Worthy thought tea parties, or any other sort of entertaining, a waste of money.

"Cut a brass farthin' in 'alf, the Major would," Mrs. Trimmer said scornfully.

So Mrs. Cole did not feel aggrieved at never being asked back, and when she met Mrs. Worthy in the Wick Provision Stores and saw how carefully she priced everything, writing down all she spent in a tattered little notebook, and how determinedly she sought out the cheapest kind of biscuits, her sympathy for Mrs. Worthy overcame her natural inertia and she asked her to come to tea the following Sunday.

As it happened, her sympathy was misapplied, for Major Worthy never grudged spending money on food which was to nourish himself, and the cheap biscuits were being bought for Jocelyn, who suffered from night starvation. But Mrs. Worthy accepted the invitation, and it was not until she had left the shop that Mrs. Cole remembered that this was the Sunday Lady Masters was coming to tea.

It was very strange, she thought, she hardly ever asked anybody to the house without consulting the girls, and yet when she did it always seemed to clash with something.

It would be awkward if Lady Masters and Mrs. Worthy were not on good terms. She told Gillian about it. But Gillian, whose life in London had blunted her to the niceties of provincial etiquette, said cheerfully that it did not matter in the slightest.

"Let them both come. Even if they don't like each other it will be stimulating for them to meet someone new. And it will give you and Laura a change of partners."

Since Gillian was not going to be there she could afford to take it lightly. But then, she always took things lightly; too lightly, thought Mrs. Cole, who was gently perturbed about Gillian's casual meeting with Mr. Greenley and her coming visit to Cleeve Manor. She was not so foolish as to suspect him of being a villain with designs on her daughter; it was simply that the whole thing was irregular. No one had introduced them; no calls had been exchanged. Aware that times had changed, she kept these thoughts to herself. In any case she did not permit herself to criticize her dear daughters, who must always be allowed to know best.

The only difficulty was that sometimes their ideas of what was best differed. She had forgotten to tell Laura that Mrs. Worthy was coming to tea, and when Laura heard of it, which was not until after lunch on Sunday, she said at once that it was a pity.

"You know how rude Lady Masters can be. I don't want her being rude here, I want her to enjoy herself."

Gillian might have said that what Lady Masters most enjoyed was being rude, but Gillian had already gone upstairs to change her dress and do things to her hair and face.

"I want Mrs. Worthy to enjoy herself, too," said Mrs. Cole.

"Well, yes," said Laura, as if that did not matter so much, "is she bringing Jocelyn?"

"Dear me. I hope not. Oh, you mean that boy?"

"Yes, Mummy, you mustn't get them mixed up. We are sure to hear a great deal about both of them."

She was quite right. Mrs. Worthy had plenty to tell them about Curtis, and although they had heard most of it before, this did not prevent them from encouraging her, with questions, exclamations, and sympathy, to relate in every detail the glories of Major Worthy's military career, the praises of the General whose name she had unfortunately forgotten, the horrid catastrophe of the sunstroke in India, and the long pilgrimage from doctor to doctor in quest of health.

"And sometimes I think I was wrong to persuade Curtis to retire so young, of course I meant it for the best and as I said to him at the time health is more important than wealth. It's your *health* that matters, Curtis, I said, never mind about being a colonel—of course, he ought to have been promoted long before that, it was a great disappointment to him, but as the General said—the same general whom we knew so well in Rawalpindi, oh dear, it's strange I should have forgotten his name when we knew him so well and I used to darn all his socks for him . . ."

Mrs. Worthy, with none but encouraging interruptions, paused only to draw breath and take little sips of tea. She had the time of her life, Laura said afterwards; really Lady Masters was wonderful; she sat there lapping it up as if Mrs. Worthy had been a lady-in-waiting telling her about royalty.

But at the time Laura was rather worried about Lady Masters. The party had begun well. Not only were the guests acquainted, but Lady Masters was obviously well disposed towards Mrs. Worthy. It was only later, when they had settled down, that Laura became aware that something was wrong.

If it had been anyone else one would have said that she was depressed, but Lady Masters had never been known to be depressed. She was a woman who appeared impervious to common ills, and her habit of simply ignoring disagreeable events made you feel that as far as she was concerned they did not exist. As the mistress of Endbury, the biggest house in the neighbourhood—for Cleeve Manor, which surpassed it, had stood empty for many years before Mr. Greenley's arrival—she had become accustomed to take the lead wherever she went. She liked to direct the conversation, and would ruthlessly disregard or talk down any garrulous stranger who strayed from the chosen path. It was for this reason that Laura had felt so dubious about having Mrs. Worthy to tea on the same day.

Yet now she was positively glad of Mrs. Worthy's presence. For Lady Masters was strangely silent. She did not want to talk; she was quite content to sit there and let Mrs. Worthy do the talking—a proceeding so unnatural that Laura wondered if she could be ill. But she looked in perfect health. Then she wondered if it could be Toby who was ill. But no, his mother would have mentioned it, and in any case her constant care for Toby's health had never been known to interfere with her management of a tea party.

From wondering about Toby's health Laura was led on to wondering if he had done something to upset his mother. Since their talk together at Endbury she had known that Lady Masters was worried about Toby, and now, the more she looked at her, the more certain she felt that her silence, her unusual patience with Mrs. Worthy, were due simply to her being preoccupied with some problem which she could not ignore. It seemed to Laura that Toby was the only person who could create such a problem. Presently Mrs. Worthy, having completed the history of Curtis's life, began to talk about her nephew Jocelyn, and then Laura noticed that Lady Masters showed a more positive interest, especially when Mrs. Worthy complained that Jocelyn had no sense of responsibility.

"Of course, he's a dear boy. Curtis is very fond of him, and so am I. Curtis has done a great deal for him, as his father, Curtis's brother Armitage, died when he was quite a baby—Jocelyn, I mean, not, of course, Armitage—and my sister-in-law was left badly off. So as I was saying, Curtis is quite prepared to help him to get a job. But Jocelyn will keep on changing his mind, really he doesn't seem to care *what* he does, or whether he does anything at all."

"Young people can be very difficult," Lady Masters observed, and Laura thought she detected a note of genuine sympathy in this commonplace statement.

"Indeed they can."

Mrs. Worthy was about to inquire after Toby Masters, then she thought better of it, for an inquiry at this moment might have seemed rather pointed.

"I have been meaning to ask your nephew over to Endbury," said Lady Masters. "When I saw him at Box Cottage I told him I would telephone and arrange a time. I hope he has not thought me very remiss."

It was difficult for Mrs. Worthy. To say yes would be impolite, to say no would imply that Jocelyn did not care whether he went to Endbury or not. She murmured something unintelligible.

"My son will be at home next week-end," Lady Masters continued, "and I hope to have tennis. Perhaps your nephew can come then. Will you ask him to let me know? He can telephone in the morning, before eleven o'clock. I have a committee meeting in Bramworthy at half-past eleven." Having thus avoided the expense of a telephone call, she turned to Laura and invited her and Gillian to join the tennis party.

Laura accepted. She did not play tennis very well, but the Endbury tennis was not of a very high standard; she had only once met a good player there, and he having been so ill-bred as to complain of the softness of the balls had not been asked again.

Hearing that there were other difficult young people in the world, even in the restricted world of Bramton Wick, seemed to console Lady Masters. She began to talk to Mrs. Cole about the garden, praising it in quite a liberal way; she even asked to see it, and accompanied her hostess to the very edge of the boggy bit, where she stood for some time with her eyes screwed up visualizing the changes which were to be made next winter.

Meanwhile, Mrs. Worthy confided to Laura that Jocelyn was anxious to meet her and her sister. She had found this out only that morning, when Jocelyn had expressed an unusual solicitude for her safety and had offered to come and fetch her home from Woodside in the car.

"So I said to him, Don't be silly, Jocelyn, it's only just down the road, hardly a walk at all—and then I realized that he *wanted* to come."

"And is he coming?" Laura tried to express polite interest, but she felt inwardly that he sounded rather dull and she was glad to hear that Mrs. Worthy had said, No, Jocelyn, it would simply be a waste of petrol.

"But I wonder if you would be very kind, you or your sister, but I somehow feel that you would be best—of course, I'm sure he would be delighted to take you both, but then he can hardly take two partners, can he? The trouble is, I have only one ticket at present," said Mrs. Worthy obscurely, "but I'm sure I can get another. Why, of course, how silly of me, I can get one from you. It was you, wasn't it, who brought the tickets round? Curtis meant to buy two, but I'm afraid in the end, by some mistake, he only got one."

Laura said gravely that it was kind of Major Worthy to have bought a ticket at all, for he had told her that he did not care for dancing.

"Oh, but we shan't be going," said Mrs. Worthy. "Our dancing days are over. No, no, he bought it for Jocelyn, but as I said to him, poor Jocelyn can't dance by himself, and after all, it's his birthday next month and this dance will do as a little celebration, if only we can find him a partner."

Laura reflected that it was typical of all she had heard of Jocelyn that he should wait for his aunt to find a partner for him, and apparently be ready to accept whatever sort of partner she produced. She also foresaw that it would be herself, not Gillian, who would accompany Jocelyn to the ball. She had no excuse ready and the ball was some time ahead. Gillian would have wriggled out of it, but Laura was not such a quick thinker as Gillian and her habit of feeling sorry for people was an additional handicap.

At this moment Mrs. Worthy noticed the time, and like Cinderella she started up in dismay. To be sure it was not the stroke of midnight, but it was past the hour at which she had promised Curtis to be home. So the plans for celebrating

Jocelyn's birthday were left undecided. In a very short time, or at any rate in a shorter time than usual, Mrs. Worthy had expressed her thanks, taken leave of her hostesses, and set off up the hill. Lady Masters soon followed her, having only waited to explain to them that it was no good her offering Mrs. Worthy a lift as she could have taken her only to the crossroads, where she turned off for Endbury.

"She has not far to go," Lady Masters said, "and the exercise will do her good. I am always telling people they should take more exercise. Till Saturday, then, Laura dear." She got into her car and backed it swiftly out of the gate with a regal disregard for any other users of the lane. Fortunately the lane was empty. Laura walked back to the house, and as soon as she got indoors Gillian came tiptoeing down the stairs.

"Hist—have they gone?" she said.

Laura said yes, Lady Masters and Mrs. Worthy had gone.

"I got back twenty minutes ago, but I made him drop me at the gate and crept in by the back door. What a long time they stayed."

"Yes, I think it was quite a successful party. But tell me about yours. Was he nice? What's the garden like?"

"As dull as can be," said Gillian. "All exquisitely neat, not a weed anywhere, speckless gravel paths, unnatural grass, and hardly any flowers. Of course, he's terribly proud of it. It's full of rare plants and shrubs from all over the world—so rare and so delicate, poor things, that they look as if they might die at any moment. Some of them have to live under glass cloches and some have little straw igloos to tuck over them at night."

"How touching."

"Come on, I'll help you wash up."

"Tell me more. What's the house like, and is there a butler?"

"A rather sinister-looking man called Schmid—I think it was Schmid, but Mr. Greenley had a cold. Not a bit like a real butler."

Gillian was in high spirits. In spite of the sinister-looking butler and the dull garden, she had enjoyed herself.

"What did you think of him?" she asked. "His name, you know, is Thomas. Isn't he exactly like a Thomas?"

Laura had seen Thomas for only a few minutes, when he had arrived to fetch Gillian. He had been a little late. She had brought him in to be introduced and had then hurried him away almost at once, to get him out of the way of the tea party. It was difficult for Laura to say much about him after such a short interview, but she thought it safe to comment on his clothes.

"I *told* you," Gillian protested. "I warned you they'd be frightful. Worse today, actually, than when I saw him before. This must be his Sunday suit."

Giggling over Mr. Greenley's Sunday suit and listening to Gillian's gay description of his country house furniture (very black oak in the hall, very loud chintzes in the drawing-room, and an all-electric log fire in the library), Laura soon decided that Mr. Greenley need not be taken seriously. This was a relief to her. It was not that she had disliked him, but at their brief meeting he had impressed her as a person whom it would be easier to laugh at than to love, and it would have been awkward if Gillian had shown any symptoms of loving him.

But as a diversion, a new interest, he would do very well. Gillian, who always knew at once what was best for other people, was now planning a campaign by which his taste was to be radically reformed. He was to be re-educated, re-dressed, and made to take his proper place in the community. For he was really quite a nice creature, she insisted; and it was a shame that so much wealth, and such a fine estate as Cleeve Manor, should be devoted to the ridiculous purpose of making plants grow where Nature had not intended them to grow.

"Cleeve Manor is really a lovely house," said Gillian. "It's as beautiful as Endbury, and, of course, historically much more important. It's really absurd that it should all be wasted."

She gave Laura a mischievous look.

"It would do Lady Masters good to have a little competition, wouldn't it? She's never had to compete with anyone, with Cleeve being empty all these years and Miles not having any money."

"I can't quite see Mr. Greenley as a rival to Lady Masters."

"Oh, not for a long time," Gillian agreed gaily. "He would need a great deal of re-education first."

It did not occur to Laura that, for Cleeve Manor to compete with Endbury, Mr. Thomas Greenley would also need a wife.

CHAPTER NINE

THE SUMMER HAD obligingly come to stay, as Mrs. Trimmer put it, and a succession of fine hot days pleased everyone in Bramton Wick except a few dissidents, mostly farmers and besotted gardeners for whom the weather is never ideal. Mr. Greenley's gardeners had only to turn on the sprinklers and connect up the hoses, since Mr. Greenley had installed an elaborate irrigation system at Cleeve, but Mrs. Cole trudged backwards and forwards every evening between the water butt and the water-loving plants (which were all at the furthest possible distance from the water butt), and insisted on her daughters' doing the same.

When the garden was concerned she could be adamant. Gillian said that no one who was familiar with Mrs. Cole in her role of doting Mama would believe it possible she could speak so harshly to a child who had neglected the sweet peas, and Laura protested that it would have been better to have planted the marrows in the boggy bit where they could have drunk their fill, but Mrs. Cole only smiled and told them not to forget the delphiniums.

Major Worthy, whose gardening reflected his methodical mind, used Jocelyn as a labour-saving device. He had a large water tank on wheels, which could be filled by a short hose connected with the kitchen tap. Mrs. Worthy filled the tank, Jocelyn pushed it to where it was needed, and his uncle applied the water to the plants. Then Jocelyn went back for more water, while Major Worthy rested and smoked his pipe. This plan worked very well; not only did the garden get thoroughly watered, but it gave the boy something to do.

"Lucky you're not in South Africa," Major Worthy said, when Jocelyn showed signs of rebellion. "Driest place in the world,

I'm told. Have to do this sort of thing all the time there. Draw it out of a well, too. No kitchen taps on the veldt."

At Bank Cottage, Miss Selbourne and Miss Garrett were also lamenting the drought, though not on account of the garden. In theory they were both gardeners, but in practice they had long ago given up the struggle. They had no money for it, no time, and far too many dogs. When they had first come to Bank Cottage the paddock at the back had been set aside for the dogs' exercise ground, and the garden had been enclosed with wire netting and a neat little gate, to keep the dogs out. The previous tenants had left them a handsome legacy of wallflowers, daffodil bulbs, marigolds, and clipped box edgings to the beds, and for some time they had lived, as it were, on their capital, telling one another how lovely it was to have a garden, and taking the trouble to close the gate behind them each time they went up to the kennels.

But almost without their noticing it, the lovely garden grew full of weeds, the box edgings straggled, the wallflowers died. Soon afterwards the gate took to sticking and had to be propped open, and then the wire netting rotted away and they had no money to replace it. The dogs definitely preferred to take their exercise in the garden and had dug up most of the flowers, while the few daffodil bulbs which Miss Selbourne had lifted and put to dry, with the intention of replanting them in a window box out of reach of the dogs, had unfortunately been cooked by Miss Garrett, who mistook them for onions.

It was the railway embankment, not the garden, that made them hate droughts. It had not rained since the day of the dog show and the grass was now in a perfect condition for being set on fire by passing trains. They kept a bucket of water by the back door and two more near the kennels. After a train had gone by Miss Selbourne walked from end to end of the domain searching for signs of fire, while Miss Garrett abused the railway company, or alternatively their landlord, Miles Corton. It was a damn fool place to build a house, said Miss Garrett fiercely; he jolly well deserved to have it burnt down. But really neither she nor Miss Selbourne worried about the house. It was the dogs that mattered.

On Saturday, which was market day in Bramworthy, Miss Selbourne usually did the shopping. Housekeeping was not their strong point, but Miss Selbourne was the more domesticated. However, on this particular Saturday Miss Garrett woke up with a bad back. To Miss Selbourne's morning call of "Tiger, Tiger!" she responded with only a loud groan, which was the agreed signal for her friend to bring her cup of tea to her bedside.

"Oh, poor Tiger—not your back again?" she asked anxiously. Miss Garrett nodded and groaned and rolled her eyes, then, heaving herself up in bed, she stretched out a feeble hand for the tea. After she had drunk two or three mouthfuls her power of speech was restored, and she said gloomily that it had been giving her hell all night.

"You should have called me."

"No, old thing, you've got your hands full already. The house and this beastly fire danger, and only an old crock to help you."

"And it's Saturday," said Miss Selbourne, missing her cue. There was no food in the house, Tiger had forgotten the bread when she went into Bramton yesterday to get the dogs' meat, and they had opened the last of their emergency tins on the Sunday following the dog show.

"I'll do the shopping," Miss Garrett said nobly. "Yes, Bunty, I'll manage somehow, don't you worry. You stay here and watch the embankment."

It was obvious that Miss Garrett, crippled with a bad back, was in no condition for firefighting.

A little later she hobbled downstairs, dressed to go to Bramworthy. She was wearing her best corduroys, which were a bright mustard colour, and a green shirt which had once belonged to Toby Masters and which she had bought at a parish jumble sale. Unfortunately it had proved a little too small, for she was a big woman, so she had been forced to cut the sleeves short and wear it open-necked. As it was summer she had put on her sandals and her straw hat instead of gum-boots and a beret. The hat was perfectly plain and round, like an old-fashioned beehive, and made her appear even taller than she was.

"Are you sure you'll be all right?"

"Now don't you *worry*, Bunty. Tiger's an old campaigner. Tiger can take care of herself." Wolfing the last of the week's eggs, Miss Garrett seemed remarkably cheerful, so that Miss Selbourne had a moment's fleeting doubt about the bad back. It was a chronic complaint and any over-exertion would bring it on, but it usually needed hot-water bottles, hot whisky, and a day in bed to send it away again. A passing train deflected Miss Selbourne's thoughts, and when she returned from the inspection of the embankment Miss Garrett was about to depart.

"The ration books, Tiger!"

"I've got them. But I'll want some money, old girl. Better give me three quid, in case I see anything we need."

Anything we need for the dogs, she meant. Miss Selbourne fetched the money from her secret store. The trouble was, Tiger would never keep accounts, and money had a way of slipping through her fingers with nothing to show for it.

But Tiger looked so happy, sitting at the wheel of the shabby old car with Agnes and Leo beside her and her beehive hat cocked jauntily askew, that Miss Selbourne had not the heart to preach economy. Poor Tiger, she thought, she does so enjoy shopping, it's mean of me not to let her go oftener. And she quite forgave Tiger her little deception of the bad back.

"Tally-ho!" Tiger said joyously. Agnes and Leo gave tongue. The car roared away down the lane, and Miss Selbourne went back to clean up the kennels and brush and exercise the other dogs.

Just at the gates of Marly House, Miss Garrett overtook Laura Cole on her bicycle. She stopped to offer her a lift. It was not her habit to offer lifts to people, but the Coles, since Gillian's good deed on the day of the dog show, had been established in her mind as decent sorts and useful people to know.

"This way for the Skylark!" she boomed cheerfully. "Penny a mile, any distance! Tiger'll take you there and bring you back. All aboard!"

It was a hot morning and Laura was already regretting having to go to Bramworthy. It was one of the days when she wished very much they could afford a car. She was glad to accept Miss Garrett's offer.

After a moment's thought she wheeled her bicycle through the Marly gates and left it behind the hedge out of sight of the road, since this seemed a better plan than leaving it at Box Cottage and having to talk to the Misses Cleeve.

"Off we go!" said Miss Garrett, and off they went. The hedges bounded by, Agnes and Leo snuffled eagerly, the car rattled and rocked as Miss Garrett set herself to pass everything in front of them. Since it was market day there was more traffic than usual on the road. But as Miss Garrett remarked, they were a lot of old dodderers, half-asleep most of them—put them to drive an ambulance and they'd be sunk, abso-bally-lutely sunk. Half-asleep they might have been, thought Laura, but not by the time Miss Garrett, with loud blasts on the horn and fierce stampings on the accelerator, had hustled past them.

Mrs. Worthy, rudely chivvied from her position on the crown of the road, swerved so violently that she nearly ended up in the ditch. "A typical woman driver!" said Miss Garrett, observing the incident through the back mirror. Evidently she did not think of herself as a woman driver.

They were at the outskirts of Bramworthy when their progress was seriously impeded by a car which was going rather too fast to be overtaken but not fast enough to draw away from them. This was what Miss Garrett liked; this was what she had been waiting for. As a tiger, weary of thin chickens, might bestir himself to stalk a man, so did this Tiger set herself to stalk the blue car ahead.

Her chance came—providentially, Laura thought at first— outside the Bramworthy Hospital, when the blue car slowed down. Miss Garrett pulled out; with a roar and a hoot she thrust past it, only to find herself in imminent risk of collision with an ambulance which was turning across the road to enter the hospital gates. Laura, who had been taught that passengers should never scream, shut her eyes. When she opened them the danger was past; the ambulance, the hospital, and the other car were fifty yards behind them, and Miss Garrett was stopping for the coloured lights.

"That was Corton," Miss Garrett announced. "Silly ass, pulling up like that and not signalling."

"But he did signal," Laura said sharply.

"Flapped his hand up and down—how was I to know that meant an ambulance? If I hadn't kept my head—!"

Like most people who have had a fright, Laura found herself tense with unreasonable anger. It was not Miles's fault, and she resented the brusque way in which Miss Garrett spoke of him as Corton. But as she turned to denounce her she was suddenly struck by something deflated and oddly pathetic in Miss Garrett's appearance. The beehive hat no longer looked jaunty, the green shirt betrayed its second-hand origin. Miss Garrett sagged. It was plain that her fierce words were just a bluff, and that she knew she was in the wrong.

Laura's kind heart could not but be touched by Miss Garrett's humiliation. She changed the subject, and by the time they reached the market place she had succeeded in restoring her companion's good humour.

They arranged to meet at twelve o'clock, outside the library; or if she wasn't there, said Miss Garrett, Laura would find the car in the car park at the back of the Lamb and Lion.

Shopping in Bramworthy on a market day was a slow business. Apart from the crowded shops, you constantly had to stop and exchange greetings with friends and neighbours. It would have been better, thought Laura, if they could all have come to an agreement not to speak to one another on Saturday mornings, but no such agreement existed or was likely to exist in a community which included Mrs. Worthy and Pussy Cleeve. She managed to avoid Mrs. Worthy, but she could not avoid old Mrs. Hesford from Endbury Almshouses, who had been Mrs. Cole's cook in the days when she still lived at Endbury and employed a cook. At Endbury Mrs. Hesford had reached the peak of her career, and she spoke of it as an ex-monarch, from the depths of his dull exile, might speak of the palace where he once reigned.

"I hear her ladyship is going to make a flat in the west wing," said Mrs. Hesford.

Laura could not imagine why Lady Masters should want a flat in the west wing, but she knew that Mrs. Hesford, whose nephew was second gardener at Endbury, was extremely well informed about everything that went on there.

"I should think it would make a very nice flat," she said cautiously.

"In your grandfather's day, Miss, they used to say the west wing was haunted."

"So I've heard. But I never heard of anyone seeing a ghost."

"Oh, I don't say there's a ghost there *now*," said old Mrs. Hesford, plainly implying that no ghost would put up with her ladyship. "But I for one wouldn't care for to start pulling down walls and turning boudoirs into bathrooms that was built for them that's dead and gone."

Perceiving that Mrs. Hesford did not approve of the scheme, Laura said hurriedly that she was playing tennis at Endbury that afternoon.

"Yes, Miss, my nephew told me. Young Wallis mowed the lawn yesterday. In the old days, when your father was alive, it was always mown on the day. Most particular, your father was."

It was difficult to be nice to Mrs. Hesford without seeming disloyal to Lady Masters, and Laura was glad when the chiming of the Town Hall clock reminded the old woman that she had a bus to catch. She hurried through the rest of her shopping, fearful of being late for her rendezvous with Miss Garrett, but when she got back to the library Miss Garrett was nowhere to be seen. She waited until well after twelve, and then went off to look for the car behind the Lamb and Lion.

Inside the Lamb and Lion, comfortably installed in the saloon bar where they didn't object to dogs, Miss Garrett was celebrating a meeting with a dear old pal whom she had not seen for nearly thirty years. She had bought about half the things on the shopping list and the rest would have to wait, for a reunion like this did not happen every day. Right out of the blue, just on the corner of Hallgate, where she was about to cross the road, a voice had cried: "Tiger!" At first, seeing a grey-haired stranger waving to her from a passing car, Miss Garrett had looked blank, but the next instant the sound of her own name, coupled with that brief glimpse of a face framed in a Dolly Sister bob with a heavy fringe over the eyes, had touched a spring in her memory.

"Shrimp!" she yelled happily, causing twenty heads to jerk round for another glance at the fishmonger's bare slab. With a smart tug at the dogs' leads she made after the car, dragging Leo away from a lamppost at what must have been a highly inconvenient moment. The car had already pulled up, but as it had pulled up in the middle of the street their first excited cries were soon interrupted by impatient hootings and tootings from the cars behind. "Can't park here, old bean," said Miss Garrett. She opened the door and heaved herself and the dogs inside. "Drive on, Macduff," she cried. "All aboard for the Lamb and Lion. This needs celebrating!"

So here they were, happily celebrating on whisky and ginger ale. It was certainly Miss Garrett's lucky day; not only was there whisky in the bar, but she had the money to pay for it. And her dear old pal Shrimp Fisher looked distinctly prosperous, and was just as ready as ever to cry: "This one's on me!" No hanging back, no keeping the whisky locked up or saying they couldn't afford it.

"D'you know who I'm living with?" she asked, when she had made this comparison in her mind. "Bunty Selbourne."

"Not *our* Selbourne?"

Those who hadn't had nicknames had only had surnames. It was perhaps by an extension of this habit that Miss Garrett spoke of her landlord as Corton.

"Tiger, how simply fantastic! I'd simply love to see Selbourne again."

"So you shall, old thing. She'd never forgive me if I didn't bring you along."

"Gosh, the last time I saw Selbourne must have been in Rouen. . . . Do you remember those awful French billets?"

"Do you remember when Spotty Kempson stayed out all night . . . ?"

". . . No, no, Tiger, this one's on me!"

While all this was going on, Miles Corton came into the bar to have a drink with a man he knew well but seldom met, a man who also farmed his own land but who lived nearer Bramchester than Bramworthy. It was in its way a reunion, but as they were both hard up they drank beer, and they talked of crops, cattle, and the Ministry of Agriculture, without once recalling the days when they had fished or shot together, or the more remote days when they had enjoyed the Spartan discomforts of the same public school.

Since they were both farmers they had been forced to remain on their farms during the war, and although this had been classed as essential service it did not provide them with a store of reminiscences, picturesque and practically inexhaustible, such as were now being exchanged between Miss Garrett and her friend. The room was quite full, and although Miss Garrett was sitting almost at Miles's elbow she did not observe him; she had embarked on the story of her life, and was telling Shrimp all that had happened to her since 1919.

But Miles noticed her. Indeed, it would have been difficult to overlook Miss Garrett and her friend in their present mood of hilarity. He noticed that they were drinking whisky, and could not avoid hearing allusions to ambulances, convoys, and damn good drivers.

Laura had been sitting in Miss Garrett's car for over half an hour when she looked up and saw Miles Corton coming towards her. He wished her good morning and asked, rather unnecessarily, if she was waiting for Miss Garrett.

"Yes, I am. I can't think what's happened to her. She said she'd meet me at twelve."

"She's forgotten you."

"Well, she can't have forgotten the car."

"My dear Laura, she can. She has. She's sitting in there having a wonderful session with a woman who is, I'm thankful to say, a total stranger to me."

"Not *Tiger*?" Laura exclaimed. "Oh, Miles, I'm sure you're wrong. I don't think she drinks."

Gillian would have known better, but Laura was thinking of the spinsterish, dog-ridden interior of Bank Cottage. The corner cupboard had never been unlocked for her, and she imagined that Miss Selbourne and Miss Garrett lived on bread and jam and cups of cocoa.

Miles laughed and said he would hardly be likely to mistake anyone else for Miss Garrett.

"Well, I wish I'd known. I might have gone in and joined them instead of sitting out here all this time."

"I think you'd have felt a little out of it. They're in full cry after the splendours of the past."

"The war?"

"The last but one."

"That's what I meant. Miss Garrett is always reminiscing about it. It's rather pathetic."

"Nonsense, Laura," he said, smiling. "Amusing, if you like, or tedious for an impatient man like myself. But not pathetic."

"I suppose you would agree with Gillian. She says I waste my time being sorry for people."

"I only said you need not be sorry for Miss Garrett. And if you're in a hurry to get home you'd better come with me."

"Perhaps I'd better. It's very late, and we're playing tennis at Endbury this afternoon."

Although Miles declared that Miss Garrett would not miss her, Laura felt bound to run back to the Lamb and Lion to tell her she was going. Tiger greeted her heartily and asked her to have a drink, but it was evident that Miles was right and that she had forgotten all about their arrangements and was in no hurry herself to return to Bank Cottage.

"I take it all back," said Laura, settling herself in the car beside Miles. "Goodness, if you hadn't been there I might have sat waiting for her till closing time."

"And faced a dangerous journey afterwards. Or are you quite inured to dangerous journeys by now?"

"Oh, dear, I hoped you hadn't noticed that."

Miles said grimly that he couldn't help noticing it, and added that it was not the first time either. Laura herself had been angry and frightened, but now, with perverse feminine loyalty, her sympathy swung back to Miss Garrett.

"Poor thing—" she began. 'Oh, well, I suppose not poor thing. It was a bit careless of her. But truly, Miles, it was just an accident."

"Very nearly an accident, and no thanks to her that it wasn't. Don't accept any more lifts from that woman, Laura. She's not safe."

"Well, she's been driving for years, and nothing's happened to her yet."

"Something will happen to her one of these days, and I don't want you mixed up in it," he said.

Laura was a little surprised that he should show such concern for her safety.

CHAPTER TEN

"I WISH WE had a car," said Laura. It was not far to Endbury, and the road was level except for one hill approaching the lodge gates. It was while they were pushing their cycles up this hill that Laura wished they had a car.

"We might have cadged a lift from Jocelyn," said Gillian. "I suppose Mrs. Worthy will let him have their car to come in."

"I don't like cadging lifts."

Gillian laughed. She had already heard about the expedition to Bramworthy. "Well, you didn't cadge that one," she said. "It was thrust on you. Think of the pleasure people get from giving us lifts. It makes them feel superior and noble-hearted."

"It's not their feelings I'm thinking about, it's my own. Somehow, getting a lift always seems to involve me in some awkwardness."

"I haven't noticed that myself," said Gillian, who never noticed awkwardnesses anyway. "Of course, it's sometimes alarming. Mrs. Worthy goes too slowly, and Miss Garrett much too fast. Miles is a good driver, and so is Toby. Miss Selbourne's all right, and I suppose Lady Masters is really, though she's a bit ruthless sometimes. You'd better avoid Miss Garrett if she makes you feel awkward."

Laura looked at her sister and said nothing. They reached the top of the hill and turned into the Endbury drive.

The rest of the tennis party was already assembled by the lawn. Lady Masters came forward to meet them and introduced them to Jocelyn, who was so exactly what they had supposed him that the introduction seemed almost superfluous. The rector's daughter from Bramworthy, and the young curate to whom she was engaged made up the party. The rector's daughter was a girl called Isabel Lumley, and people who could not think what to say about her fell back on the declaration that she was very clever and capable. She looked as if she would make a good wife for a parson, and her fiancé, who was evidently devoted to her, was generally held to have made a wise choice; for not only was Isabel clever and capable, but she was the niece of a bishop.

"You four begin," said Lady Masters. "Isabel, Laura, Henry, and Captain Worthy."

Jocelyn opened his mouth to disclaim the captaincy, but his hostess had turned away. The chap called Henry, taking it for granted that he would partner the girl called Isabel, was spinning a racket. "Heads," said Jocelyn. "Rough, I mean." It was smooth. Henry said he would serve, and Laura, knowing that Jocelyn was a stranger to the territory, made the choice of ends. It seemed to Jocelyn that no one was paying the least attention to him, and for this all too familiar situation he had a ready-made phrase, a phrase which he now repeated to himself as he followed Laura across the court.

"Just my luck," he thought, thereby absolving himself from the need to take action—except, of course, the action necessary for the game. He was partnered by Laura and not by the pretty Gillian; and Gillian was, as he had surmised, the married one.

He had lost the toss. He had been mistaken for a captain—probably Aunt Gwennie's fault—and had missed the chance of putting things straight.

These reflections, although they did not distress him, disturbed his concentration. None of the players were very good, but Henry had a fierce, commanding service which looked much better than it was. Jocelyn quite failed to master this service, and he and Laura were severely beaten.

"Chap's not much good," Toby observed to Gillian, who was sitting beside him in a swinging hammock. "Keeps giving me dirty looks, too."

Gillian had already noticed that Jocelyn admired her, and she correctly interpreted his frequent glances at Toby as indicating envy. It was pleasant to be admired, it passed the time and added to the lustre of the summer day. She thought Jocelyn a callow and undistinguished youth, but not impossible. By this she meant not incapable of improvement. He needed tidying up, he needed to be taught manners, and not to sit with his mouth open. With quite disinterested motives Gillian resolved to teach him these things.

Like Gillian, Isabel Lumley believed that people were capable of being improved. But unlike Gillian she was direct, downright, and impatient for quick results. As soon as the set was over she approached Jocelyn and told him that he had a good forehand but that his backhand was all wrong.

"You take it off the wrong foot," she said. "I used to do it that way myself, until Henry taught me. Don't mind my telling you—I tell everyone, because it's such a simple thing and it does make all the difference."

Isabel was used to instructing and advising people. She adopted a bluff, friendly manner that could not cause offence, and behind this shield she advanced steadily, armed with remorseless arguments. Gillian and Laura, and even Toby, felt rather sorry for Jocelyn, but it took Lady Masters to say boldly:

"Come here, Isabel dear, and leave poor Captain Worthy in peace. He's not a wolf cub."

Isabel at once stopped showing Jocelyn how to place his feet and came quite meekly to join her hostess. She had perhaps forgotten that Lady Masters could do all the instructing that was wanted at Endbury. A new set was soon arranged, which left Jocelyn and Isabel to sit out, but Lady Masters sat between them and directed the conversation.

Presently it was time for tea. They would have tea in the dining-room, said Lady Masters; men always preferred it—they hated balancing cups and plates, and Toby was quite a menace in a drawing-room. She spoke in affectionate mockery, but she gave him a look which was not at all affectionate. Had Toby been a less dutiful son he might well have described it as a dirty look, but he grinned amiably and suggested that his mother had better revive the custom of nursery tea, with bibs for messy feeders.

"There's something about nursery tea, don't you think, Laura? Downstairs bread and butter never tastes the same. And Nannies have such a wonderful knack of combining discipline and gaiety."

They were walking back across the lawn. Laura looked up at the two windows on the top floor with their nursery bars. She and Gillian had not liked Toby's Nannie, who had been strict and fussy and dignified, but she knew that Toby had been very fond of her. And Nannie, for all her strictness, had adored him. Even as a child Laura had understood that. Toby in the nursery had been important, the centre of his world, and probably he had been spoiled and petted to his heart's content, when other children were not present to remind Nannie of her position.

Thinking of this, while she chatted to Toby about nursery teas, Laura realized that although Lady Masters adored him too, it was a very different sort of adoration. Lady Masters was the centre of her own world, and the only importance Toby had was as a sort of accessory to Lady Masters's importance. No wonder he was in love with the past.

The dining-room was the worst room in the house, high and narrow, and overshadowed by a fine cedar which had been planted much too near its windows, but which was now too big to move and too famous to destroy. It was a panelled room, and at one end was a massive sideboard loaded with silver. Ponderous tankards, salvers designed for a stalwart butler, a loving cup heavily and hideously embossed, suitable for a banquet, and numerous smaller objects were crowded together on the sideboard without much attempt at arrangement. Lady Masters was very proud of these emblems of prosperity, which she had inherited from her papa, and she was not pleased when Jocelyn, with a misplaced effort at politeness, asked Toby if he had won all those cups and things. She answered before Toby could speak, and her sharp scorn imposed a gloom on the party which even Henry's hearty laugh could not dissipate. After tea she punished Jocelyn by leaving him to sit out and watch the tennis by himself, while she carried Laura off for a walk round the garden.

As soon as they were alone Lady Masters became much more genial. She dismissed Jocelyn, with a laugh, as that poor ignorant boy, and even went so far as to admit that she had perhaps been rather hard on him.

"Young people of his sort have no chance to learn about old things," she said. "You have only to look at Mrs. Worthy's house. Ugly, machine-made stuff, art pottery, and all those vulgar Indian gods! The name alone—! Imagine calling a house Tor Quay when it isn't even in Devonshire, and nowhere near the sea!"

Laura agreed that it was an unsuitable name.

"Now you, Laura, are fortunate. Although Woodside is so damp, and such small rooms, you have been brought up among beautiful old things. Your taste has been properly formed."

"But I'm afraid it hasn't. I'm terribly ignorant about furniture and china. Gillian says it's because I'm so bad at dates."

"My dear child, I'm not talking about dates. Expert knowledge—Chippendale, Hepplewhite, all that sort of thing—is not necessary, unless you propose to keep an antique shop. What *is* important is to know the good from the bad, to be able to appreciate the difference between some horrid little suburban villa and—all this."

It would be difficult to confuse them, Laura thought, following the imperious sweep of her hostess's arm. The house, from this aspect, appeared very large. The west wing, which was the surviving part of an earlier building, made an angle with the main block, and an old vine covered half the sheltered wall, enhancing the beauty of rose-red bricks and stone mullions. They gazed at this beauty in silence. Laura was gratified to know that Lady Masters thought her sufficiently cultured to appreciate Endbury. After all, Endbury had once been her home.

"The west wing is in some ways the most satisfying part of the house," said Lady Masters.

"Is it true that you're turning it into a flat?"

It was the demon in Laura who said this, the demon who spoke before she was ready to speak, and whose speech almost invariably involved her in awkwardnesses. The demon's words were always loud and clear, so that it was impossible to disown them. Lady Masters turned and stared at her.

"And who told you that? Pussy Cleeve?" She looked so angry when she mentioned Pussy's name that Laura was terrified. But when she spoke of her meeting with old Mrs. Hesford, Lady Masters calmed down.

"Mrs. Hesford is a great gossip," she said, "but one can't blame her, poor old thing. After all, she simply lives for Endbury."

"I'm afraid you must think me a gossip, too," Laura said unhappily.

"No, no, dear child, why should I? And it's quite true that I'm thinking of turning this wing into a separate dwelling. Not a flat, Laura, it would have an upstairs and a downstairs. The whole wing, do you see?—from there."

"It would be charming," said Laura. She was dying to know more.

"But nothing is decided yet. I had an architect down the other day, my sister's architect, much better than the Bramchester man, and I showed him what I wanted and asked him to get out an estimate. He told me I should need a licence, but I don't suppose there'll be much difficulty about that." Lady Masters, who was accustomed to getting her own way in everything, waved her hand to show how easy it would be to get the licence.

"And if you do build it, will you—I mean, are you going to let it?"

Laura would not have dared to ask the question if she had not felt that she was being invited to ask it. Lady Masters had spoken quite freely, and it seemed as if she were anxious to say more. She had quite got over her anger, which had been directed solely against Miss Pussy Cleeve, and now she took Laura's arm and drew her gently but firmly towards a wooden seat at the end of the terrace.

"Let's sit here in the sun."

When they were settled, Lady Masters looked rather mysterious. "Now, Laura," she said, "I don't want this to go any further, but Toby is thinking of giving up his bookshop."

"Is he?" Laura could not forget that she had recently urged Toby's mother to make him stick to his job.

Lady Masters remembered it too.

"Yes," she said, "but you are quite right. Toby will have to settle down. It is a pity that the bookshop will not do."

"But wouldn't it? If he just—"

"No. The bookshop is quite unsuitable. Young people like you and Toby are not always the best judges, Laura. I blame myself in the first place for allowing him to take it on. His partner is quite brilliant, but my dear, such a dreadful little man. And such dreadful friends—whom poor Toby, of course, has had to get to know and pretend to like. Quite, quite unsuitable!"

Laura made a sympathetic face.

"The other day," Lady Masters continued blandly, "he brought some of them over here. Andrew Baker—that's his partner—and his aunt, and a cousin of his, who works in a pet shop near Toby's shop. I can see that he had to ask her, as she is Andrew's cousin. Quite a pretty little thing, and probably excellent at her work, but at Endbury—no!"

Remembering how Jocelyn had been treated, Laura could not but feel sorry for Andrew's cousin.

"As you know, Laura, I do not believe in interfering with young people. I am not possessive. I want nothing but Toby's happiness. But I must say that after seeing these people I was upset. It seemed to me that Toby was in the wrong environment. He's so easygoing—so ready to like anyone."

"He is certainly very easy to get on with," said Laura, feeling that she ought to say something for Toby.

"I was upset. I thought it over for some time, and finally I talked to him about it, on Sunday night before he went back to Bramchester."

Lady Masters paused. She was evidently reviewing the talk she had had with Toby.

"He admitted that he found the bookshop rather boring," she said. "I think you knew that, didn't you?"

"Well—he said something about it once, but I wasn't sure if he meant it. He talked, then, about farming."

Lady Masters gave her a quick appreciative nod, as if she had said something exceptionally intelligent.

"Exactly, Laura. He mentioned it to me. I would never have suggested it, for I am the last person to force my ideas on anyone. But what could be better? The Home Farm is let at present, but I expect I can come to some agreement with Manley. Toby will live at Endbury, which is as it should be, and yet he will have something to do, which he needs. All men need something to do, Laura. It is very bad for them to be idle."

"It sounds an excellent plan," said Laura. So it did; but it did not explain why Lady Masters was thinking of making a dwelling in the west wing.

"I am glad to have had this little talk with you," Lady Masters said affably. "I know you will keep it to yourself for the present. It will all be public when we come back from Scotland."

"Are you going to Scotland?"

"Yes. I had not meant to go away again this year, but poor Toby is quite distressed because Andrew Baker objected to his giving up the bookshop. Toby is very sensitive, you know, and it would do him no good to go on working there in such an uncomfortable atmosphere. So I am taking him up to stay with my sister at Glen Bogle, while my solicitor deals with what do you call it—dissolves?—the partnership. I wrote to her last week, and we shall be starting on Wednesday."

Laura could not help admiring Lady Masters. Her solicitor was not the only person who could deal with things. She could not help feeling, too, that this conversation marked a great advance for herself. It might be that Lady Masters merely needed a confidante, but it was gratifying that she should have been chosen for the role.

"I think it's a very good plan," she repeated. "I do hope Toby will like farming."

Lady Masters laughed in a remarkably good-natured way.

"You mean, you hope he'll stick to it. Oh, but he must. I can't have Toby making himself ridiculous."

Laura had the feeling which she had had once before, that Lady Masters was hurt, as well as annoyed, by Toby's frequent failures and new beginnings.

"I'm sure he'll settle down now," she said encouragingly.

"I hope so, too," said Lady Masters. "I hope he'll settle down, and perhaps get married. I think it would be a very good thing for Toby."

By this time they were walking back towards the tennis lawn. Without waiting for a reply, Lady Masters began to speak about the roses; the roses, she said, had done very well indeed this year, but then there were no roses anywhere like the Endbury ones. Laura answered quite at random, and her praise of the Endbury roses was perhaps a little over-zealous. For she had suddenly been given the reason for the alterations to the west wing.

Either Lady Masters herself, or Toby and his bride would inhabit it.

Lady Masters thought of everything.

"Rather a dull party, wasn't it?" said Gillian. "Still, the tea was better than usual. Poor Jocelyn, I copied your example and felt quite sorry for him."

"Did you? Oh—because he got snubbed."

"He certainly did get snubbed. She was in great form today."

"I suppose she was."

Gillian looked sharply at her sister. "Wake up," she said, "you're making me ride in the ditch. What was she talking about, all the time you were with her after tea?"

But Laura was spared having to answer this, for as they turned into their own lane they saw a large, opulent-looking car parked outside their gate.

"Thomas!" Gillian exclaimed. "I wonder how long he's been here." She got off her bicycle and rummaged in her bag for her powder compact.

"Poor Mummy—having to talk to him."

"Don't be silly, Laura. Thomas isn't poison."

Reassured about her appearance, which was remarkably attractive considering that she had played tennis all afternoon and cycled home from Endbury, Gillian advanced towards her home.

CHAPTER ELEVEN

SEPTEMBER WAS A quiet month. Strangers might have thought that all the months were quiet, but for residents the seasons were distinguishable. In summer there were tea parties, tennis parties, and picnics, also the dog show, the local flower show, and the County Agricultural Show at Bramchester. In winter the tea parties continued, with due allowances for the weather, and there were occasional concerts and other entertainments got up for charity at Bramworthy, and the annual all-grades party at Endbury, which took place at the New Year.

September marked the division between summer and winter activities. The dog show was in the past, the harvest festival to come. In the meantime, with Lady Masters in Scotland and the Worthys at Eastbourne for a fortnight, things seemed quieter than usual.

It was at this time that Miss Cleeve decided to have a garden party. By having it now she avoided having Lady Masters, and yet was able to send her an invitation and so cancel the debt for three peaches, two baskets of strawberries, and several pounds of black currants, which Lady Masters at various times had delivered at Box Cottage.

Miss Cleeve was in the habit of repaying her debts by hiring a car and making a series of calls, once a year, on those of her neighbours who deserved the honour. The garden party was an innovation. She had read in the local paper that Mr. Thomas Greenley had consented to open the gardens at Cleeve Manor to the public, in aid of the district nurse, and this had reminded her of the garden parties there in the old days, when she was a young girl.

A garden party in those days had been a great occasion, and people had come from everywhere within driving distance. She remembered the long, fluffy dresses, the parasols, the marquee, and the band of the Volunteers playing on the lower terrace, with herself and Myrtle and Matty in white silk frocks and black boots, speaking only when they were spoken to, but enjoying themselves very much. She thought about it for a long time, and then she announced to her sisters that she would give a garden party at Box Cottage this year.

Pussy and Miss Myrtle made no difficulties. Pussy enjoyed talking to people and Miss Myrtle welcomed the chance of collecting some money for the cause nearest her heart. (When the great day came Miss Cleeve took the collecting-box away and hid it under her pillow, but naturally Miss Myrtle could not foresee this.) Neither of them remembered so clearly as Miss Cleeve the glories of former garden parties—the band, the marquee, the ice-cream—and it seemed quite reasonable that they should give one at Box Cottage. A garden, something to eat, and a fine day: what more was needed? They left it all to Miss Cleeve, who wrote the invitations in a sloping, spidery hand and posted them herself in Bramworthy.

She could not ask as many people as she would have liked. Box Cottage had only a small garden, a narrow lawn in front, with two flower beds, and at the back another lawn, seldom mown, with a clothes post at each side and a line stretched across it for the washing. Beyond this was a small enclosure which had once been an orchard, where some old apple trees and an uninhabited tumble-down henhouse took up much of the space. Miss Cleeve limited her invitations to people in the immediate neighbourhood. Lady Masters, of course (but she would not be coming), the Vicar of Bramton and the Rector of Bramworthy, the Coles, the Worthys, Miles Corton, and one or two more. To these she added a few remembered names, familiar to her in the past, of old acquaintances whom she had not seen for a long time.

Some of the people to whom she sent invitations did not reply, because they were dead or had long since left the district. "Very rude," said Miss Cleeve, crossing them off her visiting list for ever.

The invitation to Mrs. Cole included both her daughters. Gillian laughed and said it would be terrible, she couldn't bear it; Mrs. Cole and Laura might go if they pleased, but they must refuse for her. But the next day she went over to Cleeve Manor again, to meet Mr. Greenley's sister who was staying there, and when she came back she told Laura that Mr. Greenley had been asked to the garden party.

"How odd," said Laura. "I'm sure they've never met him."

"I suppose he was asked because he lives at Cleeve Manor. Anyway, he has accepted."

"But will he like it?"

"I warned him it might be rather peculiar. But he wants to see them. He's beginning to take an interest in the neighbourhood now, because I've told him so much about it."

"Did you tell him what to wear?"

Gillian laughed. "Give me time. Thomas has hardly reached the stage of trying to please me yet."

Had she overheard these words, Mrs. Cole might have found something to worry her. But Laura had come to think of Thomas simply as a new occupation for Gillian, a worthy cause like missions or the organ repair fund, only more amusing for Gillian who did not care for impersonal causes. In any case, Laura now had an interest of her own which rather blinded her to other people's interests.

Mrs. Cole was only told that Gillian had changed her mind. Luckily, she had forgotten to post her reply to Miss Cleeve, so she was able to tear it up and write a new one.

It was now only a week to the garden party, and Miss Cleeve began to make preparations. She wrote out a list of the people who had accepted. She sent Pussy and Myrtle up to the attic to unpack a trunk that had stood undisturbed for more years than they cared to remember. She interviewed Mrs. Trimmer and told her to send Trimmer up to attend to the garden, and she also told her that she would be needed for four whole days the following week instead of just Tuesday and Friday mornings.

If it had been anyone else, Mrs. Trimmer would have refused, but she was Bramton born and the name of Cleeve still meant something in Bramton; besides, the garden party had now begun to be talked about and she liked a bit of excitement. So she gladly agreed to all Miss Cleeve's demands, and quite forgot to inform her other employers of the new arrangements.

Finally, Miss Cleeve made a special visit to Bramworthy. She would not trust her sisters to go, and anyway, by this time they were much too busy.

Pussy and Myrtle had not realized, when they agreed to having a garden party, what a lot of work it would entail.

For her visit to Bramworthy, Miss Cleeve hired a car. The man who drove it, like Mrs. Trimmer, was Bramton born and had been brought up to respect the name of Cleeve, but his respect was sorely tried when she proceeded to buy pots of plants—chrysanthemums, variegated evergreens, late roses, and asters—and had them all loaded into his precious car without a thought for the upholstery. Protected by her deafness, impervious to sarcasm or protests, she sat beside him, looking more like a toad than ever, while the back of the car grew to resemble a florist's van. At each shop she sent him in to fetch the manager, for she was lame and did not intend to tire herself by walking about, nor would she condescend to do business with any underling. If the manager was engaged, they waited.

When he finally got her back to Box Cottage the driver's spirit was broken, and he made no further protests when she told him to unload the plants and parcels and carry them round to the back door. Having paid for the car, Miss Cleeve herself went in at the front door, and five minutes later Miss Pussy Cleeve came out and gave him threepence for his trouble.

On Wednesday it rained, but Thursday, the day of the garden party, was fine, warm, and settled-looking. The Misses Cleeve, like royalty, were lucky in their weather.

"I shall wear my printed silk thing," said Gillian. "And you'd better wear yours too, Laura. They'll expect it."

Mrs. Cole was persuaded to discard her shawl and put on tidy clothes, a dress Laura had bought for her in Bramchester and which Mrs. Cole privately disliked, and a black straw hat trimmed by Gillian to go with the dress.

"It's as warm as July," Gillian said firmly. "You can't possibly be cold." Mrs. Cole both could be and was, but she agreed that the Misses Cleeve would expect one to dress up. The formal invitation, the stately term "garden party," made it clear that this was a special occasion.

"Unique, I should think. I can't remember them ever giving a party before."

"I once had tea with them," said Mrs. Cole. "Early in the war. You must have been still at school, Laura."

"But this is a *party*, Mummy. They've asked quite a lot of people."

Gillian, though she was ready to do her duty by the Misses Cleeve, refused to expect anything out of the ordinary. "Tea in the garden, that's what it will be. They've asked a lot of people and there isn't room for them in the house. That's why they call it a garden party."

As it was not very far, they walked to Box Cottage, down the lane, under the railway bridge, and up the hill to the main road. Miss Selbourne and Miss Garrett, happily engaged in white-washing the kennels, waved to them as they went past. Dressed in dungarees, with their heads tied up in dusters, they were evidently too busy to go to the garden party; or perhaps they had not been asked. "What an enormous behind Tiger's got," Gillian observed. "She ought never to wear trousers." Mrs. Cole, who prided herself on tolerance where her personal affections were not engaged, defended trousers as being practical, economical, and warmer than skirts, but she was quite pleased when Laura sided with Gillian in denouncing them as hideous. She sometimes thought that Laura did not take enough interest in clothes.

Two or three cars, which had brought people to the garden party, were standing in the drive leading to Marly House. Box Cottage, on the other side of the road, had nowhere to park cars. As they reached its little gate the Coles were struck by the gay, unusual appearance of the front garden, where chrysanthemums flourished in the flower beds and two large, highly polished brass pots, one on each side of the front door, held two evergreen shrubs in full and exotic bloom. When they got up to the door they saw that these were artificial blossoms, made of crêpe paper and wired on to the shrubs. "Just look," whispered Mrs. Cole. "They must have taken a lot of trouble."

Mrs. Trimmer, almost unrecognizable in a black frock and starched white apron, led them through the house to the back garden, where the Misses Cleeve were receiving their guests. Here, engaged in disjointed and awkward conversation—perhaps overawed by the unexpected splendours around them—a dozen or more people were clustered in a small group on the lawn. The three Misses Cleeve were drawn up in order of seniority just outside the back door, and from her first startled glance Laura realized that all their own efforts to do justice to the occasion were hopelessly inadequate. They might just as well have come in their everyday clothes, for any chance they had of living up to the Misses Cleeve.

Smelling strongly of moth balls, roped with feather boas, bowed down by huge elaborate hats, and seriously hampered by parasols, the three hostesses extended their gloved hands and graciously bade their guests welcome. Each wore a different colour, but otherwise their dresses were much the same, long and full-skirted, with leg-of-mutton sleeves and high, tight net collars held up by bits of whalebone. The dresses were encrusted with lace, or patterned with insertion and pearl buttons; they had deep flounces and, as was seen when they moved away from the door, short trains. They had obviously come from some ancient hoard, and alas, they no longer fitted their owners. Safety pins, half concealed by sashes, bridged awkward gaps at the waist. The net collars were all split open at the back.

Presently, as the Misses Cleeve began to circulate among their guests, the soothing rustle of their progress was marred by mysterious pops and crackings, as if all the long seams and tucks and pleats were disintegrating from old age. But in spite of these symptoms of decay the general effect was very striking; like strange relics from a bygone civilization, the Misses Cleeve were both grotesque and impressive.

Laura and Gillian were so hypnotized by the appearance of their hostesses that it was some time before they began to examine the garden. The front garden had seemed unusually gay when they approached it, but the back garden was even gayer. Whole groves of flowers had sprung up in the most unlikely places, and the old apple trees, and the ivy mantling the hen house, had burgeoned into paper blossom. The garden was also furnished with chairs, not canvas or wicker, but respectable upholstered ones looking rather out of place, as if they were on their way to a remover's van.

On a mahogany table, partly hidden by a baize screen, stood an old-fashioned gramophone with a red trumpet, and presently a small Trimmer child was brought out by Mrs. Trimmer and set to work on it. Waltz tunes, varied by an occasional hymn tune, floated on the air.

As if the scene were a clockwork toy, imprisoned in a glass case and set in motion by a spring, everything now became animated. The guests began to talk more loudly, the Misses Cleeve left their post and moved from one group to another, a breeze rustled the paper flowers, and the Vicar of Bramton embarked on a funny story.

"Look," said Gillian, "they've forgotten to take away the washing."

But when they looked more closely they saw that what had seemed to be a sheet hanging over the line was really a small tent, or canopy, just big enough to enclose a table and two chairs.

"That's the marquee," said Laura.

"Marquee?"

"Don't you see, Gil? A marquee, a band, garden-party dresses—they've thought of everything. Oh, dear, it's so funny, but it's rather sad too."

Gillian opened her mouth to tell Laura not to be morbid. But Pussy Cleeve was making her way towards them.

"Well, Laura," she began, speaking in the fluting voice which betokened intense curiosity, "it's nice to see you safe and sound. Now do tell me what really happened. I hear that Garrett woman is going to be summonsed."

"But I don't know that anything has happened to Miss Garrett."

Pussy looked round-eyed and incredulous.

"But you were with her!" she cried. "Weren't you with her? When she had a lot of drinks at the Lamb and Lion and then ran into Miles Corton?"

Mrs. Trimmer appeared at the back door and announced Mr. Greenley. Pussy's attention was diverted. Rustling, crackling ominously, she trailed away to join Miss Cleeve in receiving this new and hitherto unknown guest.

Laura turned round and found herself face to face with Miles.

"Good afternoon, Laura," he said. "Who had a lot of drinks and then ran into me?"

For some reason she had not expected to find Miles among the guests at Box Cottage, and she told him so, adding quickly that Pussy was talking about Miss Garrett and must mean the time with the ambulance. Miles sorted out this information and then said that Pussy was not so far wrong either, except that Miss Garrett had had the drinks afterwards.

Laura might have argued about that, but she let it pass. Whenever she had seen Miles lately they had argued about something, or there had been misunderstandings leading to the confusion of feeling she described to herself as "awkwardness."

But today she did not want to argue with him. She was feeling particularly happy; the garden party, for all its absurdities, had begun to exert a delightful charm, and even the Misses Cleeve appeared only slightly pathetic.

"I wonder what Mr. Greenley if making of it," she said. "Do you see him? Over there with Miss Cleeve."

"Is that who it is? The first time, to my knowledge, that he's been seen outside the gates of Cleeve Manor."

Miles gazed with interest at the newcomer, and Laura could not resist telling him of Gillian's plans for Mr. Greenley's reform. It was a long time since she had been on such easy terms with Miles, and she was quite sorry when Mrs. Worthy and Jocelyn came up and interrupted them.

Other people, less fortunate than Laura, were beginning to find the garden party a little tedious. The Vicar of Bramton and his wife, who were still comparative strangers, drifted into a corner of the orchard and consulted together about leaving. "They're bound to have tea soon," she whispered, "and then I'll say you've got a meeting." The vicar agreed, and looked about in a harassed way for someone else to talk to; he had already had one long conversation with Miss Myrtle and did not want another. Everyone was thinking about tea; and when Mrs. Trimmer reappeared at the back door there was a general turning of heads, and the talk fell away into an expectant pause.

Through this pause two conversations continued undisturbed. Miss Cleeve, sitting in her sheet-marquee, was cross-examining Mr. Greenley about the present use and decoration of every room at Cleeve Manor. "Speak up," she said more than once, "I can't hear people who mumble." Mr. Greenley was not accustomed to being told he mumbled, but he had already pigeonholed his hostess as "eccentric—needs humouring," which meant that he need not take offence. On the other side of the lawn Mrs. Cole and the Rector of Bramworthy, two enthusiasts who seldom met, were engrossed in a discussion of the best way to drain rock gardens. But everyone else was surreptitiously or openly watching Mrs. Trimmer, who looked rather flustered and was obviously trying to attract her employers' attention.

Miss Cleeve was screened by the marquee. Miss Pussy had her back to the door, and Miss Myrtle had disappeared. After a minute or two Mrs. Trimmer gave it up and went back into the house.

A fresh burst of talk sprang up, but it was now clear to most people that something had gone wrong. The vicar cast indignant glances at his wife, who suggested that the gas, or the electricity, had failed. Mrs. Worthy remembered hearing a crash; probably Mrs. Trimmer had broken the teapot or dropped the milk—just the same thing had happened the last day of their holiday at Eastbourne, only it was the bread and butter.

Gillian, who had been talking to Jocelyn, giving him, without his knowledge, a first easy lesson in good manners, saw out of the tail of her eye that Mr. Greenley had had enough of Miss Cleeve. She gently discarded Jocelyn and walked across to the marquee, picking up on the way a solitary guest, a woman with a gushing manner who had lived at Bramton Wick for years, but was seldom seen in public.

"Miss Bailey is so interested in your parasol," said Gillian to Miss Cleeve. "She wonders where you got it."

Miss Bailey had just whispered to Gillian that the clothes must have come out of a museum. But as if to make up for it, she went into raptures over the parasol. Before she knew what had happened, she was enjoying a tête-à-tête with her hostess in the marquee, and Gillian had removed Mr. Greenley to look at the garden.

Time passed. Gradually, without discussion, without comment or explanation from the Misses Cleeve, it became understood among the guests that this garden party, peculiar in so many ways, had a final peculiarity up its sleeve. There was not going to be any tea.

By the time the more optimistic of them had given up hoping, the less indulgent had taken their departure. The Worthys went first; Major Worthy had not come to the party and Mrs. Worthy had her usual excuse, that she must get back to Curtis. The Vicar of Bramton said good-bye with a sad, forgiving air, saving up his reproaches for his wife on the homeward journey. A few people who had come from the other side of Bramworthy spoke vaguely of the long distance they had to go; Isabel Lumley detached her father, the rector, from Mrs. Cole and carried him off.

Mrs. Cole was now left a prey to Pussy Cleeve, who said with a gleam in her eye that she had no idea Gillian knew Mr. Greenley so well. "We thought we were to have the honour of introducing him to the district," said Pussy, "but I see that Gillian has forestalled us. Did she meet him in London?"

Mrs. Cole, minimizing Gillian's acquaintance with Mr. Greenley and trying to evade Pussy's questions, was conscious of her daughter's gay laugh, and of a more raucous sound that must be Mr. Greenley's laugh, coming from the end of the garden. At Woodside, Mr. Greenley had been dull, solemn, and a little pompous; like Pussy, she had not known that they were on such friendly terms.

"I really must have a chat with your sister," she said, seeking a way of escape.

Pussy did not ask which sister, for no one ever contemplated having a chat with Miss Myrtle, who in any case had abandoned the party and retired to meditate upstairs. "Oh, Sarah's got someone to talk to," she replied, and following her glance, Mrs. Cole saw Miles and Laura talking, or at least listening, to Miss Cleeve.

"That reminds me," Pussy continued brightly, "of the last time I saw them together. One couldn't help noticing that Miles has quite a penchant for dear Laura. I'm afraid he made it a little too plain, and she rather resented it. But then she's got other plans for her future, hasn't she?"

The various implications of this speech crackled in Mrs. Cole's ears like the small explosions of a Chinese firework. Without replying—for no reply seemed possible—she stood up and said quietly, in a good imitation of her normal placid voice, that it was later than she had thought and they really must be going. Pussy, who was not deceived, gave her a very sweet smile and said she must come again some time, when they could have a really long talk.

CHAPTER TWELVE

MRS. COLE FOUND herself outside the gate of Box Cottage without quite knowing how she had got there, as if she were moving in a slightly agitating dream.

"You look tired, Mummy. Didn't you enjoy it?" asked Laura. It was well known to them that the things their mother didn't enjoy always tired her.

"*I* enjoyed it," Gillian said decisively. "It was peculiar, but nice. Except, of course, not having any tea."

They were walking along the road and might now be considered out of earshot of the Misses Cleeve. Looking round to assure herself of this, Mrs. Cole realized that both her daughters had brought their escorts with them. She felt certain that Pussy Cleeve was watching them from an upstairs window.

"It's not too late for tea. Come back and have some with me," said Miles Corton, speaking to Mrs. Cole. He was surprised when she gave him a quick blank stare as if she were seeing him for the first time. Laura, who thought her mother must really be overtired, said it was a good idea, they'd love to come; at the same moment Gillian announced that Thomas had offered to drive them over to Bramworthy to have tea at that place on the river.

Mrs. Cole was now in a quandary, since her daughters wanted different things.

"Oh, it's much too late to go to Bramworthy," said Laura, thinking of her mother and trying to convey to Gillian that it would be better for her to have a rest. "The place will be shut by the time we get there."

"No, it won't, it stays open all the time. Thomas thought we might go on to the cinema afterwards."

Laura noted that Mr. Greenley, who had been Thomas when they talked about him in private, had now become Thomas to his face.

Mrs. Cole noted it too.

"Well, you go," said Laura. "And Mummy and I will have tea with Miles." She gave Gillian a meaning frown: not the cinema—can't you see she's tired?

Gillian in her turn looked at Mr. Greenley. "Do you really want to go to the cinema?" she asked.

Till this moment he had not wanted it. He had suggested it on an impulse, and he was so unaccustomed to making impulsive suggestions that he felt he was not being true to himself when he did so. He felt that it had been Gillian's idea, not his own; that he had been coaxed, humoured, or jockeyed into suggesting it. To a man of his temperament this was an alarming thought. But when she asked him if he really wanted to go he realized that he had misjudged her. He was not being coerced; he was free to make his choice. He had only to say "No," and that would be that.

"Love to," he answered promptly. "I hardly ever get the chance, you know. Too busy most nights in the week."

"I hope you don't think this afternoon has been a dreadful waste of time," Gillian said laughingly.

He was about to reply that he had felt it his duty to visit the late owners of Cleeve Manor, when he remembered admitting to Gillian that he did not suffer from a sense of duty. He caught her eye, and laughed.

Miles Corton found something disagreeable about Mr. Greenley's laughter. He was by no means blind to the faults and absurdities of the three old Misses Cleeve, but they were an institution; it was not for a newcomer to patronize them. Certainly the new owner of Cleeve Manor, in Miles Corton's opinion, had no business to laugh at the family he had supplanted. Thinking these uncharitable thoughts, he found himself being urged to enter Mr. Greenley's ostentatious car, which had been parked at the entrance to Marly House.

"I'll just run you up to the house," said Mr. Greenley benevolently. "Save Mrs. Cole the walk."

Laura had feared that Miles's cross old housekeeper would be annoyed at having to provide tea at this late hour, but Mrs. Epps, it appeared, was expecting them. Or at least she was expecting Miles. Mrs. Epps had been across to Box Cottage to see if she could give Mrs. Trimmer a hand—or not to miss the fun—and had found Mrs. Trimmer in quite a state.

"Miss Cleeve told her the tea was ordered from Malley's," said Mrs. Epps, "and Mrs. Trimmer being what she is, never gave it another thought. Not till it had gone half-past four, and nothing come nor any signs of it coming. Then she did begin to wonder. I said to her, 'You'd better ring them up and find out what's happened.' So she did!"

"And what had happened?"

"Why, they'd never had no order. Knew nothing about it, they told her." Mrs. Epps looked at them with a sort of gloomy triumph. "Miss Cleeve's getting to be an old lady," she said. "I suppose it slipped her memory."

Laura thought it strange that Miss Cleeve should have forgotten the tea, when she had remembered everything else.

"Anyway, it was a nice party," she said. "The garden looked so pretty and gay."

"It may well have done, Miss. Mrs. Trimmer says they spent days getting it ready, and then there were all the pot plants to put in, and the paper flowers to tie on—"

"Were all those plants in *pots*?" Mrs. Cole asked with interest.

"Why, yes, M'm. Miss Cleeve fetched them from the big florists in Bramworthy, and then Trimmer dug the holes for them. Very pretty and gay, as you said, Miss Laura, but not the same thing as a cup of tea, is it?"

"No, indeed."

This reminded Mrs. Epps that the kettle would now be boiling, and she went off to see to it. Mrs. Cole and Laura, who had been taken upstairs, had a final glance at their faces in the large, dusty looking-glass, and Mrs. Cole gazed rather sadly at the large, dusty room. "This was Mrs. Corton's room," she said. "Really, I think Mrs. Epps must be very incompetent. Just look at those cobwebs."

"Oh, well, just look at the house. She hasn't got time," said Laura.

Mrs. Corton had been killed in a hunting accident when Miles was five or six, and before Laura was born. Neither of them therefore could be expected to take it to heart that her bedroom should be dusty and neglected. But Mrs. Cole took it to heart. It was a long time since she had been in this room, and it sent her thoughts winging back to the past. She remembered Miles as a solemn, handsome child, sitting on his mother's knee. She thought about Mr. Corton, who had been one of her oldest friends.

It was a pity, in a way, that Miles was so much older than Gillian and Laura. He had never been a playmate for them. When they were small children he was already at school, he spent most of his holidays with some aunts in Devonshire, and it was only since his father's death that he had come to take his father's place in her mind. That is to say, she had grown to look on him as a friend, someone who could be consulted about matters beyond her own comprehension and who could be trusted to look after her interests.

Apart from this, Miles was not a good substitute for his father. Old Mr. Corton had known her in the days of her youth, and to the end of his life he had not altered his opinion that she was a very beautiful woman. His admiration had been her last link with the golden, vanished world of the past; and it was not to be supposed that Miles could replace him in this respect.

Thinking of old Mr. Corton and of the sad changes in Marly House, Mrs. Cole walked slowly downstairs. Laura looked anxiously at her and thought that she must be very tired indeed, but Mrs. Cole was not tired, only preoccupied. Miles was waiting for them in the hall, and took them into the library, the only room, he said, that was in use.

"Oh, but the drawing-room," said Mrs. Cole. "Don't you use it at all?"

"I prefer this room."

"But the drawing-room is charming," she said plaintively, beginning to pour out the tea. "Such a pity not to use it."

Miles agreed politely, but pointed out that it faced north and was too large and much too cold to be comfortable.

"Do you think the Miss Cleeves noticed that there was no tea?" Laura asked. She thought her mother was about to launch into reminiscences of the past. Laura had no real objection to reminiscences of the past, but it seemed a pity to remind Miles that he was so much worse off than his father had been.

"I thought not. They didn't appear concerned. But why was there no tea—surely it's usual to have it?"

"Didn't Mrs. Epps tell you?"

Laura repeated the story Mrs. Epps had told them upstairs.

"And just think," said Mrs. Cole, "all those plants were in pots."

"I knew that, Mummy. I saw a bit of a pot sticking up out of the soil."

"I was quite deceived; I thought they'd grown them all."

"Pussy Cleeve told me they had."

"My dear Laura, if Pussy told you that, you might have guessed at once that they were in pots."

"Oh, no, Miles. Haven't you noticed that Pussy's stories aren't quite, quite false? There's always a fraction that's true."

"An extremely small fraction, in most cases."

When Miles spoke, Mrs. Cole was instantly reminded of her own conversation with Pussy. In a sense she had been thinking of it all the time; it had been at the back of her mind when she entered Marly House, when she observed the cobwebs in the bedroom and spoke of the drawing-room's charm. Till now she had thought of Marly House as the home of old Mr. Corton, who had been her friend; now, being a mother, she could only think of it as a possible future home for her daughter Laura. Brooding over Pussy's words, she kept giving quick surreptitious glances at Miles, who was talking to Laura about the garden party.

"Miles has quite a penchant for dear Laura."

This was not the worst thing Pussy had said, but it distressed Mrs. Cole to think that, if there was any truth in it, she had not noticed it for herself.

Of course, if one believed Pussy, Laura had no intention of marrying Miles (Mrs. Cole did not put it quite like that; she shied away from the definite verb and told herself that Laura was "not interested"). But what could Pussy know about it? She was imagining things, making it up, enjoying herself in her own way by upsetting other people. Alas, as Laura had remarked, Pussy's stories, although magnified and perverted, had often a basis of truth, and it was not possible to dismiss this one as pure invention.

And when had Pussy seen Miles and Laura together? Mrs. Cole cast her mind back. She remembered that Laura had met Miles in Bramworthy, the day she had gone there with Miss Garrett, but she could not remember another occasion.

By this time they had finished tea, and Miles offered to drive them back to Woodside, but Mrs. Cole said firmly that they could perfectly well walk.

"We could go through the park," she said, "and across the railway by that little gate just above Bank Cottage."

"Oh, yes, I haven't been that way for a long time."

"The last time I went that way," said Miles, "I found that Miss Selbourne had put up a sort of barricade at the foot of the embankment on her side of the railway, to keep people out of the paddock."

"Very high-handed of her. What did you do?"

"Told her to take it down. The path's a right of way. She had no business to close it."

"But no one ever uses it," said Mrs. Cole.

"Oh, but they do, Mummy. At least they use the continuation of it on our side of the river."

"Only because the footbridge is there. If you were to take away the footbridge, Miles, people would soon learn to go round by the road."

"The path," he repeated, "is a right of way."

But Mrs. Cole, who had been told this so often, did not believe it. She had a hazy idea that a right of way meant a path which was absolutely necessary, the only route between one place and another, and there were alternatives to this particular path. It was hardly any farther to go round by the road. Therefore it could not be a right of way, and Miles was only being obstinate in refusing to close it. The Cortons were a stubborn race; old Mr. Corton, in his way, had been quite as obstinate as Miles. But in him it had been an excusable weakness, since it had always operated in her favour. In Miles it was a grave defect. Laura would not be happy with Miles, if ever . . .

Mrs. Cole collected her straying thoughts, for her dear daughter was speaking to her.

"Miles thinks we'd better go by the road, in case Miss Selbourne hasn't taken the barricade down."

"But I should like to walk across the park. I'm sure Miss Selbourne will let *us* through the paddock."

Laura was surprised that her mother should express so decided a preference; she could not know that Mrs. Cole had resolved to oppose Miles in all things, great and small.

"Very well, darling," she answered. "But you won't be able to say that no one uses the path."

The garden lay at the back of Marly House and the footpath ran just outside the boundary wall. It overlooked the garden, just as it overlooked the garden at Woodside, and could be reached by a wicket gate at the end of a grass alley. Miles walked down to the gate with them. There he said good-bye and went back to deal with an accumulation of correspondence and accounts, the inevitable accompaniment of modern farming, and most of it already a little overdue. His rooted distaste for outside interference made it a matter of principle for him to keep all civil servants waiting as long as possible for an answer. But there were limits to this game, and the limit had nearly been reached.

Laura and her mother walked through the park, along the edge of the larch plantation, and down the hill to the railway. It was a warm, still evening, the trees cast their long shadows on the grass, and grazing sheep lifted their faces to stare blandly at the strangers. "How I like sheep," said Laura. "They can look silly and dignified at the same time." But Mrs. Cole thought the sheep looked only silly. "Like milkmaids in a palace—quite the wrong setting," she murmured, fishing out of her memory some half-forgotten fairy tale.

"No jeering at milkmaids. Don't forget that I was a milkmaid once."

"Oh, Laura, that was different. In the war, I mean."

"Well, I quite enjoyed it—except getting up early on winter mornings."

"You were so far away."

"Mummy darling, Sussex isn't really far. Though it does seem odd that I should have had to go and milk cows in Sussex when I could just as well have milked them here."

"Whose cows?" Mrs. Cole asked suspiciously.

Laura looked surprised. "Well, anybody's. Miles's cows, or old Cayman's, or Manley's over at Endbury. I shouldn't have liked that, though; Lady Masters was awfully interfering with the land girls they had there. Always hauling them off to do things for the war effort or reporting them for staying out late. She was most unpopular."

"I'm sure Lady Masters meant it for the best," said Mrs. Cole. "I expect she felt responsible for them."

This puzzling and quite uncharacteristic tribute convinced Laura that her mother had something on her mind. Probably she was worrying about Gillian and not thinking of Lady Masters at all. To divert her from sad thoughts she began to talk brightly about the garden party.

They crossed the railway. A steep sloping path down the embankment brought them to the stile which led into Miss Selbourne's paddock. But when they reached it, it was evident that Miss Selbourne had paid no attention to her landlord's command, for a crude but effective barrier of furze branches and barbed wire prevented anyone's getting over.

There was no one in sight. The whitewashing of the kennels was finished, Miss Selbourne and Miss Garrett had retired into

Bank Cottage, and although the dogs were barking, they barked so frequently and with so little reason that their owners were perfectly accustomed to it and never thought of looking out.

"We must go down to the house," said Laura. "Perhaps there's a way through, lower down."

Certainly there was a well-marked track along the foot of the embankment, and when they neared the house they saw there was a new stile there, close to the back door. Mrs. Cole, whose sympathies on the question of public footpaths were all with Miss Selbourne, felt that she had done wrong to come this way, and talked of going back. But Laura was firm; she pointed out that it was Miss Selbourne's fault that they were forced to trespass in her garden. They climbed over the stile—so rickety and precarious that it was obviously the work of Miss Selbourne and Miss Garrett themselves—and walked quietly past the house towards the gate.

At this moment, from within the house, a fearful uproar broke out. The yelping of one or more dogs, the crash of broken glass and the clang of falling metal, the loud booming voice of Miss Garrett and the shrill agitated voice of Miss Selbourne combined to suggest that murder was being done, or at least that some major domestic calamity had occurred. Mrs. Cole and her daughter paused; then, as the noise began to subside, they both decided that it would be more tactful to go on. But they had been seen. The back door opened and Miss Selbourne appeared, uninjured but looking a little flushed.

Mrs. Cole hurriedly began to explain why they were there. Miss Selbourne said they had been forced to block up the stile because people might come in that way by night and steal the dogs. She did not say that Miles Corton had told her to remove the barricade. She seemed not to know or care that it was a right of way. Mrs. Cole felt that Miss Selbourne was a very nice woman, in spite of the dogs and her dreadful dungarees. She resolved to ask her to tea.

Miss Selbourne glanced rather anxiously through the open door behind her. "Will you come in?" she asked. "Or perhaps, if you don't mind, you'd better not. We've just had rather an upset."

Mrs. Cole looked sympathetic, and Laura said they had heard it.

"Yes, it must have sounded very alarming. Tiger trod on one of the dogs, and then she dropped the tray."

"I don't believe it," Laura said a few minutes later, when they had parted from Miss Selbourne and were walking up the lane. "It sounded much more as if she'd *thrown* something at the dogs. But she'd never do that. Perhaps she threw it at Miss Selbourne and hit a dog by mistake."

"What nonsense! Everybody drops things; what could be more natural—especially with dogs getting under one's feet?"

"But she was swearing, and the curses and the crash came first, before the yelps of injured dogs."

Mrs. Cole laughed indulgently. Nice people did not throw things at one another, or curse and swear.

Laura said, "Poor Miles."

Mrs. Cole stopped laughing and asked her daughter what she meant.

"He's a good, kind landlord, but he's got such peculiar tenants. It seems bad luck. I'm sure the Misses Cleeve never pay any rent, and Miss Selbourne blocks up his right of way, and we're always coming on him for advice and help."

"It's very easy to say 'poor Miles,' and feel sorry for people," said Mrs. Cole, speaking rapidly and rather incoherently as she always did when she presumed to criticize her daughters, "but you mustn't let it get into a habit, Laura darling. I've noticed you do and so has Gillian. There's no reason whatever to feel sorry for Miles Corton. He has everything he needs, and I can't see that he's a better landlord than anyone else. He takes very little trouble—not a bit like his father. Please don't call him 'poor Miles.'"

CHAPTER THIRTEEN

AUGUST, SEPTEMBER—how fast the days went by! Soon it would be October. Next Tuesday—no, next Wednesday! Mrs. Worthy picked up a pencil and scratched out yesterday's date on the kitchen calendar. Long ago, like every other schoolgirl, she had hastened the end of term by making calendars on squared graph paper and ticking off each day as it ended, and she still kept up the habit, although there was now no holiday, no festival, to look forward to. Three months—longer—since Jocelyn's arrival, and here he was still, and here he would stay, she felt, forever, unless Curtis turned him out of the house, which he would never do because, after all, Jocelyn was poor Armitage's son and blood was thicker than water.

"Gwennie!" shouted Major Worthy from the hall. "Gwennie!"

When Mrs. Worthy got there she found him standing tense and alert, like a well-trained police dog, above a muddy pair of shoes, a damp golf jacket, and a disintegrating ball of string. "What's all this?" he asked. "That young feller left it here?" He had lately taken to speaking of Jocelyn in this way, as if he was some stranger billeted on them.

"I'm afraid they must be Jocelyn's. Yes, they are, I remember now, it was raining when he came in this morning and I said to him, Jocelyn, leave your wet things outside. Of course I meant in the porch or the lobby, but he doesn't think. Now what did he want the string for?" said Mrs. Worthy, beginning to wind it up. "I remember he asked me for some string. He came into the kitchen and—"

"Young feller ought to be in the Army," said Major Worthy.

"But he's *been* in the Army, Curtis."

"Lot of good it did him!"

Mrs. Worthy saw that he was seriously upset. The effect of having Jocelyn to live with them was cumulative, every now and then something happened which reminded Major Worthy of all he had had to put up with; if he appeared unduly annoyed it was because it was really a retrospective annoyance, divisible among numerous causes. Mrs. Worthy perfectly understood this, and she listened patiently while he said what he thought of his nephew's untidiness, his bad manners, his everlasting slouching and shambling.

"Needs to be made to work," said Major Worthy. "Work or starve. Phui!"

But Curtis was too good-natured to say these things to Jocelyn himself. He said them instead to his wife. And after it was all over Jocelyn would still be there, slouching and shambling and eating more than his rations. It did no good. And it was positively bad for Curtis to get so excited; he was a delicate man and the doctors all said he was not to be worried. Having pacified him, Mrs. Worthy went back to the kitchen, where she rescued a cake from the oven and decided that Jocelyn must be made to work. Any work, never mind about fruit farming or engineering, they would take too long to get started and the important thing was that he should start at once. Any work—for even if he had to live with them, he would be away all day if he was working—and surely there must be work, even driving a van or sweeping the roads.

Just before tea she saw Jocelyn going past the window. She tapped on the glass and beckoned him into the kitchen.

"New cake for tea?" Jocelyn asked amiably. When food was the subject of conversation he could be quite animated.

"Where have you been? I wanted you to post my letters."

"Sorry, Aunt Gwennie. I've been down at Woodside. They're digging up the garden."

"Well, your uncle has often asked you to help him with the digging here—only yesterday I heard him telling you about the herbaceous border. I must say—"

"Aunt Gwennie, you remember about the dance?"

"Don't interrupt me."

Jocelyn goggled; he perceived, dimly, that his Aunt Gwennie was angry with him. "Sorry," he repeated, "but you see, it's about the dance."

"What dance?"

Jocelyn explained that it was the Conservative dance at Bramworthy. She had told him she would find him a partner and get another ticket, but now he had found a partner for himself. He had asked Gillian to go to the dance.

"So about the ticket, Aunt Gwennie. Have you got it yet? Because it's next Saturday. And I'll have to have the car, because they haven't got one."

If Mrs. Worthy had not been so angry she would have remembered that this was to be his birthday treat. But Curtis had been seriously upset, her own afternoon interrupted, and here was Jocelyn simply assuming that he could have the car.

"No," she said, "you can't have the car. And if you want another ticket you must buy it for yourself. I'm sorry, Jocelyn, but you must remember that your uncle and I are not rich people—that is, we can't afford to throw money away. Not that I grudge you anything, I know young people like dances and so on, and I've no objection to them myself. I'm sure this will be a good dance—"

"But Aunt Gwennie! I've *asked* her. And I haven't any money to buy a ticket."

"That's your own fault," Mrs. Worthy told him. "You must get a job. And don't stand there gaping."

After tea Gillian announced that she had done enough gardening for one day. "I shall walk down to Bank Cottage and see if they're throwing things," she said. "Come with me, Laura."

Ten minutes after they had gone Mrs. Cole looked up and saw Jocelyn Worthy standing on the footpath and making signs to her across the fence. Jocelyn had already spent most of the afternoon at Woodside, leaving only when it was quite plain that he was not going to be asked to tea ("We've had him often enough," Gillian had said firmly), and as she made a point of not fraternizing with people who used the footpath, Mrs. Cole only waved her hand and called out that the girls had gone to Bank Cottage. Jocelyn seemed to have something to say, but whatever it was it could not be shouted, and she stayed where she was, until he gave it up and walked on.

"Just my luck," he thought morosely. Earlier in the day his luck had seemed to be on the turn; he had discovered that Gillian was not married after all, or at least that she was a widow, which was almost the same thing, and she had agreed to come to the dance with him. And now he would have to say that he could not take her.

There was, of course, a faint possibility that Gillian might offer to buy a ticket for herself. Other girls went Dutch treat; but such was Jocelyn's luck that these generous types never came his way. However, the possibility existed, and it was because of this that he had come back so promptly to explain things.

Gillian and Laura seldom crossed the bridge without stopping to look down at the river. The river was quite insignificant, a shallow stream half hidden by willows and brambles, but they had known it all their lives and, like other old friends, it could not be ignored. They leaned their arms on the parapet and stared down at the sliding waterweeds.

"I've snatched Jocelyn from you," Gillian said. "He asked me to go to the Conservative dance."

"Goodness, how enterprising of him. Do you want to go?"

"Well, I said I would. It will be something to do. I expect I shall have to show him how to dance."

Laura had none of the reformer's zeal and she was quite content that Gillian rather than herself should be the one to show Jocelyn how to dance.

"But I thought Thomas was taking you out on Saturday," she said.

"Thomas left it open. A bit too open," Gillian replied candidly. "Just as well to have another date sometimes."

"I thought you liked Thomas."

"Oh, I do. I think he's sweet. But *he* thinks he can drive over here and collect me whenever he feels like a visit to the cinema." Gillian laughed. "You know, he's getting madly addicted to the cinema, but he has to pretend that I'm the one who likes it. He's brightening my dull life."

"Oh," said Laura. She thought about Thomas. He was rich, he was good-natured, he knew a lot about alpines and orchids, he was generous to his relations. But was he sweet? If they had been like the sisters in books she could have asked Gillian for more details, but Gillian had a way of discouraging what she called "nosiness." Laura decided that it would be better not to question her about Thomas, but she went on thinking about him, until Gillian said, "Come on," and moved away from the bridge.

"Don't look back, but I think I see Jocelyn on our tracks. Coming down the footpath."

"Perhaps he's just out for a walk."

"I don't think he's given to walking," Gillian said. "He hasn't seen us. We'll take refuge in Bank Cottage."

Walking briskly, they approached the refuge. The elms along the roadside hid it from view, but they could hear the dogs barking and the sound of voices raised, as it seemed, in argument.

"They're at it again," Gillian whispered. "Hammer and tongs! How glad they'll be to see us. It will give them a chance to stop."

She opened the gate and walked boldly up the path. As soon as they were inside they realized that Miss Selbourne and Miss Garrett were not quarrelling with each other, but saying exactly what they thought to Miles Corton. All three were standing in front of the house, Miles with his back to the gate and his tenants side by side, united against a common enemy. Both ladies were speaking at once. At the sudden appearance of Gillian and Laura their voices died away, and Miles turned round to see what was happening.

Gillian's prediction was incorrect. Nobody was glad to see them; it was quite obvious that they had come at the wrong moment. But after a brief struggle Miss Selbourne forced a welcoming smile to her face.

"Good evening," said Gillian. "We thought we'd walk down and see how you were getting on. How are the dogs?"

This was the right thing to say. The health of the dogs was more important to Miss Selbourne and Miss Garrett than their own health. Miss Selbourne pulled herself together and began to talk about the dogs. They were all well, there was a new litter that looked remarkably fine, and Blue Girl was expecting.

"Fat lot of good that will do us," Miss Garrett interjected, "if we go up there some morning and find them all missing."

Laura remembered Miss Selbourne's fears that thieves might come over the stile and steal the dogs. She guessed that Miles had been ordering the removal of the barricade. But Gillian, who had not been told about the thieves, was for once at a loss.

"Missing?" she echoed.

"Stolen," said Miss Garrett. She glared at Miles Corton and muttered something which ended in "and I should know where to look for them."

The atmosphere was tense with antagonism. Miss Selbourne seemed to think that her friend had gone too far; she grew rather pink and asked Gillian to come and look at the puppies. Gillian obligingly said she would love to, and they moved away towards the paddock. Miss Garrett went into the house and banged the door behind her. Laura looked at Miles.

It was difficult to see him as a dog-stealer. The idea was so preposterous that she could not help smiling. But she realized almost at once that he was not in the mood to enjoy being laughed at.

"Oh, Miles," she said impulsively, "don't be angry."

"My dear Laura, I'm not angry. But don't start being sorry for them, or I shall be."

"Am I always being sorry for people? I suppose I am. Mummy and Gillian say so—Mummy was quite cross with me the other day when I said I was sorry for—" She broke off abruptly.

"Whom were you being sorry for, the other day?"

"Oh, I don't know. I forget."

"Not, by any chance, for me?"

"Yes," said Laura in a small voice.

Miles looked at her for a moment in silence.

"Were you?" he said slowly. "Why were you sorry for me, Laura?"

Just for a few seconds she could not remember why. Her memory of the other scene, the conversation with her mother, was overshadowed by her sudden conviction that the present conversation was becoming tremendously important. It was as though, beneath the casual words, something else was being said.

"For the wrong reasons, I expect," she answered at last.

"But all the same, I'm not ungrateful."

"Don't be grateful. It was horrid of me. So patronizing."

"You don't think—"

But what she was not to think was left unsaid, for at that moment they both realized that someone was standing at the gate and making efforts to attract their attention. It was, of course, Jocelyn; like Gillian and Laura before him, he had arrived at the wrong time, but unlike them he did not notice it. His appearance anywhere had never provoked great enthusiasm, and he needed no more than a temperate greeting, a slightly absent-minded smile, to make him feel quite at home.

Having obtained the smile and the greeting from Laura, Jocelyn opened the gate. "This is Bank Cottage, isn't it?" he began, speaking to Laura and ignoring Miles, who had given him no greeting at all beyond an exasperated stare. "Your mother said you'd be here."

"Well, I am here," Laura said kindly.

"Oh, good. Yes. Actually, it was Gillian I really wanted."

"She's here too. She's gone to look at the new puppies."

"Actually, you'd do. I mean, you could tell her." It had occurred to him that it would be better to ask someone else to tell Gillian. Then if she was vexed she would have time to get over it, and perhaps to think about buying a ticket for herself. He thought Gillian was marvellous, but he realized that she might also be difficult; marvellous girls, in Jocelyn's experience, were always difficult, it was a sort of natural law which frequently operated to his disadvantage.

"Tell her what?" Laura asked. Like Mrs. Worthy she felt unreasonably angry with him, though he had done nothing worse than interrupt a conversation, and she resented being used as a messenger. "But she's here," she went on, before he had time to give the message. "You can tell her yourself, whatever it is. I'll show you where the kennels are."

There was really no need to do this, since the kennels were in full view at the far end of the paddock, but Jocelyn was the sort of person who had to be shown.

Before she could carry out her intention, one of the upstairs windows in Bank Cottage was thrust open and Miss Garrett's head and shoulders appeared, looking strangely out of scale and much too large for the house. She glared at them with majestic disapproval, like an aggrieved and implacable goddess.

Laura had quite forgotten Miss Garrett's angry retreat, and was startled by her sudden reappearance. She could not think what to say to her.

"This is Jocelyn Worthy," she said at last, since neither Miss Garrett nor Jocelyn showed any sign of recognizing one another. "Jocelyn, this is—"

"Where's Bunty got to?" Miss Garrett asked abruptly, addressing herself to Laura and taking no notice of the others.

"She's up at the kennels with Gillian."

"Cut up there and tell her I want her, will you? And then come in for a drink. You and your sister."

Miss Garrett withdrew her head and closed the window. Jocelyn stared open-mouthed at the place where she had been. Never before, perhaps, had he been so aggressively ignored.

Laura looked at Miles. She would not now have blamed him for being angry, but she was relieved to see that he was not angry at all. His expression showed more than the absence of anger; it had a positive and settled good-humour, as if Miss Garrett's behaviour no longer had the least power to disturb him. She found herself wishing that Jocelyn would go away so that she could continue talking to Miles, but since that was not possible she merely stayed where she was, without giving another thought to Miss Garrett's command.

"Well . . . I suppose I'd better be getting back," Jocelyn said doubtfully. He looked from Laura to Miles, and then up at the window where Miss Garrett had made her sudden brief appearance. He frowned, for even to an indifferent observer like himself it was plain that something peculiar was happening.

"I suppose . . ." he repeated, scuffling his feet on the gravel. Miles laughed and said to Laura: "You had better do as you were told."

"What? Oh, fetch Miss Selbourne. Yes, I will." She remembered that Jocelyn had a message for Gillian, and invited him to accompany her. Jocelyn, with a wary eye on the window, said that actually tomorrow would do.

"Oh, come along," Laura said briskly, speaking in the kind but authoritative manner so many people adopted towards Jocelyn. Miles said cheerfully that there was nothing to fear; he was the chief offender, anyway.

"They'll forget it," Laura replied.

"They had better not forget to take down the barricade."

"I wish I knew why doubtful characters are expected to come that way. There's nothing to stop them coming up the lane."

"You must ask Miss Garrett about that. I'm sure she has her reasons."

Jocelyn, who had been listening in a baffled way to this talk of barricades and doubtful characters, wondered why they laughed.

"I must be off," said Miles, "before I'm thrown out. Good night, Laura." He nodded to Jocelyn, who muttered a sulky good night in reply.

"Good night," said Laura. She turned away to go to the kennels, but Gillian and Miss Selbourne were walking back across the paddock.

By now Gillian had heard all about Miles Corton's tyrannical behaviour, his ridiculous mania for preserving rights of way, and his utter inability to understand a dog-lover's feelings. The recital of her wrongs had been a great relief to Miss Selbourne, who gradually grew calmer and was even led to admit that a compromise might be reached. The stile could be freed from its barbed-wire entanglement and fitted with a burglar alarm set to ring in Tiger's bedroom. Neither Gillian nor Miss Selbourne understood the mechanism of burglar alarms, but it seemed quite feasible, and surely no one could object to it. (Gillian wondered if Miss Garrett might object, but Miss Selbourne was happily confident of Tiger's power to tackle any burglar.) This reasonable solution of her difficulties so pleased Miss Selbourne that she asked Gillian to come in for a drink.

"And Laura, too, of course," she said. "But I really can't ask Corton. We'll go in through the back door and then you can call her from the window."

Miss Selbourne was considerably less bloodthirsty than Miss Garrett.

"It's all right, he's going. Look, he's walking down the lane."

"But she's talking to someone."

They were half-way across the paddock, but Miss Selbourne was short-sighted. Gillian said that was Jocelyn Worthy, Major Worthy's nephew.

Jocelyn was relieved to find that Miss Selbourne greeted him in a normal manner, shook hands, and asked him in for a drink. Laura, of course, was quite a normal type (besides being Gillian's sister), but tonight she kept forgetting to listen to him. Miles Corton had not listened to him either, and as for that redfaced woman at the window, she was bats. Having reached this comforting conclusion he was able to forget that the redfaced woman had pointedly not asked him to have a drink. He followed the others into the house.

"Poor darlings!" cried Miss Selbourne, opening the sitting-room door and releasing Agnes and Leo, who had somehow been overlooked when she and Tiger flew out to do battle with their landlord. The poor darlings had whiled away their captivity by chewing a cushion to bits, but this sort of thing happened so often that she hardly noticed it. Stuffing the remains of the cushion behind a chair, she unlocked the corner cupboard and fetched out the drinks.

"I can see you are fond of dogs," she said approvingly to Jocelyn, who was crouched on the floor with Agnes and Leo, pulling their ears and tickling their tummies.

Jocelyn looked up and said, Yes, he was, rather. Seeing that his hostess had the right ideas about drinks, he added that this kind of life would just suit him.

It was not only the sight of a bottle of gin being lavishly dispensed that made him speak so ardently. Ever since entering Bank Cottage he had felt curiously at home. In this house no one fussed about scorch marks on polished tables or tobacco ash on carpets; in this house the dogs were lively companions instead of staid old codgers like Binkie, and neither dogs nor humans would be reproved for crossing the hall with muddy feet. Even the red-faced woman upstairs was obviously an easygoing type when it came to housework.

Gillian asked: "What about Tiger?" and Laura said she was upstairs. Miss Selbourne went off to find her, and was gone a long time. Jocelyn now remembered why he had followed Gillian and Laura to Bank Cottage. He had been indulging in a happy dream of a place of his own just like this, famous prize-winning dogs to supply him with a comfortable income, and no one (by which he meant no Aunt or Uncle) to badger him. It was hard to have to abandon this dream and explain to Gillian that he could not take her to the dance at Bramworthy.

Gillian did not offer to buy her own ticket, but she spared his feelings. She was not at all vexed, and if she was amused she did not show it. But like his Aunt Gwennie—though in a kinder manner—she said that he ought to get a job.

"What do you want to do?" she asked.

"Well, I'd like to breed dogs. Of course, you need some capital to start anything like that."

"You need some experience, too," said Laura. "Have you ever kept dogs?"

"Actually, I've never had the chance. But I've always wanted to." It seemed to Jocelyn that this was true. He had had many ideas for his future, and dog-breeding had surely been among them. The more he thought of it, the more attractive it appeared.

Gillian looked at him thoughtfully. She suspected that his enthusiasms were short-lived, but dog-breeding might suit him as well as any other occupation. It was not a bad idea at all; and she tucked it away in her mind for future consideration.

Miss Selbourne returned from her long absence upstairs, and Gillian saw at once that Miss Garrett had not taken kindly to the plan for a burglar alarm.

"Tiger's got a headache," said Miss Selbourne. "She's gone to bed." She picked up the gin and poured out another round of drinks, even more generous than the first, and when Laura expressed sympathy for Miss Garrett she answered curtly that Tiger was always getting headaches.

CHAPTER FOURTEEN

LIKE MOST VILLAGES, Bramton Wick had a speedy and efficient bush telegraph, and the information that Lady Masters had returned from her visit to Scotland reached Woodside from two different sources on the very evening of her arrival. Mrs. Worthy had been shopping in Bramworthy and had seen the Endbury chauffeur on his way to the station, and the boy from the Wick Provision Stores was later than usual with Mrs. Cole's groceries because he had had to make a special journey to Endbury; her ladyship's cook, said the boy bitterly, had clean forgotten the wholemeal bread her ladyship always had for breakfast.

Unknown to each other both Mrs. Cole and her daughter Laura took a particular interest in the news. Laura had frequently assured herself that the talk she had had with Lady Masters on the afternoon of the tennis party was not really at all important. But she could not forget it. If Lady Masters had not gone to Scotland, if the new intimacy begun that afternoon could have continued without a break, she might by now have succeeded in persuading her, as she had once hoped to do, of her own merits as a daughter-in-law.

It was still possible to succeed. It was, she thought sometimes, almost alarmingly possible.

For the weeks of separation had made a difference, and Laura was no longer so certain that it would be a good thing for her to marry Toby.

She liked Toby; she had always liked him; nothing had changed. But that was just it. She could not say to herself that absence makes the heart grow fonder; in her it had had the reverse effect, for she had scarcely thought about him. She had thought about Lady Masters, about Endbury, about the alterations to the west wing and the bars on the nursery windows—about everything but Toby himself.

Laura had never been seriously in love, and did not expect to be, but she felt there was something wrong here. She believed that she needed more time, an untroubled interval in which to examine her own mind. She hoped very much that Lady Masters would not be in too much of a hurry about finding a wife for Toby.

Mrs. Cole, on the other hand, was waiting quite impatiently for her next invitation to Endbury. She had never liked Lady Masters, but for Laura's sake she was prepared to make the best of her. A marriage between Laura and Toby would be the fulfilment of her long-cherished dream. Even thinking of it—and she thought of it a great deal—made Lady Masters seem more tolerable. As for Toby, she had always been fond of him; and from the worldly point of view it would be a very good marriage. She was not so mercenary as to wish her daughter to marry for money, but she could not avoid making the comparison between Endbury and Marly House, between Toby and Miles Corton.

Mrs. Cole had been brought up in an extravagant world where everyone had enough money, and although she had long ago grown used to being poor she could not forget the agreeableness of being rich. Miles Corton was not rich, and never would be, and if Laura were to marry him she would have to live in that hideous house and scrimp and save to the end of her life. But if she were to marry Toby she would have the comfort and ease she deserved.

Above all, she would have Endbury.

In the watches of the night, when her daughters supposed her to be peacefully asleep, Mrs. Cole lay awake shaping and enlarging her dream. She had told herself so often, and so sincerely, that she was not a match-making mother, that she was quite surprised to discover in herself reserves of tact and cunning. They would be needed; for somehow, without alarming Laura or making Gillian suspicious, she must establish a friendship with Lady Masters. Mrs. Cole saw clearly that without her approval nothing could be done, but she saw no reason why Lady Masters should disapprove. She thought that Lady Masters, like herself, must often have played with the idea of such a marriage. It was so obvious, and so suitable.

The more she thought of it, the easier it grew to persuade herself that Laura really wanted to marry Toby. Perhaps there was already an "understanding" between them; perhaps there was only Toby's dependence on his mother that prevented an open engagement. This part of her wishful thinking was based entirely on Pussy's words. Pussy had said that Laura had "other plans for her future," and although she had no business to say it, and did not deserve to be listened to, she certainly had an uncanny way of knowing the very things people most wished to keep to themselves.

Mrs. Cole could not disregard Pussy's words. She did not want to disregard them. She lay awake, picturing Laura in white satin and her own Brussels lace, worrying over the problem of how Lady Masters was to be dislodged from Endbury and made to live elsewhere—for though the house was large it would be better for Laura to reign alone—and occasionally sparing a thought for Gillian, who would now have to be the prop and comfort of her old age.

Towards the end of the week she received a note from Lady Masters asking them all to luncheon on Sunday. She read it to her daughters at breakfast, keeping a discreet watch on Laura to see if she appeared pleased.

"Gracious," said Laura. "All three of us?"

"Perhaps she brought back a haunch of venison from Glen Bogle and finds it wants eating."

"Gillian, don't be silly," Mrs. Cole said gently. It was no use, her daughters were off at their old game of pretending that they never got enough to eat at Endbury. Laura said that venison would be a nice change from Snippets *à la mode*, and Gillian retorted that she never got snippets anyway—only snippet in the singular and a thin snippet at that.

"Children, children!" said Mrs. Cole. "It's kind of her to ask us, and I shall accept. I haven't been to Endbury for a long time," she added hastily, feeling that she must make some excuse for accepting an invitation without so much as asking them if they wanted to go.

A little later, while they were making the beds, Gillian asked Laura if she had noticed anything peculiar about their mother at breakfast.

"No, I didn't. Had she got her dress on back to front?"

"Not that sort of peculiar. She looked at us very oddly, especially at you. Rather furtive—as if she was up to something."

"Something for our good?"

Gillian thought it over. "Yes," she said, "it was like that. Something for our good, or perhaps more for your good than mine."

"Poor Mummy, we must cooperate if we can, but I hope she won't go to a lot of trouble to get us something we shan't like." Gillian began to laugh. "I hope it's not husbands," she said. Both of them were so convinced that Mrs. Cole was not a matchmaking mother that Laura had no hesitation in laughing too. Gillian pointed out that this theory exactly explained the furtive look, directed more to Laura than to herself, for she had already had a husband and Laura had not.

"You first, then me. If Mummy starts talking about a round of visits we shall know that's it."

When Gillian left school she had been sent on a round of visits and she had never forgotten it. She had visited an aunt in Brighton, an aunt in North Wales, and some cousins in the Midlands. The aunts and cousins had proved dull company, but on the way home she had got into conversation with a young man who was anything but dull; this was William, whom she subsequently married.

Mrs. Cole had been given to understand that Gillian met her beloved at her aunt's house in North Wales; a round of visits might therefore appear to her a profitable enterprise. Her daughters amused themselves in elaborating this theory, but they did not discuss the possibility that Mrs. Cole might be looking for husbands nearer home. Laura wondered if her mother had considered Thomas Greenley as a candidate for Gillian. Gillian remembered that in addition to giving them furtive looks, Mrs. Cole had shown an odd determination to visit Endbury. But they kept these thoughts to themselves.

It was Mrs. Trimmer's day for "doing" the brasses and the kitchen floor. Mrs. Trimmer was niece to Lady Masters's old parlourmaid and had cycled over to Endbury to see her the previous evening. She seldom visited her aunt, and when she did so it was only from a sense of duty; there was no enjoyment in it because enjoyment, for Mrs. Trimmer, meant a long cosy gossip, and her aunt disapproved of gossip.

"Sit there till kingdom come, she would, and never utter," Mrs. Trimmer would say. "Too fond of 'erself by 'alf, and looking down 'er nose at me for going out daily."

But this morning Mrs. Trimmer arrived brimming over with news. Yesterday evening old Mrs. Hesford had walked over from the almshouse, as she did about once a month, to have a look at the Endbury kitchen and irritate the reigning cook by talking of the old days. Mrs. Hesford might be irritating, but she was a privileged person, an ex-monarch who was entitled to a little gossip if she fancied it, so Mrs. Trimmer was able to congratulate herself on having chosen that evening for her own visit.

The family had had bad weather at that Scotch place; it had rained all the time and her ladyship had caught a cold. "Scotland's not the place for me any more," she had said to Cook. "I shall never go back to Glen Bogle." ("Like a Jacobite lament," Gillian commented later.) Her ladyship's sister, the one they had been staying with, had travelled back to London with them and was coming to Endbury for the weekend, and her ladyship said she was to have the bedroom over the library because it had a fine view and her sister was very fond of views.

"But that's such a cold room," said Mrs. Cole. "We only used it for bachelors."

"Yes, M'm, me aunt says to 'er ladyship it was a cold room. But 'er ladyship says that 'er sister liked cold rooms, she was used to them at Glen Bogle."

Mrs. Cole sighed, for the thought of cold rooms depressed her, and Glen Bogle must have been cold indeed if Lady Masters had noticed it.

"*And* I hear Mr. Toby's going to be a farmer!" said Mrs. Trimmer, who had been saving this up to the last. It fell rather flat, for Mrs. Cole's conscience overcame her curiosity and she decided that she really could not discuss Toby's career with Mrs. Trimmer. So she said that they would probably hear all about it on Sunday when they lunched at Endbury, and made an excuse for following Gillian and Laura into the sitting-room, leaving Mrs. Trimmer to work off her disappointment on the brasses.

However, there was no reason for not discussing it with her daughters, and she promptly told them what Mrs. Trimmer had just said.

"If that's true he must be giving up the bookshop. How stupid!"

"I don't think he liked the bookshop much anyway."

"Yes, Laura, but just think of all the things Toby has tried and failed at since he came out of the Army. He'll be running out of careers soon. It's quite ridiculous."

"Poor Toby. It's just that he can't settle down."

"Poor Toby—bosh!" Gillian said unkindly. "He's a poor little rich boy, that's what's the matter with him."

"Children, children!" said Mrs. Cole. But only one child really deserved the rebuke. The other, she was pleased to see, was sticking up for Toby.

That afternoon Toby called at Woodside. He explained that he had to drive into Bramton and wondered if any of them would like to go too. No one wanted to go to Bramton, but Mrs. Cole remembered that there were some papers to go to the Misses Cleeve. "You could give Laura a lift to Box Cottage," she suggested.

"But he doesn't go that way, Mummy. He always goes by Wick."

Toby protested that he could just as easily go by Marly House and Box Cottage, and Laura went off to fetch her coat, a little annoyed because she had planned to darn all her stockings that afternoon.

Toby had left his car at the gate, and she noticed that he had turned it round.

"I was quite right," she said. "You meant to go by Wick."

"If you're not in a hurry we can go that way. You can come into Bramton with me and then we'll come back by Box Cottage."

Laura agreed to this. They drove back to the crossroads and along the old Bramton road, past Major Worthy's house with its neat white gate, past Miss Bailey's house with its high impenetrable hedge, till they reached the top of Gibbet Hill. Toby stopped the car.

"This is why I like to come by Wick," he said.

Bramton lay below them. In the foreground was the New Bridge, mellow with age and of a pleasing design, and beyond it the houses were huddled together on rising ground, which had once been surrounded by marshes, with the square tower of the church dominating the picture. It was certainly very charming.

"Do you come this way to look at the view?" Laura asked.

"It's pretty good, isn't it? Pure eighteenth century. Nothing to remind one of the ghastly present."

"There's the railway," she objected. She understood what he meant, but she could not resist pointing out the railway.

Toby said it hardly counted—it was as much a thing of the past as the water mill below the bridge. But Laura held stubbornly to the opinion that a railway was an anachronism in an eighteenth-century landscape. Toby started the car again and they drove on in a rather unsympathetic silence.

While she waited for him in Bramton Laura's kind heart began to get the better of her literal mind. She did not blame him for preferring the past, but it struck her that his attitude to the railway was like his mother's attitude to anything which conflicted with her own opinions. Such tiresome intrusions went unobserved, or were said "not to count." But Toby was not, like his mother, insensitive to criticism; on the contrary he was all too sensitive. His feelings were easily hurt, and she had hurt them that afternoon when she had laughed at his cherished view.

By the time Toby got back to the car Laura had quite repented of her churlishness. He was still using his "hurt" voice, but it did not take long to persuade him that they were the best of friends. As soon as he felt sure of this he cheered up and took her to have ices at the Sunny Teashop.

When they got there they were told that it was too late in the year for ices. Toby said they would have tea instead.

"We ought to get back," said Laura, sitting down at a table in the window. "Won't Lady Masters be expecting you?"

"Well, I can always eat another tea when I get home." He looked at her and laughed. "I shall have to, too. You know how Mama feels about food being wasted."

"Yes," said Laura. This was the second time that Toby, whom she had formerly thought of as a mother-worshipper, had criticised the author of his being. She propped her elbows on the table and said boldly:

"Toby, you're grown up. Don't you think you ought to take a stronger line?"

She half expected that instead of taking a stronger line he would take refuge in hurt feelings, but he answered her quite seriously.

"How can I? Mama can be very difficult. And then, you see . . . well . . ."

"Well—what?"

"Well—she has the money."

She was perfectly aware of this, but it was a shock to hear him say it. It implied that criticism of Lady Masters could be carried to almost any lengths. But before she could reply, the waitress arrived with the tea.

"Lovely, gaudy cakes," said Toby, reverting to his ordinary manner. "Look, Laura, they're like childhood's dreams come true. I only know one place better than this for gaudy cakes, a café in Bramchester quite near the cathedral. I used to go and gorge there."

Bramchester reminded Laura of something else.

"Is it true that you're going to be a farmer?"

"Perfectly true. Who told you?"

"Mrs. Trimmer told Mummy."

"All those Trimmers could make their fortunes in spy rings—they have an absolute genius for sleuthing. They find out everything long, long before it's made public."

Laura agreed. She could not say that she had known about the farming long, long before Mrs. Trimmer brought the news.

"I think I shall like farming. Don't look so guilty, Laura, I was only joking about Mrs. T. It's all fixed up now, and I've finished with the bookshop. Have another cake?"

It was clear that the bookshop had become a mere interlude in Toby's past and that all his thoughts were centred on his new career. He began to talk of farming with great enthusiasm, and although Laura listened and laughed and encouraged him, she could not help remembering that he had been just as enthusiastic about his other careers.

Miles Corton had also driven into Bramton that afternoon, to see the local builder about some repairs to a cottage. He had noticed Toby's car parked near the Cleeve Monument, and now, on his way back to his own car, he happened to glance through the window of the Sunny Teashop and saw Laura and Toby laughing and talking within. He had already had a depressing interview with the builder, who had a hundred good excuses for not knowing when he would be able to start the job, and he did not care much for Toby Masters at the best of times. He paused, and gave him a disapproving look, a look which said: "Why aren't you working in your idiotic bookshop?" But neither Toby nor Laura had a glance to spare for the passers-by in the street. Their heads were close together and they were engaged in animated conversation, as if they had something particularly pleasant to discuss.

Miles walked on to his car. He looked up at the statue of Sir Alexander James Cleeve, then he looked at Toby's car, so much newer and better kept than his own. He sighed, and drove out of Bramton at a speed which he would have found deplorable in another driver.

Shortly afterwards Toby and Laura followed him, also driving rather too fast; they had not noticed the time and now it was late and they still had to call at Box Cottage.

"You'll be far too late to have tea when you get home," said Laura.

Toby grinned at her. "Never mind. Perhaps this is where I start taking a strong line."

Miss Pussy Cleeve was standing at the gate of Box Cottage, looking up and down the road with an air of casual indifference. She was lying in wait for Mrs. Epps, who had been into Bramworthy and might be expected back by the next bus, but the arrival of Toby Masters and Laura quite put Mrs. Epps in the shade. She seldom saw Toby, and it was a long time since she had had the pleasure of comparing him with his dossier.

"Come in, come in," she cried gaily. "Or are you too busy, Laura dear? I am sure Mr. Masters is not too busy. I hear he's a man of leisure these days."

Toby was slightly nonplussed. Laura, faced with a choice of sympathies, chose to be sorry for Toby and said firmly that they could not come in.

"We've been into Bramton," she said, "and we were detained. We simply must get back."

Pussy deliberately looked puzzled, and indeed she might, for there was nothing to detain anyone in Bramton. Then her puzzled expression changed to one of all too intimate comprehension. "Well, well," she said meaningly, "I won't keep you. I'm sure you have better things to do than talk to three old women."

Both Laura and Toby became embarrassed; embarrassment or fury were the common reactions to conversation with Pussy. Laura leaned over the back of the seat to get the papers. Toby said in a voice rather louder than usual that he was not going to be idle for long—he was going to set up as a farmer.

"How interesting. Like Miles Corton—or more successful, I hope. Poor Miles, I believe, is thinking of selling up."

"First I've heard of it," Toby said guilelessly.

"Oh, he doesn't want it known. He's an arrogant creature, and obstinate, like all the Cortons."

"Here are the papers," said Laura, thrusting them into Pussy's hand. By this time Pussy was outside the gate and standing so close to the car that it was impossible to drive away without hitting her. She was determined not to let them go, and she began to make tender inquiries after Lady Masters and Mrs. Cole— inquiries which Toby and Laura disposed of with brisk assurances that they were in the best of health. Toby put his hand to the ignition switch. Pussy asked gently if he was going to do his farming at Endbury.

"It will be nice for your mother that you are to live at home," she said. "She is so devoted that she will be glad to have you under her eye. Bramchester is not very far away, but I'm sure she used to worry about you. One hears such strange rumours, you know. All quite false, I can see, but worrying."

She smiled sweetly at Toby, whose sensitive nature was now betraying itself in pinkness and silence.

"Good-bye," Laura said firmly. Like one released from an evil spell, Toby started the car, revving up so fiercely that Pussy stepped back out of danger.

"Good-bye . . . come again . . ." Her parting words were lost in the speed of their departure.

"We're going the wrong way. You'll have to turn round."

"Oh, hell," said Toby. "I'll go round by Barton Mill. It's not much farther."

By common consent they began to talk of things that had nothing to do with Pussy, or farming, or devoted mothers. It was a little difficult to keep the talk from drifting back to these forbidden subjects, but luckily Toby had just returned from a holiday; the Scottish scenery, even though it had been continuously shrouded in rain, had so impressed him that he found a great deal to say about it.

CHAPTER FIFTEEN

MRS. COLE FOUND the luncheon party rather disappointing. It was formal and dull and gave her no chance of beginning a new relationship with Lady Masters. She hoped there might be some significance in their having been asked to meet Toby's aunt, but it was difficult to be sure of this because the Vicar of Bramton and his wife had also been asked. The aunt herself was dazzlingly arrayed in Scotch tweed, but otherwise inconspicuous. The food was as mediocre as usual. There was no haunch of venison, but as a concession to the vicar there was a small bony savoury after the sweet.

"Your husband is too thin," Lady Masters told the vicar's wife. "He wants feeding up." And she gave her the name of a bedtime beverage which needed neither sugar nor milk, only a little water, and was far more nourishing than tea or cocoa.

Mrs. Cole could not pretend that she had enjoyed herself, but when Gillian made fun of the bedtime drink and Laura insisted on cutting extra bread and butter for tea, she rebuked them. This time they both noticed it. Laura felt uneasy; for an awful moment she wondered if her mother and Lady Masters could have talked things over and arrived at a secret understanding, but then she realized that this was not only improbable, but impossible. Mrs. Cole had not had an opportunity to talk to Lady Masters alone.

Mrs. Cole's tact and cunning were no match for Gillian's perspicacity. Gillian saw clearly that her mother wished them to think more favourably of Lady Masters, and she also saw the reason for it. But she was not certain if it was herself or Laura who was destined to be Toby's bride.

The week following the luncheon party was wet and stormy. This was unfortunate, for the next Sunday was Harvest Festival and the decorations for Bramton Church came mostly from people with gardens but no greenhouses. There were greenhouses at Endbury, but the head gardener could seldom be induced to part with anything but a few insignificant ferns. The hothouse fruit which he grew to perfection was sold at a handsome profit in Bramchester and could not be spared for church decoration, and the chrysanthemums were never ready in time. Mrs. Cole usually had plenty of outdoor chrysanthemums, but now the rain had dashed them all to pieces, and Mrs. Worthy's were just as bad.

"It is too bad of the vicar to have the festival so late in the year," said Mrs. Worthy, who had called at Woodside to ask after Mrs. Cole's chrysanthemums. "In the old days I'm sure it was always in September. Curtis says he will have nothing fit to send except a vegetable marrow. It's a beautiful marrow, quite one of the largest I've seen, but then, everyone sends marrows."

Gillian and Laura, who had been asked to help to decorate the church, agreed that there was always an abundance of marrows. After Mrs. Worthy had left, Gillian said she would write to Thomas. "Of course, he wouldn't part with any of those alpines and things," she said, "but that's just as well, because they're all hideous. He might have something large and showy and not at all valuable tucked away in those greenhouses at the back. I'll ask him."

She wrote to Mr. Greenley in London, since he came down to Cleeve only at week-ends. Being a busy man he did not answer her letter, but on Saturday morning a van arrived at Bramton Church with a handsome collection of plants as large and showy as anyone could desire. Gillian was gratified; everyone else was deeply impressed. Mr. Greenley's contribution made the End-bury ferns look stunted and necessitated their removal to a less prominent place in the church. It was perhaps fortunate that Lady Masters was not present.

Gillian and Laura had been given a lift into Bramton by Mrs. Worthy, who was also helping to decorate the church. When the decorating was finished she remembered that she had to go on to Bramworthy to collect a parcel from the station and speak to the laundry about Curtis's shirts, so she drove out by the Bram-worthy road and dropped them at the corner of Wick Lane. They would get wet, she protested; if only it wasn't for the petrol she would have run them home, but what with having to fetch the fish on Wednesdays because that was the best day for fish, she was always short. But she hated to think that they would get wet. She begged them to come with her to Bramworthy.

Gillian and Laura were quite accustomed to wet weather and they were both wearing mackintoshes, so they managed to per-suade Mrs. Worthy that the rain would not hurt them. Watching her drive slowly away down the Bramworthy road, Gillian re-marked that they would not have got so wet if they had not had to stand there in the rain arguing.

"I like Mrs. Worthy," said Laura. "She's got a kind heart. And she must have a wonderful character, too, to put up with Major Worthy and that dreary Jocelyn."

"I grant you Jocelyn. But she doesn't put up with Curtis—she simply adores him."

"I suppose so." She could not help feeling sorry for anyone who had nothing better to adore than Major Worthy. Even the dog or the parrot with which Gillian had once threatened her would be preferable to that.

"It's a very successful marriage," said Gillian. "But it's a pity they don't do something about Jocelyn."

"They've tried to. At least, she has. She went to the Labour Exchange and put his name down. But there didn't seem to be anyone who wanted to employ him."

"Gracious," said Gillian. "She's more determined than I thought. Do you mean she would push him into any sort of job, however menial?"

"I think so. She was telling me about it when we were tying the corn stooks round the font. He gets on Major Worthy's nerves."

"We must find him a job. Now, what could he do?"

Discussing Jocelyn's capabilities, they walked slowly downhill under the dripping trees. At the foot of the hill was the railway embankment. The lane went through a narrow arched opening under the embankment and then made a sharp turn to run parallel with the railway, past Bank Cottage, to the bridge across the river. The arch under the railway and the blind corner beyond it were considered very dangerous, but fortunately there was little traffic on the road.

It was a pity, Gillian said afterwards, that they had not been there a little earlier. Then they would have witnessed the grand parting scene between Miss Selbourne and Miss Garrett, and might even have been able to intervene and prevent it. But perhaps, she added, it would really turn out for the best.

Miss Selbourne had slept badly, and the sight of yet another wet morning did nothing to cheer her up. She had a cold, Tiger had a cold, one of the puppies had something which might be distemper. She rose at the usual hour and went through the usual routine of letting out the dogs, lighting the oil stove, and making a cup of tea.

She called, "Tiger, Tiger," in a hoarse croak from the foot of the stairs. But she did not wait for the response; instead she went back to the kitchen and sat down in the rocking chair, as near the stove as she could get. The rain pattered on the window. Agnes and Leo were barking to come in. But through these sounds there was faintly audible another sound, the prolonged groaning which was an indication that Miss Garrett was too ill to get up. Miss Selbourne paid no attention to the groans. She sipped her hot tea and wondered if she should take the puppy to the vet.

Presently the kitchen door opened and Miss Garrett appeared in her dressing gown. It was a man's dressing gown, very thick and hairy, and made her look rather like a large grizzly bear. She gazed reproachfully at Miss Selbourne. Then she poured out a cup of tea and perched herself on the edge of the table.

"Good morning, Tiger," said Miss Selbourne. "How's the cold?"

When she had drunk her tea Miss Garrett said huskily that the cold was no better. Miss Selbourne replied that she was sorry to hear it.

"I shall hab to hab anudder day in bed," Miss Garrett announced abruptly. She fished a repellent-looking handkerchief out of her pocket and blew her nose with great violence. Miss Selbourne helped herself to a second cup.

"I couldn't sleeb," said Miss Garrett. "Nod a wink."

Miss Selbourne stood up. "I couldn't sleep either," she said. "I've got a cold, too."

If it had not been such a wet morning, if she had not had a sick puppy to worry about, and if above all she had not been suffering from a cold, she would have spoken more kindly. Even as it was she meant only to remind Tiger that they were both in the same boat. But her voice had a sharp edge to it, and the words seemed to hang between them like a challenge. Miss Garrett responded to the challenge by another outburst of nose-blowing and coughing, plainly designed to show that her cold was much worse than her friend's, and at the end of it she looked up and said mournfully:

"Id's no good, old thing. I'mb just an old crock."

Formerly, whenever Miss Garrett denounced herself as an old crock, her friend had been wont to reassure her, or to offer the sort of assistance that an old crock needed to help it on its way through life. But latterly the phrase had begun to irritate Miss Selbourne. She found herself listening for it and noticing how it popped out whenever there was anything disagreeable to be done. Being an old crock was rapidly becoming, for Miss Garrett, a whole-time occupation. The sympathy and help which Miss Selbourne had given so freely in the past had now become mechanical responses, and the mechanism worked with increasing stiffness and reluctance.

This morning, for the first time, the mechanism did not work at all.

Without replying, Miss Selbourne went to the back door and flung it open. For the last ten minutes Agnes and Leo had been scratching and whining outside, and now they came bounding in and at once began to shake themselves, sending showers of muddy water all over the kitchen.

"By cold!" rasped Miss Garrett. "Shud the door."

Miss Selbourne shut the door, found the dogs' towels, and knelt down to dry them. When she had finished with the dogs she turned her attention to her friend. Tiger had moved to the vacant rocking chair and was sitting there with her eyes shut.

"I'm going to get dressed now," Miss Selbourne said. "I'll light the sitting-room fire and then we can have breakfast there."

Miss Garrett gave a prolonged groan. When this dismal sound had ceased Miss Selbourne heard her own voice proclaiming that it was quite time Tiger pulled herself together.

She had not intended to speak so harshly, but having begun she could not stop. It was not the first time they had quarrelled, but never before had they quarrelled so bitterly or said so many unkind things. The previous quarrels had usually begun by Miss Garrett's wanting something she could not have, a bottle of whisky, a new car, a larger establishment; this one was different, it concerned their life together—the way Tiger moaned and groaned and pretended to have headaches, the way Bunty clattered up and down stairs and thought only about money.

At the climax of the quarrel Tiger burst into tears and announced that she was off; she'd stood a lot from old Bunty, but this was the limit, dragged from her bed and expected to work when she'd be damn lucky if she hadn't got pneumonia. Coughing, weeping with rage, and groaning, Tiger stumbled out of the kitchen and retreated to her bedroom, ostentatiously locking herself in.

Then Miss Selbourne remembered the precious dogs, whose health mattered so much more than her own (or Tiger's), and she too retired upstairs. When she was dressed she made a hurried breakfast of stewed tea and cold porridge; if Tiger wanted breakfast she could get her own. As soon as she had finished she went out to the kennels. The puppy seemed better, but there was the usual feeding and grooming to be done, and then she discovered a leak in one of the roofs and had to attend to it. She was not a good carpenter and it took her some time to contrive a little patch of roofing-felt and nail it on with battens. While she was doing this she remembered that it was Saturday and that she ought to be in Bramworthy getting the rations. And there was nothing for lunch.

She felt her anger returning. It was cold on the roof of the kennels, the rain was trickling down her neck, the nails would not go where she meant them to, and she had to keep stopping to blow her nose. Tiger was warm and dry in the house. She would stay in her room all day, sulking, and then behave as if nothing had happened.

If she had not been so occupied with her carpentry she might have noticed that something *was* happening. Bank Cottage was a scene of much activity. Doors banged, drawers and cupboards were opened and shut, and a watchful face appeared several times at the bathroom window, which overlooked the kennels. Agnes and Leo barked excitedly, reminding Miss Garrett that she had more possessions than a few clothes. She could hardly bear to leave her dogs behind, but the important thing was to get out—just to go, which would show Bunty what she thought of her. She could send for the dogs later.

She had not much time to think about where she was to go, but there were at least two possibilities, an unmarried brother whom she had not seen for five years, and her old pal Shrimp Fisher. Miss Fisher seemed the more promising, for she lived only a few miles beyond Bramchester—and had she not implored Tiger to come over and look her up, any day, any time? Shrimp would listen and sympathize and give her a drink. Miss Garrett decided that Shrimp would be the right person to go to.

It occurred to her that it would be much easier if she took the car. Strictly speaking, the car belonged to Bunty, but she could jolly well do without it for a few days. The car lived in a shed which opened on to the lane; she carried her luggage downstairs and then went back to the bathroom and peeped out to make certain Bunty was still busy at the kennels. Then she regretfully shut Agnes and Leo into the sitting-room, for their delirious joy at the prospect of a drive would certainly attract Bunty's attention. She crept out and stowed her luggage in the car, started it, and drove out into the lane.

Just as she was about to drive out of Miss Selbourne's life forever, she remembered that she had not got her ration book.

Miss Garrett had often found herself in difficulties through having left her ration book at home when she went shopping, and she saw at once that it was essential to have it with her now. Even Shrimp might not welcome a guest who arrived without one. She stopped the car outside the wicket gate and hurried back to the house to retrieve it.

The wind and the rain and the noise of her own hammering had prevented Miss Selbourne from hearing the car. She was still on the roof, nailing down the last of the-battens, when she happened to glance up and saw Miss Garrett walking quickly up the path to the house. Though she was short-sighted she could not fail to recognize that bulky figure, and she also saw the car at the gate. She might have supposed that Miss Garrett was trying to make amends by going off to do the shopping, but apart from the unlikelihood of such behaviour there was something unnatural about the scene. Something out of the ordinary.

Then she realized what it was. The dogs were not there.

Miss Selbourne slithered down the roof and jumped to the ground. The absence of the dogs made it plain that Miss Garrett was trying to do something by stealth. She ran back across the paddock, and as she ran she saw Miss Garrett come out of the house. "Stop, stop!" she cried.

Far from stopping, Miss Garrett began to run too, a heavy lumbering run that was a poor match for Miss Selbourne's athletic strides. But Miss Garrett had only a short distance to go. By the time Miss Selbourne reached the gate she was already in the car, wheezing but triumphant, with the engine running and her hand on the brake.

"Stop!" Miss Selbourne repeated. "What are you doing?" The words were a waste of time and breath, for now she could see the luggage piled on the seat, topped by a spiky German helmet which was Tiger's dearest treasure.

"My car!" she screamed. "You can't have my car. Come back!"

But the car bounded forward and shot away down the lane, leaving her standing there in a haze of blue smoke and diminishing noise.

The triumphant glory of her departure went to Miss Garrett's head like strong drink, causing her to drive even faster than usual. She was going so fast that when she came to the sharp bend before the railway arch she was forced to take it very wide, and as she swung round it the German helmet was thrown off her suitcase and hit her on the shoulder. At the same instant she realized that another car was coming through the arch towards her.

Whether she was confused by the blow from the helmet, or whether she wished at all costs to avoid a collision, is uncertain; what happened was that Miss Garrett drove straight off the road, over a bank, through a hedge, and slap into the railway embankment. The car hit the embankment with great force, hung there quivering for a moment, and then turned over on its side. The hideous clatter and roar of its unorthodox progress ceased abruptly. There was no sound but a tinkle of breaking glass and the patter of falling rain.

Gillian and Laura were at the other side of the railway arch. They heard, rather than saw, Miss Garrett's swift departure from the road. The baker's van which had just overtaken them pulled up suddenly and the driver leapt out and ran to the gap in the hedge.

"Come on," said Gillian, running too. Laura had no wish to face a scene of carnage and destruction, but she followed unwillingly. When she got there it was not so bad as she had feared, there were no corpses or blood to be seen, and Miss Garrett was plainly still alive, though imprisoned within a car which looked as if its career was ended. The hoarse booming voice of Miss Garrett proclaimed that she was all right, and went on to babble confusedly of the steering and a beastly Hun helmet. But when they had extricated her—which took a little time—it was apparent that although she had had a marvellous escape from death she was not entirely undamaged. She had broken or wrenched her wrist, and had a cut forehead, and was badly dazed.

"Blimey, you was born lucky," said the van driver, when he saw it was no worse.

But Gillian said that Miss Garrett probably had concussion and ought to be taken straight to Bramworthy Hospital. Bank Cottage, she said with truth, was a place very ill-suited to invalids.

While she was telling the van driver that he should drive Miss Garrett into Bramworthy, and he was protesting that he had all his Saturday round to do, as well as having to report this little lot to the police, the problem was solved by the arrival of an ambulance. Among the audience—for by now there was quite a large audience—there had been an officious person who had run to Bank Cottage to tell Miss Selbourne that her friend was bleeding to death down the road, and Miss Selbourne's first action had been to telephone for the ambulance. So Miss Garrett was wrapped in blankets and borne away to Bramworthy Hospital. The little crowd dispersed, the van driver, having assured everyone that it was not his fault, went on his way, and Gillian and Laura walked back up the lane with Miss Selbourne.

Miss Selbourne had put in a belated appearance at the scene of the accident and had not offered to accompany her friend in the ambulance.

It was not far to Bank Cottage, and Gillian asked her if she hadn't heard the noise of the crash.

"Yes, I did," she replied. "At least, I think I did. I was so upset, you see, and so angry. I had the hammer in my hand when she left, and I hit the gate with it. Then I realized what I was doing, and I ran back into the house . . . I was going to telephone to the police about the car. . . . But something stopped me."

These intriguing words opened the way for more questions, and five minutes later they were sitting in the kitchen with Miss Selbourne and hearing the whole story of Tiger's unpardonable behaviour.

CHAPTER SIXTEEN

THE HIGHLY DRAMATIC departure of Miss Garrett (who was now languishing in Bramworthy Hospital) gave everyone something to talk about. A rumour got round that Gillian or Laura or both of them had been in the car with Miss Garrett, but their appearance at the Harvest Festival next morning, without bandages or bruises, soon corrected this. When the service was over Lady Masters came up to them in the street and wanted to know exactly what had happened. While Gillian was telling her about it—suppressing the fact that Miss Garrett was running away, and not mentioning the suitcases—Laura found Miles at her side.

"I suppose you are congratulating yourself on being right," she said, seeing that he was listening intently to the tale of the disaster.

"Being right? In what way?"

"Well, you said she was a dangerous driver. Do you remember?"

"I remember telling you not to drive with her, and I'm glad you took my advice."

Laura was about to reply that she had never been offered another lift by Miss Garrett, when he continued:

"I heard last night that you were in the car. I went over to see Miss Selbourne, to find out if it was true."

"Oh," said Laura. She remembered that Miss Selbourne and her landlord were not on good terms. She allowed herself to suppose that Miles had been anxious about her. But then, he had known them all their lives; it was quite natural that he should be anxious.

Toby Masters, who had been talking to his mother and Gillian, turned round to say that he had a wonderful plan, he had just been telling Gillian about it but, of course, he particularly wanted Laura as well, next Wednesday if that suited them.

"It's like this," he began, and then, seeing that she was not attending, he said rather possessively: "Now listen, Laura." Conscious that Toby had been speaking for some time and that she had not heard a word of it, Laura assumed an expression of sparkling interest.

Miles Corton bade them all good morning and walked over to his car, where the Misses Cleeve were already installed.

Gillian and Laura had come with Mrs. Worthy. It was lucky that Major Worthy and his nephew were not church-goers, for this gave Gillian the opportunity she wanted of speaking to Mrs. Worthy about Jocelyn's future. On the way to church she had encouraged Mrs. Worthy to talk of her husband's health and the strain it was having Jocelyn about the house all day, and on the homeward journey she propounded her plan.

"Jocelyn seems very keen on dogs," she said, "and Miss Selbourne really needs some help. She can't possibly look after all those dogs and run the house on her own. Do you think she'd like Jocelyn to help her?"

Mrs. Worthy was always a slow driver, but now she took her foot off the accelerator and let the car chug along at a snail's pace. "Do you mean every day—all the time?" she asked incredulously, screwing up her eyes in the manner of a pilgrim who glimpses the promised land. "Oh, but that would be—well, it would be just what he needs. Of course, Curtis and I are both devoted to Jocelyn, but we do feel he needs something to do. As I was saying to Curtis, it would make all the difference if he only had something to do—Jocelyn, I mean. It would use up his energy and then he wouldn't always be standing up and sitting down and fidgeting in the evenings, when Curtis wants to be quiet."

All the way home they discussed it. Gillian said there would be plenty for Jocelyn to do. Mrs. Worthy was doubtful about this, for at home there were few tasks which kept him occupied for long. But Gillian said it would be different if he was working for someone else, and Mrs. Worthy was only too anxious to believe her.

"But what about wages?" she asked. There was nothing about Bank Cottage to suggest that it could support a full-time assistant.

Gillian pointed out that if they sent Jocelyn to South Africa or set him up in any other career it would cost them a lot of money, and that dog-breeding was just as much a career as fruit-farming or engineering.

"You can't expect Miss Selbourne to train him for nothing," she said. "Some of the well-known kennels want a very big premium from their pupils, but I'm sure Miss Selbourne would take him cheaply because she really needs someone."

"Oh, dear!" Mrs. Worthy said. "I don't know what Curtis will say about that. I shall have to ask him. Of course, he has always promised to give Jocelyn a start, but then Jocelyn keeps changing his mind, and naturally Curtis does not want to waste his money paying for something that isn't going to last."

But, of course, in reality it was her own money which would pay for Jocelyn's training, and the thought of having him out of the house, all day and every day, was a powerful argument in favour of paying Miss Selbourne a small premium for employing him.

"You're wonderful, Gil," Laura said when they were alone.

"I'm sure Jocelyn will suit Miss Selbourne beautifully; the more I think of it the more I see how well they'll get on."

"I've still got to persuade her to have him. I'll go down this evening and have a nice cosy chat with her."

"Do you think, when Miss Garrett recovers, that they'll make it up?"

"I shouldn't think so. I believe Miss Selbourne has been wanting to get rid of her for ages. She'll be an awful fool if she has her back."

"But poor Tiger! What will she do?"

"She'll find someone else," Gillian said confidently. "The Shrimp woman perhaps. People like Tiger always find someone to scrounge on."

"I think I'll go over to Bramworthy and visit her."

"That would be a good deed. People in hospital seem to have an absolute craving for visitors. If I were ever ill," said Gillian, who never was, "I should want complete privacy. I couldn't bear people to see me looking bloated, or shrunken, or swathed in bandages. But I've noticed that most invalids appreciate an audience."

"I'll go on Wednesday, if she's well enough for visitors by then."

"You can't go this Wednesday. Have you forgotten Toby's wonderful plan?"

Laura had forgotten it, and she said crossly that she did not see anything particularly wonderful in having tea with Toby.

"Not just tea, darling. A picnic."

"It's the middle of October—much too late for picnics."

"Autumn's the loveliest time of the year; why shouldn't we go and look at it?" Gillian chanted, in a good imitation of Toby's enthusiastic voice. In her own voice she added: "Thick coats, fur boots, pink noses, cold tea—it will be heaven!"

"Oh, dear," Laura said, "are we being horrid?"

"If by horrid you mean non-enthusiastic, I must say I expected a little more zest from you. I've never pretended to enjoy these revivals of childhood's customs, but I always thought you did."

"Well, I do, in a way. The trouble is, I sometimes feel years older than Toby. I never used to feel like that."

"You must be growing up," Gillian said kindly.

On the day of the picnic they were forced to admit that they would not need their winter coats or their fur boots. It was a warm, cloudless afternoon, and the brilliance of the sunshine quite made up for a slight breeze. Toby's plan was to drive over to Bramworthy and go out on the river; they would row upstream, he said, and picnic in the beechwoods above the old abbey.

The picnic was not really a revival of childhood's custom, but a substitute for the blackberry picnic, which would have taken place in September if he had been at home. Even Gillian agreed that it would be fun to go out on the river, which they had never been able to do as children because there were no boats in those unenterprising days. The newly opened Riverside Café was the first establishment to provide boats, and these were intended to be used on the short reach of navigable water between the café and the Bramchester bridge, where there were no obstacles and no danger.

The proprietor of the Riverside Café looked doubtful when he heard that they meant to go up beyond the abbey.

"It's all shallows, and full of snags," he said. "You might get up to the abbey, but you can't go farther than that."

"Very well," said Toby. "We'll go to the abbey."

When they had embarked he explained to them that the chap was just nervous about his precious new boat. "The river's big enough for six boats," he said cheerfully, pulling away with great vigour and sending splashes of water into the air and sometimes into the boat. "He thinks we'll wreck it or something."

Both Gillian and Laura had a strange and touching faith in Toby's ability to manage a boat, but presently Gillian observed that they were not getting along very fast.

"It's the current," Toby explained. "It's much stronger than you think." He redoubled his efforts, and gradually they left the houses behind them and moved between green fields. A bend in the river hid the town, and ahead they saw the ruined walls of the abbey and the hanging beechwoods in their bright autumnal beauty. Gillian and Laura exclaimed with admiration, Toby turned round to look, and the boat swung sideways in the current and grounded gently on a submerged bank.

Seeing how difficult Toby found it to get away from the bank should have warned them, Gillian said afterwards. But at the time they thought nothing of it. The sun was shining, it was warm and pleasant in the boat, and they were all in a good humour.

Presently, after touching two more mudbanks, they drew level with the abbey. Getting there had taken much longer than they had expected, and they all agreed that it was time for tea.

"We'll land here," Toby said, "and then we can go on afterwards."

He turned the boat towards the shore. It had no rudder and his companions could only direct him by shouting warnings of visible hazards.

"Higher up!" Gillian cried. "You're coming in where there's nothing but mud!" Too late, for Toby had hit the mud. Ten minutes later, when he had managed to free the boat, it became wedged in a hidden tree trunk. After that there was more mud, and then a long wire running out into the river to prevent cattle getting into the abbey grounds. All these obstacles, like magnets, drew the boat into their clutches, and from all of them it could be released only with the utmost difficulty, with many ominous scratchings and scrapings along its bottom, and with a lavish distribution of mud and muddy water over its occupants.

"Good heavens, Toby," Gillian said. "Have you ever been in a boat before?"

"Often and often. But this is rather a difficult boat."

"*Now!*" cried Laura, who had been posted in the bow as a look-out. "Straight in there—it's deep all the way to the bank. Keep straight!" Toby bent to the oars, the boat shot lightly over some minor obstacle, and they hit the bank with a bump which upset the tea-basket. But everyone was too glad to have arrived to worry about one of the cups' being broken.

After tea Gillian said firmly that she for one was not going any farther in the boat; the homeward journey would be as much as her nerves could stand. Toby, who had got wetter and muddier than either of them, was secretly relieved to hear her say it; he was beginning to feel cold and his hands were blistered. The bank where they sat was now in shadow, and he suggested that they should climb up to the mound and explore the abbey ruins. The abbey stood well above the level of the river and the sunlight still glowed on its crumbling walls.

"We shall get nice and warm scrambling about up there," he said.

"You should have worn your winter woollies," Gillian retorted mischievously. Toby had once told them that he had three different grades of underwear, summer, spring-and-autumn, and winter, and since Gillian herself was a person who sacrificed comfort to elegance and wore the flimsiest possible garments all the year round she thought this very funny.

"Come on," said Laura, seeing that Toby was beginning to look extremely cold. "It will be fun. I should think we could get right up on that wall."

"Not me," Gillian protested. "You know I can't stand heights." It was a weakness she was ashamed of, but she had never been able to overcome it. To pay her out for laughing at his winter woollies, Toby now began to make fun of Gillian's vertigo. Laughing and arguing, they ascended the steep mound. This was what Toby liked—to have them both with him, to tease them a little (for luckily neither of them minded being teased), and to recapture the happiness of the past. Gillian and Laura had been the companions of his childhood; it was quite easy, with them, to slip back into nonsense and irresponsibility.

But he needed them both. Their sallies and arguments with each other provided the right atmosphere. He was fond of them both, and particularly of Laura, but the magic would not work unless they were together. Presently they arrived at the foot of the massive wall Laura intended to climb, and though he did his best to persuade Gillian that she would enjoy the view from the top, she insisted on staying where she was. "I should be sick if I went up there," she said. Toby did not want her to be sick, but he wanted the laughter and the jokes to continue. Unlike Macheath, he wanted both his dear charmers at once.

Laura had scrambled nearly to the top of the wall. Gillian stood at its base, calling to her to be careful. Between them, half-way up the crumbling buttress which served as staircase, Toby looked from one to the other. Suddenly he realized that this was a symbolic moment; it symbolized the choice which he had always known he would have to make. Thinking this, he turned quite pale, for it seemed to him that his next move must also have a symbolic importance. It was as though when he faced the necessity of having to choose he had also committed himself to making the choice there and then.

Ever since he had left the Army and come home to Endbury Toby had dallied with the idea of marriage. It had been an agreeable fantasy, perhaps all the more agreeable because of the practical difficulties in the way. Without his mother's consent it would be impossible to get married, for as Laura had guessed, he had no intention of cutting himself off from Endbury, and Endbury without his mother's income to support it would not be Endbury at all. Till recently he had felt pretty certain she would not approve of his marrying, which meant that he was free to dream and that an irrevocable decision—which was a thing he tended to avoid—could be indefinitely postponed. But lately Lady Masters had made it clear to him that her views on matrimony had undergone a change.

Toby had already succeeded in forgetting, or nearly forgetting, the particular episode which had brought about this change. It was sufficient that it had happened, and that far from impeding him, his Mama was positively encouraging him to get married.

Lady Masters had frequently insisted that she did not believe in coercion. Her horror of coercion prevented her from naming the person she wished her son to marry. Within limits, he was free to choose.

"It's lovely up here!" Laura called from above. "Come and look at the view."

"Don't believe her," said Gillian. "People who have got to the top of anything always pretend there's a better view. It's just as good from the mound."

Toby drew a deep breath. He shut his eyes, but when he opened them again the symbolic moment was still with him.

Without saying anything, he began to scramble upwards.

Unaware of the tremendous importance of Toby's action, Gillian turned away and wandered out through the broken walls. She had enjoyed the picnic, but she wished they would come down. The colour had faded from the beechwoods, the breeze had strengthened, and there was an autumn chill in the air. When she had regained the river bank she turned round, meaning to wave and call to Laura, to remind her that it was getting late.

Toby and Laura were standing close together. Toby had his hand on her arm, and they were not looking at the view.

"Dear me," Gillian said to herself, "has it come to this?" She gazed at them with interest, but they were too far distant for her to read their faces.

Toby had not intended, when he climbed to the top of the wall, that it should come to this. But finding himself at Laura's side, and still elated by his conquest of the symbolic moment, he suddenly thought how splendid it would be, now that he had made his choice, to have it settled and approved.

For a vacillating nature like Toby's, impulsive action is much easier than premeditated action, and he was quite accustomed to making big decisions on the spur of the moment. So, with no preliminaries beyond an ardent look, he laid his hand on her arm and said:

"Laura!"

Laura had been brought up to believe that you should not let a man propose to you if you did not mean to accept him. But since no one had yet attempted to propose to her she had not realized that there might be difficulties in living up to this admirable precept. She had supposed that womanly intuition or plain common sense would give one fair warning of what was coming and enable one to take evasive but tactful steps to prevent it.

Toby's behaviour gave her no warning at all, and by the time she recovered from her surprise it was too late to be tactful.

"Laura," he repeated, speaking rapidly and yet in a voice which did not lack confidence. "I've often thought about this, and perhaps you have too. I mean, I hope you have. We know each other so well, I'm sure we should be very happy. Together. Well—how about getting married?"

"No!" cried the demon who always spoke while Laura was struggling to find the right words. "No, I couldn't!"

The demon's utterances were invariably loud and clear, but never louder or clearer than in the present crisis. Laura was overcome by contrition and she at once tried to mitigate the harshness of the demon's refusal.

"Oh, Toby!" she cried, "I'm so dreadfully sorry. You took me by surprise or I wouldn't have said that. I mean, it isn't that I don't like you. I'm very fond of you. Only I hadn't thought about marrying, and I'm afraid it wouldn't do." (Untrue, untrue, whispered the demon, mocking her well-intentioned lies.) "Toby," she continued, regaining a measure of calm, "please, don't say any more now. Let's go back to the boat before Gillian comes to look for us."

Both Laura and Toby were fortunately unaware that they were silhouetted against a fine October sunset.

There was a long pause, a reproachful stillness in which the cawing of the rooks in the distant woods sounded unnaturally emphatic. Then Toby turned to climb down from the wall.

It was just as well that Laura had besought him to say no more, for at that moment he was quite incapable of saying anything. Whether he was unusually conceited or whether his dream-fantasies had unfitted him for coping with the hardships of real life, the fact remains that it had never occurred to him that Laura might reject her destiny. The choice was to be his, the approval was to come from his mother, the chosen one had only to play her part in the role assigned to her; and it was not the harshness of her words, but their incredible meaning that deprived Toby of his powers of speech.

He was more bewildered than wounded. It was as if the scene on the abbey wall had been a distorted and unrecognizable projection of the truth, and as he followed her down to the boat he was already beginning to make the changes, the small adjustments, which would be necessary to bring the picture back into focus.

Gillian had packed away the tea things and folded up the rug. "My tiny hands are frozen," she said, "and my tiny feet too. Hurry up, Toby, let's get away before the monkish ghosts appear. It's a lovely abbey in daytime, but I don't care for it when the shades of night are falling."

If that was a proposal, she thought, it has not gone according to plan, and what is needed now is a flow of sprightly conversation. Having made her diagnosis she set herself to apply the remedy. It was sometimes difficult for her to appear unaware of the frigid constraint which paralysed her companions, but she managed pretty well, and fortunately the stream was now in Toby's favour and the return journey was much quicker than the outward one.

In the car Gillian sat between them, and when they got back to Woodside she thanked Toby at great length and extolled the picnic in glowing terms, so that the meagreness of Laura's thanks went unnoticed by Mrs. Cole, who had come down to the gate to meet them.

Devoted mother as she was, Mrs. Cole could be remarkably obtuse, and neither Laura's silence nor Toby's rather hurried departure gave her an inkling of the frightful truth: that Endbury had been offered and rejected.

CHAPTER SEVENTEEN

FOR THE NEXT few days Laura could think of nothing but the extreme awkwardness of her situation. She was ready to admit that it was largely her own fault, but that did not make it more endurable.

When Toby proposed to her she had known at once that she did not want to marry him. It was a pity she had not discovered the change in herself a little sooner, instead of shutting her eyes and letting the weeks drift by. Although her plan for winning over Lady Masters had never really been carried out, it was clear now that Lady Masters must have made her own plans and must have had good reasons for supposing that she would approve of them. All this, the memory of her own scheming, the feeling of guilt, the humiliation of having behaved so foolishly, was hard to bear, but the particular sensation she described to herself as "awkwardness" made it worse.

The awkwardness came of having to continue to live as though nothing had happened, of hearing her mother talk about Toby and Lady Masters and Endbury—it was curious how often the talk got round to Endbury—of meeting Gillian's speculative glance and fending off her questions, and of fearing, when she went out, that she would meet Toby or Lady Masters.

If she had been more accustomed to receiving offers of marriage Laura might have been able to bring herself to talk about this one, or at least to put it out of her mind. As the days went by she regretted not having told her mother about it at the time, which would at least have lessened the awkwardness. But it seemed too late to tell her now; the right moment had passed, there was never an opportunity of telling it naturally, and worse still, she gradually began to suspect the truth behind Mrs. Cole's increasingly frequent references to Endbury and her changed opinion of Lady Masters. She had been wilfully blind, she told herself, not to have seen it before now.

In the circumstances it was a relief that Mrs. Cole was at present too busy with the alterations to the garden to think about tea parties.

Gillian, too, fortunately, had plenty to occupy her. Mr. Greenley, who seemed to like his holidays at very odd seasons of the year, was in residence at Cleeve Manor. With him was his widowed sister from Sunningdale, who was asked to Cleeve Manor only at such times as her children were at boarding school, children, in Thomas's opinion, being positive dangers to rare and irreplaceable plants. Gillian was invited to stay with them for a few days and to go to the Hospice Ball at Bramchester. The Hospice Ball, which was given annually by an ancient guild which now existed for no other purpose, was an important occasion in the social life of the county. Gillian recklessly extracted some money from her post office savings account and treated herself to a day's shopping in Bramchester and a new evening dress, which was so *décolleté* that only to look at it made Mrs. Cole shiver.

Gillian's clothes were always clean, pressed, mended, and perfectly ready to wear. Nevertheless she busied herself with small alterations and finishing touches, and with washing her hair and manicuring her nails; and as all this kept her upstairs in her bedroom or in the spare room where the ironing board and sewing machine were kept, she and Laura were seldom alone together. When they were, Laura avoided dangerous silences by asking questions about Mr. Greenley and his sister. She was surprised to find that Gillian was quite easily beguiled into talking about Mr. Greenley.

"Thomas is coming on wonderfully," said Gillian. "Subscribing to the Hospice Fund, taking tickets for the ball—he'll be thinking he has a stake in the county soon. And his sister is rather nice. Fat and silly, but nice."

"Is she very grand?"

"Overwhelmingly grand, in mink, to look at. Her clothes are almost as awful as Thomas's. Isn't it peculiar that women with lots of money are so often guided to buy such frightful frocks and hats? It's a sort of law of compensation."

The shortage of petrol never seemed to bother Mr. Greenley and he motored over to fetch Gillian, bringing his sister with him. Laura decided that her own views on niceness must be radically different from Gillian's. Mrs. Cartwright-Brown was a large, plump woman, older than Thomas, more gorgeously apparelled, and even duller. She had a phlegmatic disposition and showed signs of animation only when she spoke of her children; at other times she seemed to relapse into a coma, sitting perfectly still and looking out on the world with lacklustre eyes and an expressionless face. She was a widow twice over, the children were the children of her second marriage, and she appeared so fixed in middle age that it was quite a shock to be told that her eldest boy was only twelve.

It was also a shock when Gillian addressed her new friend as Trixie. This incongruous name, so ill-suited to her massive personality, amused Laura and antagonized Mrs. Cole, who decided that Mrs. Cartwright-Brown must be a very stupid woman. Anyone less stupid would have blushed to be addressed as Trixie and insisted on Beatrice, or whatever Trixie stood for.

Mrs. Cole was perhaps prejudiced, for she resented having to entertain Thomas and Trixie to tea on a day when the operations in the garden had reached a crucial stage. They were Gillian's friends, Thomas was taking Gillian to the Hospice Ball, and it was her duty to entertain them, but she did it under protest and was in no mood to make the best of them. Naturally they did not suspect this. Mrs. Cole's manners were charming, and Thomas had already pigeonholed her as "one of the old school," and Mrs. Cartwright-Brown's faculties were probably not sufficiently developed for her to suspect anyone of anything.

They had tea early, and in the midst of her pleasant, tranquil conversation Mrs. Cole kept hoping that the visitors would also leave early so that she could go out and inspect the work in the garden before it got dark.

The hired labourers who were digging the new drains did not always see eye to eye with her about how the drains should run, and more than once she had had to appeal to Miles Corton for masculine support. She was not always right about drainage, but she was sure that the labourers knew even less about it than she did. Both she and they were willing to accept Miles's advice; he had been several times, and each time she had kept him in the garden as long as possible and had been careful never to leave him alone with Laura. No Victorian chaperone could have guarded her child more zealously than Mrs. Cole. She was convinced that Laura was very much drawn to Toby, but she was not going to give Miles a chance to distract or distress her.

It was unfortunate that Miles should call today, just as the visitors and Gillian were collecting their coats and preparing to leave. It delayed their leaving; Miles came into the hall and was introduced to Mrs. Cartwright-Brown, and exchanged a few casual and not particularly cordial remarks with Thomas, whom he had, of course, met on the day of the Misses Cleeve's garden party. Gillian foolishly invited them all to come back to the sitting-room for a drink. She was in her gayest mood, and looking particularly pretty. Mrs. Cole was glad to see her happy, but she was glad too when Thomas said that they must be off. He said it kindly but firmly, and Gillian gave in at once.

Afterwards Mrs. Cole wondered about this. It was not like Gillian to be so docile. In her fond heart this virtue was attributed to Laura, while Gillian had a charming talent for getting her own way.

By the time they had gone it was almost too dark to look at the garden. After a perfunctory walk across the lawn to peer down at the trenches, the piles of earth, and the line of pegs which marked the position of the new path, she brought Miles back to the house. Laura met them at the door and reminded her that she had gone out in her thin slippers.

"They're wet through, Mummy. You'd better go and change them at once."

With misguided devotion her mother insisted that they were not wet—only the toes, and they would soon dry by the fire.

"Well, come and have some sherry," Laura said. "Come in, Miles. I haven't seen you for ages."

Knowing that both her daughters had the modern habit of making exaggerated statements, Mrs. Cole was yet a little displeased by this remark. Miles Corton came to Woodside quite often enough. She sat down by the fire and asked Laura to fetch her old shawl, which she had dutifully discarded in honour of Thomas and Trixie.

"Gillian is going to the Hospice Ball tomorrow night," Laura told Miles.

He answered coolly, "I hope she enjoys herself."

"I'm sure she will. Gillian loves dancing."

"I used to be very fond of it myself," said Mrs. Cole, looking back into the past. She thought of her admirers, and of the young girls with whom she had laughed and gossiped. Thomas and his dull sister would have made a poor showing in that company.

"Is *she* going?" she asked abruptly. Trading on her own vagueness she often managed to forget the names of people she disliked, as if to show how little they meant to her.

"Who, Mummy? Oh—Trixie. Well, I suppose so."

"Trixie," said Mrs. Cole, underlining it. Her faint air of surprise, of disbelief, made them laugh.

"Parents can't foresee the future," Miles said. "But they
ought to be more careful."

"She could change her name. People do. I knew a girl at
school who called herself Stephanie because she couldn't bear
being one Anne among so many."

Mrs. Cole thought to herself that Laura was really quite as
pretty as Gillian. When they were together Gillian outshone her
because she was more at ease, more vivacious, and Laura was always ready to let her take the lead. It was perhaps a pity that they
were so much together. But Gillian would be away till Monday.

"I really must ask Lady Masters over," she said. Her train of
thought had led her to this conclusion quite logically, and she
was slightly surprised to find that Miles and Laura were talking
of something else and seemed to regard Lady Masters as an interruption.

Laura said quickly that she was very busy just at present.
"And there's the garden, Mummy. You said you were too busy
yourself to bother about entertaining or being entertained."

The garden was important to Mrs. Cole, but her dreams for
Laura were even more important.

"The men won't be here on Sunday," she said. "I could ask
her to lunch then. And Toby too. If I write tonight, and send it
by the first post in the morning—"

"There's the meat ration," Laura protested.

"A very good excuse," Miles said, "for not having people to
lunch if you don't want them."

For some reason this annoyed Mrs. Cole very much. It certainly sounded as if Laura did not want Lady Masters or Toby
to come to lunch. That was nonsense, of course; Laura was ab-
surdly sensitive and had lately begun to shy away from discussing Toby—a very good sign, in her mother's eyes, of the special
interest she felt for him. But Miles must not be allowed to run
away with the wrong idea.

"The meat ration has nothing to do with it," she said fretfully. "It's just that Laura thinks it would be a bother for me. But, of

course, it's not a bother when it's people you like—old friends."
She gave Laura a look which was meant to be admonishing, in a
fond maternal way, but which only succeeded in adding a particular significance to the words "old friends." Never had Laura
come nearer to being one of those regrettable daughters who
engage in acrimonious public disputes with their parents. She
wanted to point out that Lady Masters, although technically an
old friend, had never been entertained at Woodside except from
a sense of duty, and that it was only in the past few months that
Mrs. Cole had promoted her from being looked-down on to being looked-up to. But it was impossible to say this, and she felt
that her protests had already given an unnatural importance
to the discussion. Afterwards, when Miles had gone, she would
have to find some better reason for not inviting Lady Masters to
luncheon.

Miles did not stay very long. He liked Mrs. Cole, but this was
one of the evenings when he liked her less than usual.

When he had gone, Mrs. Cole sat down and wrote to Lady
Masters. Laura was washing up the tea things, and when she
had finished she went upstairs to hunt for some knitting which
had been put away uncompleted at the end of last winter and
which she meant to unravel and start again. Laura's belong-
ings, unlike Gillian's, were not neatly folded and systematically
grouped, and it took her some time to find the knitting, which
was hibernating at the back of her boot cupboard. While she was
upstairs Mrs. Trimmer called to bring back the clean sheets.

"Thought I'd drop 'em in as I was passing," said Mrs. Trimmer, who did laundry work in her own cottage and at her own
convenience.

Mrs. Cole put the parcel on the kitchen table and asked if
Mrs. Trimmer was on her way to see Enid. Enid was the married
daughter who lived on the Bramworthy road.

"No, it's me aunt. Not that I'd be seeing 'er so soon after last
time if I didn't 'ave to," said Mrs. Trimmer, who always spoke
of her relatives with perfect candour, "but she asked me to get
'er some of that fine crochet cotton which they 'ave in Bodgers'
at Bramton and which can't be got, seemingly, in Bramworthy.

Wants it to make a doochess set for Christmas, so I thought she'd better 'ave it now."

"Is it for your aunt at Endbury?"

Mrs. Trimmer had several aunts, but she nodded vigorously. "There she sits, 'er and Cook, every evening, tat-tatting away, and what they do with all the stuff they make fair beats me, Christmas excepting, of course," she said.

Mrs. Cole was delighted to hear that Mrs. Trimmer was on her way to Endbury; it would save a post. Mrs. Trimmer put the letter into her capacious black bag and promised not to forget it, and to compensate her for her trouble, Mrs. Cole told her that it was an invitation to lunch on Sunday, for she knew that Mrs. Trimmer loved to know all that was going on.

Mrs. Trimmer nodded again and looked comprehending and mysterious.

"I won't forget," she said emphatically. "Shouldn't forgive meself if I forgot a thing like that." She fiddled with the lamp of her bicycle—for they were now indulging in the usual prolonged farewells at the back door—and as she turned away she said, with a mother-to-mother intonation:

"Miss Laura's looking ever so pretty these days, isn't she, M'm?"

Once again Mrs. Cole was left with the impression that other people knew far more than she did about what was going on.

Mrs. Cole was, except where the garden was concerned, notoriously absent-minded, and after breakfast the next morning, when nothing more had been said about the invitation and it was too late to catch the first post, Laura began to hope that she had forgotten about it. If she did not write today it would be too late to write at all.

At breakfast they talked about the garden; it was a fine morning, the labourers were energetically at work, and as soon as she had satisfied her conscience by doing a little dusting— because poor Laura was single-handed this morning—Mrs. Cole put on her gum-boots and hurried out of doors. There were a lot of plants to be lifted and transferred to the new beds, and plenty of other work to keep her busy and happy. Watching her, Laura felt happier too; it seemed clear that this was to be a day devoted to gardening.

It was on her conscience that she had never been to visit Miss Garrett in Bramworthy Hospital. She might go that afternoon, but it would be as well to find out first if Miss Garrett was still there, and she decided to walk down to Bank Cottage and ask Miss Selbourne. The housework was done, the lunch prepared; and she was not likely to meet Toby or Lady Masters in Wick Lane.

She walked slowly down the lane, enjoying in a melancholy way the mild warmth of the sunshine. At the gate of Bank Cottage she met Miss Selbourne returning from a walk in the other direction, accompanied by a number of dogs. All the dogs except Agnes and Leo were attached to her by long leashes and was in constant danger of being tripped up as they bounded and frisked around her. None of Miss Selbourne's dogs had ever been trained to walk to heel.

"Come inside!" she called cheerfully. "Can't stop here—they don't like it." Laura opened the gate and they went into the paddock, where the dogs were unleashed for a final scamper before being shut up in their kennels.

Laura was a little surprised to find Miss Selbourne exercising her dogs, for that had been one of the tasks considered suitable for Jocelyn. She looked about her; he was nowhere to be seen, and she wondered if his enthusiasm for dog-breeding had already waned. But she knew it would not be tactful to ask after Jocelyn or Miss Garrett before asking after the dogs. Her inquiries produced a long and detailed account of each individual dog, which was rather boring because she found it difficult to tell them apart and still more difficult to invent new expressions of interest, sympathy, and admiration. But at last the subject was exhausted, and with the aid of a bag of biscuits Miss Selbourne began to lure the dogs themselves back to their kennels.

"Can't Jocelyn help you with all this?" Laura suggested.

Miss Selbourne looked up from her task. She appeared a little embarrassed.

"Jocelyn's a great help," she said, "in other ways."

Laura supposed that Jocelyn was doing some gardening for a change. It was true that Mrs. Worthy had paid a premium for him to learn about dog-breeding, but her real object had been to get him out of Major Worthy's way. Provided she kept him occupied, Miss Selbourne was earning her money; but since she was plainly uneasy about the manner of Jocelyn's employment, Laura said no more, but went on to ask about Miss Garrett.

"She's with Shrimp Fisher, over at Copyhanger. She left hospital last Monday. Yes, quite all right, I think, but I haven't seen her." Miss Selbourne fastened the last dog into its kennel and said coldly: "I had a very rude letter from Shrimp. Obviously she believes every word Tiger says. But she'll learn."

"And what about Miss Garrett's dogs?" Laura asked. After you had spent a short time with Miss Selbourne you instinctively began to think in terms of dogs.

"Shrimp is having some kennels built. Then they are coming over to fetch them."

She added rather sadly that she would miss the dogs very much.

Laura looked at her watch and said she must go home and see to the lunch. They walked back across the paddock and as they neared the house Jocelyn came out of the back door. He was wearing a large white apron, which quite altered his appearance, and held a frying pan in his hand. He addressed himself to Miss Selbourne.

"I've found some more fat," he announced. "So we can have them fried after all."

"Oh, Jocelyn, how clever of you," she said admiringly.

There was a short pause. Then Miss Selbourne put a brave face on it and confessed that Jocelyn was doing the cooking, because it really suited both of them very much better that way.

"I have my lunch and tea here," Jocelyn explained. Then if we're late I don't keep Uncle Curtis waiting. Aunt Gwennie lets me have some rations. She doesn't mind a bit. But don't tell her I'm doing the cooking, because it might upset Uncle Curtis."

"Jocelyn's a much better cook than I am. And it gives me so much more time for the dogs."

"I do the housework too. Come in, Laura, and have a look."

In a happy chorus, strophe and antistrophe, Miss Selbourne and her apprentice extolled the merits of their new system. Laura was taken into the house and shown the kitchen, where Jocelyn had cleaned the pans and scrubbed the table and mended the dripping tap. The kitchen was no longer dominated by dogs' food and dogs' plates, and there was a new cake cooling on the dresser. She saw at a glance that the rest of the house had received little attention; there was still dust in the corners and dogs' hairs everywhere. But Miss Selbourne was used to this, and probably both she and Jocelyn preferred a cosy squalor to fresh air and furniture polish.

"You must come to tea," said Miss Selbourne. "Jocelyn's getting very good at cakes, and his drop-scones are a dream." Jocelyn accepted these compliments with a modest smile. It was just his luck, he seemed to say, that cooking should happen to be his talent.

CHAPTER EIGHTEEN

ON SUNDAYS, Major Worthy liked his breakfast an hour later than on weekdays. Afterwards, if it was a fine morning, he went for a short walk; if it was wet he inspected his greenhouse. At eleven o'clock the Sunday papers arrived, and these occupied him till lunchtime.

The duty of public worship was delegated to Mrs. Worthy, and he liked her to go to church at least once, and preferably twice, a month. This did not excuse her from her other duties of bedmaking and cooking. Mrs. Worthy sometimes wished that she in her turn could delegate some of her tasks to Clara, but it was impossible because Clara always went to Bramworthy on Sundays to visit her aged mother. Major Worthy was not unreasonable, and if she left everything ready he was perfectly willing to cooperate by putting the joint and the potatoes in the oven, but nevertheless church-going Sundays were difficult and strenuous times for his wife. Too often she arrived panting at the church door after the service had begun, and had to creep into a seat at the back because she could not face the walk up the aisle to her front pew.

This morning everything went well until the moment came to start the car. Mrs. Worthy was not mechanically-minded, but she realized that the sad little grunts the car gave when she pressed the self-starter meant that something was wrong. She went on pressing the self-starter till there was no longer the slightest response. Experience had taught her that in such a crisis it was no good appealing to Curtis, since he knew no more about cars than she did and disliked having his ignorance exposed. There was nothing for it but to give up the idea of going to church, and she walked down the drive to close the gate she had previously opened.

As she stood at the gate she saw a car approaching her and heading towards Bramton. It was nearly certain to be someone on the way to church, and almost without thinking Mrs. Worthy raised her hand in a vague gesture for help. The car slowed down, then stopped, and Lady Masters's face appeared at the window, looking benevolent but slightly annoyed.

"Get in, get in," said Lady Masters, opening the door and then setting the car in motion again almost before her passenger was safely bestowed. She was alone, and as she was a much faster driver than Mrs. Worthy they would be there in plenty of time. All the same, Mrs. Worthy felt that she had made a social error, and she continued to grovel until her benefactress relaxed and said affably that with old cars like Mrs. Worthy's one could always expect trouble.

"It is time you got a new one," she continued. "Not brand-new, of course—you wouldn't be able to get that—but a good second-hand one. It would really pay you."

Mrs. Worthy said humbly that they couldn't afford it. Lady Masters repeated, with kindly impatience, that it would *pay* them. "People are always saying they can't afford this or that, when a moment's clear thinking would show them that money well spent is an investment." They were already in Bramton, and as she drew up outside the church she nodded at another car standing a few feet away. "Look at that, Mrs. Worthy, that's what I mean. It's a disgrace—a confession of failure. If Miles Corton had any sense he'd sell that car tomorrow."

Mrs. Worthy looked at the blue car. It was certainly very shabby but otherwise there did not appear to be anything wrong with it. Feeling sympathetic towards Mr. Corton, she found herself defending his car with tactless zeal; fortunately they arrived at the lych-gate before she had time to say how much she disliked the appearance of all modern cars, and by common consent they fell into silence as they walked up the path to the church door. In a magnanimous whisper Lady Masters said that she would wait for Mrs. Worthy in the porch after the service was over.

By the time they had discussed the sermon, the peculiarities of the vicar's intonation, and the choice of hymns, they were within sight of Mrs. Worthy's home. When they reached the gate Lady Masters drew into the side of the road and switched off the engine.

"What a beautiful morning," she said, as if she were seeing it for the first time. "Quite, quite divine. Don't run away, Mrs. Worthy—a day like this is too good to be spent indoors."

Mrs. Worthy thought of the joint roasting in the oven, the potatoes needing basting, Curtis looking at his watch. "Yes, indeed, quite a lovely day," she agreed. "Quite like summer. But really—"

"You have a fine view from here. It would have been better if the house had faced more to the south. Strange that your architect did not see that, but so many architects think only of the appearance of the house, not of the poor unfortunate beings who are going to live in it."

Lady Masters gave a playful laugh, but Mrs. Worthy did not care to hear herself described as a poor unfortunate being.

"We face almost due south," she protested, "only a little bit to the west, which is better because of the sunsets. My husband designed the house himself, we did not have an architect. As I said at the time, we did not need one, as Curtis was so good at drawing and knew just what was wanted, and had lived in so many houses—being in the Army, you know, and in India. Though, of course, that was different because they were all bungalows and no stairs."

"Very different, I imagine. I have never been in India. England is good enough for me," Lady Masters said patriotically. She coughed and changed the subject, for Mrs. Worthy must not be encouraged to argue.

"And how is your young nephew? I hear that he is working for Miss Selbourne."

At any other time Mrs. Worthy would have been glad to speak of Jocelyn's career, of the difficulties she had successfully overcome, and of the merits of the present arrangement. But now she fiddled with her gloves and replied briefly that he was very well; then with her hand on the door she began her speech of thanks for the lift, interrupting herself to ask hurriedly after Toby's health, which she ought to have done sooner. "Quite settled and happy, I hope?" She tucked her Prayer Book under her arm. "Farming . . . so suitable. . . ." Out of the tail of her eye she saw Curtis standing in the porch, in an attitude of restrained impatience.

Lady Masters thanked her and said Toby was very fit except for a cold. "I am sorry you are in such a hurry," she continued. "You should learn to relax. 'What is this life if, full of care, we have no time to stand and stare?' The poets speak truth, Mrs. Worthy."

It was Major Worthy who was standing and staring. "Yes," said Mrs. Worthy, "but I have the lunch to see to. Clara—that is, our maid—goes out on Sundays. Another time—any other time—but, of course—"

"Ah, these domestic duties, how they tie us! I am fortunate today," Lady Masters said gratefully, as if she were in the habit of cooking her own meals. "I am lunching with Mrs. Cole at Woodside."

Mrs. Worthy perceived that she was being made use of. It had been a short service, and Lady Masters had some time to spare; the beauties of Nature, the pleasures of relaxation, were just so much camouflage. Shutting the door on Lady Masters in mid-sentence, she called a final and rather sharp goodbye through the window.

"Vicar lost his watch?" Major Worthy asked, as she hurried towards him.

Mrs. Cole's drawing-room was provided with a useful little window, known as the spyhole, which overlooked the front gate. Through the spyhole Mrs. Cole saw her expected guest approaching at an unexpectedly early hour, and called a warning to Laura. This gave them time to shake up the cushions, collect the scattered pages of the Sunday paper, and hide Mrs. Cole's darning inside her desk.

"She's far too early," Laura complained. "The food won't be ready for ages."

The door bell trilled through the house. "Sherry," Mrs. Cole suggested as she went off to answer it. Luckily, it was one of the times when there was sherry available.

Lady Masters's acceptance of the invitation had filled Laura with dismay. The embarrassment of meeting her again was aggravated by the fear that she had come on purpose to be reproachful, or contemptuous, or in some other way unpleasant. Though she could hardly believe that Lady Masters would speak openly of the proposal, Laura knew her too well to be able to hope that her anger would not be noticeable. Lady Masters was not a woman who believed in hiding her displeasure; and this meant that Mrs. Cole would see that something was wrong and would be sure to want to know what it was. Laura was very fond of her mother, but she had a horrid conviction that their outlook on life was quite different and that it would be far better for both of them if Mrs. Cole never discovered that her daughter had refused Toby Masters.

A prey to these disturbing thoughts, she found herself face to face with the dreaded guest. She did not know what to expect, and was almost shocked when Lady Masters greeted her as "Dear Laura" and went on to make bland and cheerful inquiries after her health.

"Such a pity about Toby," said Mrs. Cole.

Lady Masters agreed that it was a pity. But his cold was no better; she had kept him in the house for four days, and this morning she had insisted on a day in bed. It was really the only way to get rid of a bad cold.

Toby had caught his cold through being out in the rain all day with Manley. This led quite naturally to a discussion of the weather, and on to the beauties of Nature. Toby's name dropped out of the conversation, but without any obvious pause or any hint that it was a name to be avoided. Lady Masters seemed perfectly at ease, and neither in her greeting nor in her behaviour could Laura detect the smallest alteration.

The beauties of Nature and the exceptional splendour of this particular Sunday carried them through the sherry. Laura had to leave her mother alone with Lady Masters while she attended to the lunch, but when she came back it was plain that nothing had been said to upset Mrs. Cole. By the time the lunch was eaten, Laura was ready to admit that in one respect at least she had misjudged Toby. By slow degrees, passing from fear to bewilderment, from bewilderment to hope, she arrived at a state of comparative calm in which she could speak quite rationally of the garden and the neighbours.

Having been brought up on the legend that Toby always told his mother everything, she had not dared to hope that on this occasion he would keep his sorrows to himself. But now the legend receded into a sort of historical perspective; it belonged to the past and could safely be ignored. In proof of this she recalled the various occasions when Toby had openly criticized his mother. In her agitation she had quite forgotten them. She was almost ready to laugh at her unnecessary and ridiculous forebodings, but laughter was kept in its place by a new twinge of remorse when she thought of Toby. She had behaved very badly to poor Toby, and he had repaid her by behaving better than she would ever have believed.

Poor Toby, too, must be suffering from a genuine cold. Feeling quite sorry for him, Laura also allowed herself to feel thankful that if he had to have a cold he should have it now.

At exactly the same moment Mrs. Cole was thinking how sad it was that Toby could not be there; on such a glorious afternoon he and Laura could plausibly have been sent out to look at the alterations in the garden, while she and Lady Masters sunned themselves in the bay window. Sighing deeply, she said they would have coffee in the other room.

Lady Masters was in no hurry to leave. With Mrs. Cole's concurrence she had quite assumed the position of an old and valued friend. She even offered to help with the washing-up, assuring them that though neither Cook nor old Emily would let her lift a finger at Endbury she was always delighted to help her less fortunate friends. But Mrs. Cole and Laura would not hear of it; the washing-up, they said, could be done later. Both of them thought privately that to have her with them in the kitchen would be more a hindrance than a help.

"It is really a sin to sit indoors on such a lovely day," Lady Masters declared. "We ought all to go out for a long tramp. I always tell people there is nothing like a long tramp to chase away the cobwebs. I am sure you agree with me, Laura. You are so fond of walking."

"I never seem to have time, though. The house and the cooking, and then shopping in Bramworthy—"

"Ah, yes, you are like me—a slave to other people," Lady Masters said affably. Conscious that it was an honour to be like Lady Masters, Laura made a suitably humble reply.

"But this afternoon we are both free, are we not?" Lady Masters continued, as if the thought had just struck her. "And I have an errand to perform—an errand I had meant to do tomorrow, but it can just as well be done today. There is nothing like taking time by the forelock."

Laura's instinctive antipathy to the idea of going for a long tramp with Lady Masters was lessened when she found out that it was only to take them to Bank Cottage, a matter of ten minutes each way. Besides, there was no good reason for refusing, and Mrs. Cole was already saying how nice it would be for her. Mrs. Cole had no intention of going herself, and waved farewell to them with a beaming smile which reflected her secret relief at being rid of Lady Masters.

The drive to Woodside was steep and narrow, and Lady Masters had left her car at the gate. She paused there and suggested that perhaps it would be better if they went for a drive.

"Oh, but it's only just down the lane," said Laura, puzzled and suddenly apprehensive.

"Dear child," Lady Masters said, opening the door of the car, "get in. We can talk as we go."

Laura got in, feeling it would be rash to argue. A moment ago she had been certain that Lady Masters knew nothing of Toby's proposal; now she was no longer certain, but she could not believe that Lady Masters knew everything. Perhaps she suspected, or perhaps this was to be a discussion of Toby's future with veiled hints of what would be good for him. Alarmed, but hoping for the best, she looked straight in front of her and prepared to be wilfully obtuse.

When they came to the river Lady Masters commented on its beauty. With a splendid indifference to the claims of other wayfarers she stopped the car on the bridge.

"Our own river," she said, "is not nearly so picturesque."

Laura forbore to point out that it was just a different stretch of the same river. She felt that it was not for her to give topographical instruction to her companion.

"Our own river is too straight," Lady Masters continued. "Straight and uninteresting. No better than a canal."

Laura said that the old canal beyond Bramworthy was quite pretty in places.

Without warning, Lady Masters abandoned the subject of rivers and turned towards her. "Dear Laura," she said, "you have made me very happy." She laid her hand on Laura's arm, just as Toby had done on the day of the picnic. "I have to tell you this," she continued, "because I understand so well your doubts and hesitations. It is because of that—because I wanted to reassure you—that I have come here today as Toby's ambassador."

Laura gazed at her in a stupor of horror which Lady Masters appeared to take for excessive timidity.

"My dear child, there is nothing to be afraid of. When Toby told me that you had refused him—just like that—I was upset. I admit it now. But then, when we talked it over, I began to understand. When I heard all the circumstances I realized that it had come as a surprise to you."

"But—"

"As I said to him, a refusal like that means nothing. But indeed," and she looked at Laura with an arch smile, "I think he had already guessed that for himself."

"But I refused him."

"I understand young people, Laura. I know how you feel about Toby. I know your character, too; you have always been shy and reserved and—shall we say—diffident. *Good* faults, Laura," Lady Masters said kindly. "I am not surprised that you asked for more time. It was the natural answer—exactly what I should have expected from you."

"He misunderstood me—" Laura began. But her companion swept happily on.

"You told him to say no more about it—then. But now, my dear—now that we have had this little talk—I am sure you will be able to give him a very different answer!"

The bright sunlight had made the interior of the car quite hot; Laura had the sensation of being shut up in a little box—or prison—without doors or windows, of being condemned to sit side by side with Lady Masters for all eternity. Shaking herself free of this nightmare, she said in a loud voice:

"Stop, please stop! It's all a mistake. I can't marry Toby. I don't want to."

Lady Masters stiffened into a dreadful rigidity, as if she had suddenly been turned to stone. The understanding smile became a fixed grimace. She slowly withdrew the hand that had been holding Laura's and clasped it in her lap.

"A mistake?" she echoed vaguely, as if she had never heard the word before. For a moment she seemed incapable of further speech. Then she pulled herself together, visibly reorganizing her feelings.

"A very strange mistake, Laura," she said coldly. "You have treated my poor Toby very badly."

"But I refused him. And I never meant him to think—"

Lady Masters gave a high-pitched, angry sound that might have been a laugh or a snort of contempt. "I heard all about it from Toby," she said, "and it was quite plain what you meant him to think. You have behaved abominably."

Though she had hitherto been abjectly remorseful and embarrassed, Laura now found herself growing angry too, angry with Lady Masters and angrier still with Toby.

"He had no business to tell you about it," she said.

"My dear Laura," Lady Masters replied in a voice of ice, "please remember what is *your* business and what is not."

"It's your fault if he thinks I'm going to change my mind. You suggested it to him."

"You have deceived me," Lady Masters said. "I have been terribly mistaken in you. I am thankful—yes, really thankful—that this has happened. But for this mistake—as you call it—" and here she gave Laura a look so charged with scorn that it was as dazzling as a high-powered electric torch—"but for this, I might not have known until it was *too late*."

Feeling that if she did not get away from Lady Masters soon she would begin to scream, Laura fumbled for the door of the car.

"Yes, you had better go. We have nothing more to say to one another. You have been stupid, as well as heartless."

Slightly cheered by the thought that Laura would live to regret her folly, Lady Masters braced herself to make a statement which should rank as Famous Last Words.

"I have never understood you at all," she began majestically. It was a sentence of excommunication, but its effect was rather marred by the blaring of a car's horn immediately behind them. Even the right to occupy the bridge for as long as it pleased her was denied to Lady Masters, whose anger was temporarily diverted to the source of the interruption. While she was starting the car, Laura opened the door. She half sprang, half tumbled out, slamming the door behind her as the car moved away. The bridge was narrow and she had to flatten herself against the parapet, thinking as she did so how very awkward it would be to be run into by Lady Masters at that moment. She gazed wretchedly after the retreating car until it turned the corner and disappeared down the lane.

Only then did it occur to her that her behaviour must seem very odd to the people in the car behind. She looked round, striving to appear completely at her ease in case it was someone she knew.

There was only one person in the car behind, and he, far from being impressed by Laura's nonchalance, leaned out and besought her to stop crying.

CHAPTER NINETEEN

WATCHING MILES as he walked towards her, Laura thought he looked almost as angry as Lady Masters. But when he came nearer she saw that he was less angry than alarmed—and indeed anyone who had witnessed her precipitate exit from the car might well have found it an alarming sight.

Miles's presence at this moment was the last thing she would have wished for, and yet, now that he was here, she felt strangely comforted. But she still tried to behave as though nothing unusual had happened.

"I'm not crying," she assured him.

"But you were," he said. "What's happened—are you hurt?"

"I didn't fall out," Laura said. "I got out."

"The difference wasn't very obvious."

"Well, I fell out, perhaps. But I was getting out anyway." She spoke calmly, but even to her own ears it sounded faintly absurd. She had a vision of herself stumbling out of the car and clinging to the side of the bridge, looking both distraught and ridiculous. That was what Miles must have seen, and it was hardly possible to go on pretending that she had been behaving normally.

"I don't want to interfere," he said gently. "It's nothing to do with me. But—Well, was that a serious quarrel?"

Laura abandoned the pretence. "Oh, dear," she sighed, "it wasn't a quarrel at all—it was being disapproved of, and despised, and cast into outer darkness. It was horrible! And all my fault, really."

"Nonsense! Please, Laura, don't think of it like that. He's not nearly good enough for you."

Laura looked at him in bewilderment. Then she realized that he had only seen the back of the Endbury car. It was, she supposed, a natural mistake, but why should he be so quick to assume that she was quarrelling with Toby?

"It wasn't Toby," she said. "I wasn't—at least, I suppose I have quarrelled with him now, but I didn't mean to. Poor Toby—but it was his fault too. He shouldn't have told her."

Her companion seemed to be working this out for himself. There was a long pause before he said slowly: "So that's it." He spoke as if he had hoped for something else.

"He shouldn't have told her," Laura repeated crossly. Now that she had time to think of it, Toby's conduct appeared even more distressing than it had done at first. She had quite forgotten that this was exactly what she had expected him to do. It seemed now like a double betrayal, because he had discussed his mother with her and had then turned round and discussed her with Lady Masters.

"But he had to tell her sometime," Miles said. "Not that I'm making excuses for him," he added grimly.

This remark only increased her confusion. It did not make sense—for why should Lady Masters have to be told?—but it implied that Miles knew about Toby's proposal. She was assailed by a horrid fear that the whole of Bramton Wick must know about it. She said sadly:

"I wish it had never happened. She was so angry, and now, if people talk about it, it will be worse."

"Do you mean that she objected to it?" he exclaimed. "That woman—! Well, I won't say what I think of her."

Laura could not help feeling that it would console her to know what he thought of Lady Masters. But she also felt that the whole conversation was taking place in a dream, in which she and Miles exchanged remarks that sounded lucid and rational, but meant nothing. The alternative to the dream theory was that everything she said was doomed to be misunderstood and that Miles was sympathizing with her for quite the wrong reasons.

"She couldn't help it. You see . . ."

Miles waited, but Laura said no more. It was difficult to know where to begin.

"Very well," he said, "I won't abuse her. But what are you going to do now?"

"I shall never feel sorry for anyone again!" she cried impetuously. "At least, I shall never feel sorry for Toby. I ought to, but somehow I can't, because really, Miles, he made everything so much worse. What do you mean by saying he had to tell her sometime? If only he had kept it to himself we might have got over it quite easily."

This speech was not as enlightening as she had intended. Miles looked oddly unsure of himself, as if he had begun to share the feeling that it was all a dream. Realizing that something more was needed, she added hastily:

"You see, if he only hadn't talked it over with her no one need ever have known."

Miles drew a deep breath and said: "Laura, are you or are you not engaged to Toby Masters?"

"I'm not," said Laura. "I mean, I never was."

Trying hard not to blush as the implications of this question grew plain, she only succeeded in blushing more deeply. After a prolonged silence Miles said he must have got hold of the wrong idea. Laura, still blushing, said it was all her fault, and he reminded her that she had just said it was Toby's fault.

"It was my fault in the beginning."

"It's a very confusing story," he said, smiling. "And you may as well know that everyone in the neighbourhood has been telling me for a long time that you were secretly engaged."

Laura looked away. She looked at the little river, swollen and muddy after a week's rain. She heard its gentle murmur as it flowed under the bridge, a soft deceptive sound like Pussy's voice and all the other voices, muted but confident.

"You could have asked me," she said, "instead of listening to everyone in the neighbourhood."

"At first, I didn't believe it. Afterwards . . . and anyway, how could I ask you?"

Laura said she supposed not.

"Quite apart from the fact that I never saw you alone. Every time I came to Woodside—and Heaven knows I found enough excuses for coming—" He broke off, and then said in quite a different voice: "Do you know what I'm asking you now?"

"Oh, Miles!" said Laura, forgetting the rules—if indeed she had ever known them—for dealing with a proposal of marriage which you meant to accept as opposed to the proposal which had to be declined in advance.

"My dear Laura," he said, "I'm not nearly good enough for you either. But will you marry me?"

Afterwards Laura, whose memory of this momentous occasion was regrettably confused, thought she must have mixed up the rules and applied the wrong one, for it seemed to her that she had accepted in advance. But at the time neither of them noticed anything unusual. The happiness of being able to acknowledge openly what each had long acknowledged in secret, the relief, for Laura, of finding that all her worries had become completely unimportant, and the sincere pleasure Miles took in denouncing his past stupidity—this occupied them to the exclusion of all else, and time flowed by unheeded while they traced the course of their affection.

Laura dated her love for Miles from the day when he had stood in the sunlight and looked up at the Cleeve Monument in Bramton, and she had suddenly seen him for the first time. She had not realized then what was happening to her, nor even that it was peculiar to be seeing for the first time someone you had known all your life. Miles said he had loved her long before that; he had fallen in love when she came back to Woodside at the end of the war, but since he was at that time on the edge of bankruptcy he had not felt justified in asking her to marry him.

"Not that I've much to offer you now," he said. "Still, I'm solvent."

Laura laughed and said that Pussy must be getting quite out of date, as she had only just got round to the news of Miles's bankruptcy. He agreed that Pussy was losing her grip, and insisted on being told just what she had said; and then he explained that his father—whose generosity was rather greater than his good sense—had died heavily in debt, and that at one time he had thought he would have to sell Marly.

"Though how she heard of it—!"

"Poor Pussy," Laura said cheerfully. "I wonder how soon she'll hear of this."

Happily unaware of the part she had already played in alarming Mrs. Cole, they agreed that Pussy deserved to be told. Why she deserved it was not clear; it was part of their amiable benevolence towards the rest of the world, so much less fortunate than themselves.

"And, talking of telling people," Miles said, "do you think your mother will be pleased?"

"Well, of course it will be a surprise for her," Laura answered quickly. "She'll have to get accustomed to it. You know how surprises fluster her."

"My darling Laura, it's nice of you to spare my feelings. But I know more than that."

"You are too observant."

"I know she wants you to marry Toby Masters."

"Was it so obvious?"

"Fairly obvious," he said tolerantly. The long talks with Mrs. Cole in the garden at Woodside, in which questions about retaining walls and the draining of the boggy bit had been mingled with favourable allusions to Endbury and dear Toby, had made it painfully clear to him where her sympathies lay. It was Mrs. Cole's behaviour, more than anything else, that had led him to believe the rumours about Laura's engagement. But he bore her no malice for it now.

"It's because of Endbury, you see. That's the only reason—because we lived there and she still thinks it ought to belong to us."

Miles nodded, forgiving Mrs. Cole for her deception and then forgetting all about her. The mention of Endbury had reminded him of something else.

"By the way, if you weren't engaged to him and Lady Masters was not objecting to it, what was happening this afternoon?"

"Dear Miles, never mind what happened this afternoon. Come back to Woodside and we'll break the news to Mummy."

"You needn't tell me," he said, laughing at her. "I think I can guess."

"Please don't. It's a horrid, humiliating story."

When Laura did not return, Mrs. Cole thought they must have stayed to tea with Miss Selbourne. Lady Masters and Miss Selbourne were the merest acquaintances, and Miss Selbourne had never been known to ask anyone to tea (it might be different now she had Jocelyn to cook for her), so the idea soon began to seem improbable. Could they have gone back to Endbury? At the thought of it Mrs. Cole grew quite excited. She saw that Lady Masters had taken the car, which gave her good reason for thinking that they must have gone farther than Bank Cottage. She hoped that Laura would not catch Toby's cold.

However, this maternal solicitude was quickly dispelled by much more agreeable fancies; there must be some reason— some *special* reason, she thought—for Lady Masters's behaviour. The flimsy excuse of going for a walk, and then changing her mind and taking the car, the prolonged absence, it must mean something, and what could it mean but—? The significant "but" was the key to a door that opened on vistas of splendour: bridesmaids; the Brussels lace; a wedding in Bramton Church, but with the Rector of Bramworthy too because she liked him much better than the Vicar of Bramton; a spring wedding if possible, because of the flowers; as fine a trousseau as she could possibly manage. . . .

"What can I sell?" she wondered, mentally listing the furniture, the pictures, and her own remaining jewellery, and rather regretting having given her pearls to Gillian. Of course, Gillian was the elder, and had got married first, but it was a pity the pearls could not have gone back to Endbury with Laura.

At this point, conscious that her imagination was running away with her, Mrs. Cole told herself that she would not think any more about it. Perhaps it was unlucky. But even the power of superstition could not prevent her from thinking, as she carried her tea tray back to the kitchen and replaced the milk jug in the larder, how wonderful it would be if Laura should come home and announce that she was engaged.

The fine afternoon was now merging into a fine evening. Inside the house it was already dusk, and Mrs. Cole began to worry because Laura had taken only her thin coat and might be cold. She made up the fire, then she went upstairs to close the windows and draw the bedroom curtains. Her own bedroom looked out over the garden, and she stood at the window, as she did almost every night, contemplating the beauty she had created and thinking how it might be improved.

A garden, even such a small garden as this one, was an expensive form of self-expression; but then it was her only extravagance. She never thought of it as an extravagance and when she spoke vaguely of economizing it was generally because the money was needed for the garden—the garden itself being rigidly excluded from schemes of retrenchment. Now, while half her mind was occupied with plans for Laura's trousseau, the other half was considering the extension of the herbaceous border, which would mean curtailing the vegetable garden and cutting down two or three old apple trees.

It would be rash to maintain that her devotion to the garden equalled her devotion to Laura and Gillian. Nevertheless, Mrs. Cole, who ought to have been at the spyhole watching for her daughter's return, was still gazing out on an imaginary herbaceous border, and debating the exact height of an imaginary *thuya* hedge, when Laura and Miles entered the house. Hearing their voices, she went to the top of the stairs. In the fading daylight, looking down into the hall, she could see only that Laura had someone with her, and for a brief moment she thought it must be Toby bringing her back from Endbury. Forgetting that Toby had a cold and was spending a day in bed, Mrs. Cole drew a deep breath of satisfaction.

"Laura, darling!" she called in a warm, welcoming voice, hurrying downstairs towards them. But almost as she spoke she realized that it was not Toby after all; the tall man who stood there in the dusk could only be Miles Corton. The disappointment of finding it was not Toby made her greet Miles with less than her usual cordiality.

They followed her into the drawing-room. Laura said she hoped there was some sherry left, and went off to look for it. Resenting this extravagance—for though it would not have been extravagant to offer Toby a drink, there was no need to offer one to Miles—Mrs. Cole at once began to talk about the garden, which was a safe and enjoyable subject. But when Laura came back her curiosity got the better of her and she interrupted herself to ask what had become of Lady Masters, and where Laura had been all this time.

"Oh, she went home," Laura said casually. A silly reply, thought Mrs. Cole, coming strangely near to criticizing her precious child. Of course Lady Masters had gone home; where else would she be likely to go?

"But did you see Miss Selbourne? Did you have tea with her?"

Laura looked across at Miles. "No," she said, "we didn't. I—I met Miles down by the bridge."

Where she had met Miles was of less interest to Mrs. Cole than what had become of Lady Masters, and she asked fretfully:

"But what *did* you do? Did you go for a drive? I saw that you went in the car after all. I wish you had thought of bringing Lady Masters back for tea here, as you were out so long." She did not really wish this, for she had had enough of Lady Masters for one day, but Laura ought to have asked her. "She will be late getting home, and I know they always have tea at four o'clock."

"She won't be late," Miles said. "She went home a long time ago."

Whether or not these words were meant to be reassuring, Mrs. Cole took them in the wrong spirit; to her they sounded like a flippant dismissal of Lady Masters and all she represented. Almost as if he were laughing. Then she realized that if Lady Masters had gone home early then was a big gap of time unaccounted for. A more resolute mother might have continued her questioning, but Mrs. Cole, instinctively playing for time, changed the subject by telling Miles that Gillian was coming back tomorrow.

"Mummy!" said Laura, before Miles had time to reply.

Mrs. Cole looked at her daughter. Since Laura's return, since the moment when she had seen that it was Miles, and not Toby, who stood beside her in the hall, she had felt faintly uneasy. Something had happened; there was a breath of excitement—and danger—in the air. Now, while she looked at Laura, the uneasiness became alarm. For no reason—or for a most sinister reason—she found herself picturing Marly House. Ugly as it was in fact, her inward vision made it still uglier and invested it with circling winds and ceaseless icy draughts.

"And all those cobwebs," she murmured aloud. This inconsequent remark went unnoticed by Miles and Laura, who proceeded to tell her, with as much calm and tact as possible, that they wished to marry. Neither had expected that she would instantly approve of their engagement, but they were too much engrossed by their own happiness to realize how strongly she disapproved. Mrs. Cole took refuge in vagueness, in saying it was a great surprise, she had never dreamt of it, and Gillian must be told first. Outwardly she remained tolerably calm; inwardly she was extremely agitated, and Pussy Cleeve's words rang in her head like prophetic tolling bells.

She ought to have guessed. She ought to have *known*. She ought to have Done Something.

CHAPTER TWENTY

ON MONDAY AFTERNOON Gillian returned from Cleeve Manor. Thomas drove her back, but could not stay long because he was going up to London on the evening train. Laura had gone to Marly House to have tea with Miles; quite apart from a faint, wild hope that being taken all over Marly House might make her regret her choice, Mrs. Cole was glad of her absence, which would give her the opportunity to break the news to Gillian and find out what she thought of it.

The presence of a third party entailed a slight delay, for Mrs. Cole had no intention of discussing the dreadful situation till they were alone. But in spite of her restraint Gillian was soon aware that something important had happened. Her mother was even vaguer than usual, and although she chatted politely with Thomas it was quite plain to anyone who knew her that she was not listening to his account of the Hospice Ball.

"Not a bad show," Thomas said. "Not a bad show at all."

Mrs. Cole said that must have been wonderful.

Gillian wondered if it was sudden ruin, or the death of a dear old friend, or simply some fearful catastrophe in the garden. There was an aura of tragedy about Mrs. Cole which suggested that it had been something disastrous. Gillian did not care for disasters, and she was preparing herself to minimize this one when something was said that made her think it was not a disaster after all. In reply to Thomas's polite inquiries her mother said briefly and rather coldly that Laura was out. Mrs. Cole had a fond conviction that everyone must share her interest in her daughters, and it was so unlike her not to give a full, exact account of their activities that Gillian instantly perceived that whatever had happened, had happened to Laura.

As soon as Thomas had left the house, Mrs. Cole drew her back into the drawing-room and announced in tones of deepest woe that Laura wanted to marry Miles Corton.

"Does she?" Gillian said. "I thought that might be it. Has he asked her?"

"They're engaged," wailed Mrs. Cole.

"Let's have tea, and you shall tell me all about it. It's been coming on for weeks, you know."

Whatever Mrs. Cole had expected, it had not been this.

"Gillian!" she cried. "If you knew, you should have told me. We could have done something. Laura's so young . . ."

"Mummy, darling, Laura's only five years younger than I. She's older than I was when I got married."

"That was different. That was the war."

Gillian always knew what was needed, and what was needed now was a nice cup of tea. Leaving Mrs. Cole to make up the fire, which was smouldering in a dismal way as if it shared her feelings, she went into the kitchen and in a remarkably short time returned with the tea on a trolley, set out elegantly with the best china and the silver teapot. Soothing people's ruffled feelings was exactly what Gillian was best at, and it was easier in this case because she knew the reason for her mother's dismay and disapproval. But she was careful not to let the conversation get round to Endbury. Endbury would have to be mentioned, but that would come later.

To begin with she listened to a confused and agitated account of how Mrs. Cole had heard the news and what a shock it had been to her. She had already been worried and anxious because Laura had been out for so long and hadn't come back at tea-time, and had taken only her thin coat. And then Laura had brought Miles in and without any warning they had announced that they wanted to get married, and Miles had stayed the whole evening, and Laura had used all the eggs to make an omelette for supper.

Although she appeared agitated and confused Mrs. Cole thought she was giving an accurate statement of what had happened and what she had felt at the time. She could not help adding a few dramatic touches, such as her anxiety at Laura's prolonged absence, and stressing the fact that it had all come as a complete surprise to her. The destruction of her secret hopes was so painful that she felt justified in making these small exaggerations.

"I never dreamed of it," she repeated. "It's as if she'd suddenly said she was going to marry a total stranger."

"It's odd, really, that we don't know Miles better. After all, you were such friends with old Mr. Corton, and he did so much for us."

Gradually, under the influence of tea and sympathy, Mrs. Cole was lured into remembering what a good friend old Mr. Corton had been to the family. She always enjoyed talking about the past, and soon she was plunged into a flood of reminiscences, with Gillian cunningly guiding her in the right direction.

"People used to say he was stubborn," she declared, "but he was always very kind to me. And he took such an interest in the garden. Nothing was too much trouble."

"Miles is very like him. And he likes gardening, too."

Unable to deny the physical resemblance, Mrs. Cole refused to admit that Miles cared for gardening. "Oh, no," she said, "he doesn't mind what happens to Marly. I was quite horrified, last time I was there, to see how neglected it was. Weeds everywhere, and the knot garden quite ruined."

"But farming takes most of his time. It isn't that he doesn't care. Look how often he's been here to help you with the alterations—that shows he must be interested." Gillian could perceive another motive for Miles's frequent visits to Woodside, but naturally she did not mention it. "When they're married, you'll be able to help them," she went on. "Laura will want to get that garden straight, and she won't know where to begin. You'll have lots to plan and think about."

Mrs. Cole looked a little happier. Though she had not yet got over her disappointment she saw for the first time a small ray of light amid the encircling gloom. The gardens at Endbury were perfect; and even if she had wanted to she would not have been allowed to tamper with them. But the garden at Marly House, like a sad, neglected child, cried out for care and attention. There was so much to be done that it would be difficult to know where to begin.

Of course they would not have much money. It would be better to get rid of the knot garden and all those elaborate beds which needed edging and constant weeding. It would be better to grass over all that part below the terrace. And then, perhaps . . .

Watching her mother, who was gazing into the fire and twisting the fringes of her shawl between her fingers, Gillian saw that she was happily employed in reconstructing the Marly garden.

Presently they would come back to discussing Miles and Laura, but it would be easier now to persuade her that everything was really for the best.

Gillian was a kind-hearted daughter. She realized that it would take a little time for her mother to get used to the idea of Laura's marriage, and that still more time would be needed before she really began to approve of it. She had had as much agitation and excitement as she could bear. For these and other reasons Gillian decided not to speak about her own future. It was clearly not the right moment to break it to Mrs. Cole that she was to lose both her daughters, or alternatively that she was to acquire two uncongenial sons-in-law.

Even before she knew about Laura and Miles she had foreseen that there would have to be a right moment for telling her mother about Thomas, and she had pledged him to secrecy. So there was no hurry; the first thing to be done was to get her into a favourable pro-engagements frame of mind, and then in a few days' time, when she had begun to think about weddings, the right moment could be created.

While they talked, Gillian continued to lay her plans. Laura's marriage would make a difference; if Mrs. Cole continued to live at Woodside they would have to find her a housekeeper or companion; or perhaps it would be better if she left this house, which would be rather too large for her, and lived either with Laura at Marly or with herself at Cleeve. Or for six months at a time with each of them. But that need not be settled at once, it could wait until she had time to discuss it with Thomas and find out how he felt about mothers-in-law.

It was lucky, she thought, that Thomas was so rich, and then, quite spontaneously, she found herself thinking, "Dear Thomas!" For she was more attached to him than she would have cared to admit, and some of her reformer's zeal had already abated. The prospect of wealth was not unpleasant, but while she was fully aware of her good fortune she was also convinced that she and Thomas were ideally suited to one another.

Mrs. Cole, who so deplored the obstinacy of the Cortons, could be obstinate herself where her own interests were concerned, and Gillian's plan for removing her from Woodside was doomed to failure. Gillian did not foresee this, for in everything concerning her daughters Mrs. Cole had always been pliable and accommodating. Happily ignorant of the great tussle to come, they settled down to a friendly talk, in the course of which Mrs. Cole admitted that she had hoped Laura might marry Toby Masters.

Gillian sympathized about Endbury, but pointed out that marrying Toby would have meant marrying Lady Masters too.

"And being completely dominated," she said. "You know what she's like. Laura could never stand up to her."

"But if she had gone away—left Endbury—"

"Mummy, darling, can you see her leaving Endbury?"

Facing facts, Mrs. Cole could not. Now that the dream was over there was no need to continue the mental exercise of willing herself to like, or at least to admire, Lady Masters. The self-imposed discipline had been as uncomfortable as a tight pair of shoes, and it was a relief to be able to relax, to shuffle, as it were, into cosy soft slippers, and to say that fond as she was, and always would be, of Toby, she could only pity him for having such a possessive mother.

"Not like you, darling," said Gillian, building up the picture of an indulgent parent who let her daughters follow the inclinations of their own hearts.

The weather had changed since yesterday. Driving rain hid the park, and the wind was bringing drifts of leaves from the trees and howling round the ugly, solid walls of Marly House as if to show what it could do when it tried. It was not perhaps the best possible day for inspecting one's future home, but nothing could depress Laura and Miles, not even a prolonged tour of the house, which had now brought them up to the dusty and lumber-filled attics. Miles was stubbornly attached to his home and Laura was quite incapable of finding any fault with it. They both knew that other people thought it ugly and inconvenient, they were even prepared to agree that it was rather large, but neither of them wished to live anywhere else.

The tour of the house had taken a long time, for each room had to be considered on its merits. It would be impossible for them to use all the rooms, and yet it was hard to decide between them. By the time they reached the attics it was already dusk.

"It's a pity," said Miles, "that my great-great-grandfather had to go and build all this on top of what was already quite a large house."

"Oh, well, it's very useful to have a lot of storage room."

"We've certainly got that," he said. "Even without the attics."

"Perhaps we shall have a large family," Laura remarked, her mind directed to this possibility by the sight of an old and exceedingly uncomfortable-looking cradle pushed away among the trunks.

Miles said he did not think they could afford a large family. Was it reasonable, he added, to have a large family simply to fill up the empty rooms at Marly House?

"No, but I expect we should love them for themselves. And they would give us plenty to talk about, which is so important in married life."

"That sounds like worldly advice from Gillian," he said. "I can always tell when you're quoting Gillian. You speak with such confidence."

Laura laughed and protested that it wasn't true. "We have quite different ideas about lots of things, and I don't always think she's right. Do you know, Miles, I have a fearful feeling that Gil is going to marry Thomas."

"If I didn't love you so much the thought of having Thomas Greenley for a brother-in-law would quite discourage me from marrying into the Cole family."

"How absurd you are. There's nothing wrong with Thomas really, except that he's *dull*. And he can't help that—"

"And you are about to pity him for it. Very well, my love, I won't interrupt you. Go on. Say 'Poor Thomas.'"

FURROWED MIDDLEBROW

Made in the USA
Middletown, DE
13 August 2023

36603458R00119